KEPT

from

YOU

BOOK 2:4 TEAR ASUNDER

NASHODA ROSE

Kept from You
Published by Nashoda Rose
Copyright © 2016 by Nashoda Rose

Toronto, Canada

ISBN:978-1-987953-13-8

Cover by Kari Ayasha, Cover to Cover Designs
Cover Photo by Wander Aguiar Photography
Model: Nick Bennett
Content Edited by Kristin Anders, The Romantic Editor,
www.theromanticeditor.com
Editing by Hot Tree Editing , www.hottreeediting.com
Formatted by Champagne Book Design, champagenbookdesign.com
Proofing: Elaine York, Allusion Graphics LLC, www.allusiongraphics.com

Warning: *Kept from You* is for 18+ due to language and sexual content.
This is a complete stand alone in the Tear Asunder series.

*Any editing issues are my own. I'm Canadian, and on occasion I may use the Canadian spelling rather than U.S.

NASHODA ROSE

Irish Crown

Tear Asunder Series
With You
Torn from You
Overwhelmed by You
Shattered by You
Kept from You

Unyielding Series (A Tear Asunder spin off)
Perfect Chaos
Perfect Ruin
Perfect Rage

Scars of the Wraith Series
Stygian
Tyrant
Credo
Take

www.nashodarose.com

Prologue

Toronto

Savvy

FIST SLAMMED INTO THE METAL LOCKER BESIDE MY HEAD and my math book cradled in my arms slipped and fell to the floor with a loud clunk.

I sucked in a mouthful of air and froze.

The fist belonged to Killian Kane.

The Killian Kane.

Rumor was he'd been suspended from school numerous times for fighting, and the only reason he hadn't been expelled was his father donated a lot of money to the school.

And yeah, I was scared of him. You'd be stupid not to be.

Thankfully his fist indenting the locker wasn't to get my attention; it was to get Josh Clery's attention—the guy who unfortunately had the locker beside me.

"Ki… te," Josh stuttered as he turned around, his face pale, hands at half-mast.

Killian's nickname was Kite. And at first thought, the word conjured a beautiful kite flying through the air in a gentle wind.

This was not the origin of his nickname. Far from it.

Because the word Kite also meant "to prey on others." And Killian lived up to *that* nickname. Although in his defense, he did it sort of fairly.

He fought the older kids who bullied the younger ones. He banned wedgies after some kid was found in the changing room hanging on the wall hook by his underwear.

If Killian heard about shit like that, he dealt with it.

Often that meant dealing with kids older and bigger than him.

He was fearless, and there was a part of me that was awestruck by him because nothing deterred him from his purpose.

Unwavering.

Unbending.

My perception of a Greek god was pretty much Killian. One of the god's who had a temper and knew how much power he wielded and used it.

He was good looking, but that wasn't what made him attractive. It was how he drew you into him like a string on a marionette with his steady green eyes.

I'd never spoken to him, and he'd never said a word to me, which was a good thing since no one wanted Killian Kane's attention.

Although, on a few occasions when I saw him in the hallways, I swore he watched me. And when our eyes would lock briefly, he always looked away while I'd lower my head and walk away as fast as I could with my heart racing and legs quivering.

He did that to me, made me breathless, which wasn't a good thing.

Killian supposedly moved here from Ireland a few years ago, but I'd been at a different grade school than him. He was also a year ahead of me, so even though we were now in the same high school we didn't have any classes together. And I was glad because I'd never be able to concentrate with him so close.

The first time I'd witnessed Killian in action was in the cafeteria.

He was in a rock band with a few guys from school, until 'the fight'. The second Killian walked into the cafeteria that day there was tension. I'd heard the hushed whispers and the rumor that Killian had hooked up with the lead singer's girlfriend. I hadn't thought it was true because Killian had never been seen with any girls.

His band mates had stood when he'd approached, and I'd been terrified for him because there were three of them and only him. I'd wanted him to turn around and walk out. But Killian would never have done that, and he didn't. He'd walked right by them and went and got his food.

It was when he had his lunch in hand that it happened.

The lead singer stepped into his path and dumped Killian's tray on the floor.

Killian remained completely calm. But that was where his nickname came into play.

Because he'd bent, picked up his tray and now ruined lunch, then threw it in the garbage. Then he'd strode back to him.

The predator approached his prey. And there was no doubt they were prey to him.

I'd never heard the cafeteria so silent before. The only sounds were Killian's footsteps and his ex-band mate's chuckles. They'd either been really brave or completely stupid considering Killian's reputation. Maybe they'd thought since they were on school property, he wouldn't do anything.

He did.

I had no idea how Killian did it as it happened so fast, but in one move he had the lead singer on his back and on the floor. Within seconds the guy was begging. I couldn't see exactly what Killian did to him, but it was calm, controlled, and without a flicker of fear.

A new guy, Sculpt, who I didn't know except by name, had stood up from his table and moved closer to Killian. I assumed to back him up if the other band mates jumped him.

They didn't, probably because Sculpt was even scarier than Killian. Sculpt's tattooed, bulging arms and dark, almost black, intense eyes were pretty intimidating.

Ever since that fight, Killian and Sculpt hung out together, and I'd heard they started their own band with a couple of guys from another school.

And now I stood frozen at my locker, an arm's length away from Killian Kane. Afraid to move, breathe or otherwise, lest I gain his notice.

My math book lay at my feet, canvas school bag slung over my shoulder and Killian so close to me his broad shoulder brushed mine when he grabbed Josh by the T-shirt and slammed him into the locker.

My heart jumped at the loud bang of Josh's spine hitting the metal.

"I fuckin' warned you," Killian growled.

And it was a growl or maybe a snarl because he said it between clenched teeth. He tilted his body in close to Josh, and Josh had nowhere to go, trapped between furious Killian and his locker.

"I warned you what would happen if he came to my school and dealt that shit."

Dealt that shit was drugs. Josh's older brother was a big-time dealer, and anyone who wanted drugs went to him.

Josh sold them too, but not the hard stuff, and neither brother sold them at our school—until recently.

Killian landed a couple of guys in the hospital after they'd tried to sell drugs on school property. One guy had a busted nose and a broken right arm. The other had cracked ribs and lost three front teeth.

Neither kid admitted it was Killian, but everyone knew. Especially since the day after the incident, Killian had a bandage above his right eye, and his knuckles were bruised and cut up.

My best friend, Mars, whose brother Aiden was in Killian's class, said when the teacher told Killian to go to the infirmary to get checked, he told the teacher to "mind his own fuckin' business."

That got him sent to the principal's office. No one knows what happened there, but he pretty much lived in detention.

"I… I know. I told him, but"—I kind of felt sorry for Josh,

because he looked like he was going to piss himself—"...he said it wasn't *your* school," Josh stammered. "I swear. I told him not to."

It wasn't Killian's school, technically, but you still followed his rules, and one of his rules was no drugs.

Killian straightened, but he didn't release Josh's shirt.

"Where is he now?"

"He took off when he, uh... heard you were looking for him." Josh briefly glanced at me, and I half smiled. It was my small act of kindness, because even though I wasn't a fan of Josh as he and his brother were drug dealers, I sympathized with him for being on Killian's radar.

You did not want to be on Killian's radar. And exactly why I hadn't run, but kept quiet, motionless, and barely breathing. The rabbit in the hole waiting until the coast was clear for my quick escape.

Besides, I had a math test tomorrow I needed to study for so I wasn't leaving without my books.

"Tell him to meet me at the river," Killian said. "Five o'clock. He doesn't show, I'm coming for him another way, and he won't like it."

I knew exactly what meeting at the river meant. He was going to fight Josh's older brother. Older meaning he'd graduated last year.

"I swear, Kite, he won't do it again," Josh said.

Killian's voice lowered. "Too late for that. You were supposed to tell him the rules. He either didn't listen or you didn't tell him. Either way, now I have to do something about it."

Maybe it was my fiery red hair that caught his eye, or that my heart thumped so loud he heard it, but whatever it was, Killian's gaze sliced to me.

I stiffened, inhaling a quick breath and my heart fluttered.

We stared at one another.

It was the first time I'd been this close to him, and it was terrifying, and at the same time captivating and intense.

His eyes reminded me of the green Popsicles my dad used to pick up on his way home from work on hot, humid days. We'd sit on the front porch of the house and eat them before they melted, which was hard to do in the heat and we'd both end up with sticky hands.

Killian's eyes were like that. Green and cold with ice chips in them, so clear it was as if I saw my own reflection.

And they were absolutely beautiful.

Cool as ice, Savvy. He is not a nice guy.

"Breathe," Killian said.

I swayed to the side as my lungs screamed for air. I couldn't look away even if I wanted to, lost within the cool depths of his eyes.

"Jesus Christ. Breathe," he barked.

That snapped me out of it, and I exhaled.

His piercing eyes stayed on me for a second, and I swear they softened, warmth simmering briefly before they hardened again.

He shifted his attention back to Josh at the same time as a voice called out, "Kite?"

Sculpt strode down the hall toward us then put his hand on Killian's forearm. "Not fuckin' here."

"His brother was dealing drugs on school property," Killian retorted, glaring at his friend.

"I know, but not here. The school won't give you another chance and your dad—"

"Fuck him."

Sculpt tensed. "I get it, man. You know I do, but you can't risk it."

Killian swore beneath his breath then released Josh's shirt and stepped back. "Tell him to meet me."

"Yeah. Okay. Sure, Kite." Josh scrambled to pick up his books, slammed his locker and took off.

"You're going to get expelled," Sculpt said. "The principal said no more chances. If he saw that, you'd be history."

"Josh and his brother are bad news." Killian leaned up against the locker beside me, but it was as if I no longer existed because he completely ignored me.

I thought it was fairly safe to move, grab my things and slip away, so I crouched to pick up my math book.

"You're Savannah, right?"

I looked up with my hand on my book, and Killian was looking at me, but it was Sculpt who had spoken.

Ummm, why was he talking to me?

Neither guy had spoken to me before. Even when I'd seen them in a local coffee shop they hung out at with a couple other guys not from our school, they didn't acknowledge me.

"It's Savvy," I corrected.

"I'm Sculpt. You meet Kite?"

For a millisecond, I considered laughing because it was so ridiculous that he was introducing himself and Killian.

Seriously, what person did not know who they were?

Within five seconds of the first day of secondary school, I knew Kite's name. I found out weeks later his real name was Killian, and ever since that was who he was to me.

I loved his name, and I didn't like what his nickname meant. There was more to his fighting than him preying on others. It was like... he was so angry and tormented by something that he had to fight, but maybe he didn't want to. So, he fought the bullies and assholes.

Or I was just making up my own excuse for him.

"You help out the school nurse," Sculpt said.

"Yeah," I replied.

I placed supply orders, dressed the odd scrapes and wounds, nothing substantial, but I had my first aid certificate. I'd never treated Killian or Sculpt for anything.

I suspected Killian wouldn't have a nurse or anyone else treat him for minor cuts or injuries. It would have to be serious before he saw the nurse. Plus, I imagined he was accustomed to injuries and bandaged himself.

"You good at keeping your mouth shut?" Sculpt asked

What kind of question was that? I wasn't outspoken by any means, or prone to gossip. Actually, I only had a few friends to gossip with anyway. "I'm not going to say anything about this, if that's what you're asking."

"Nope. Wasn't asking for that reason," he replied.

Killian's eyes narrowed and his back stiffened, but he remained silent.

Even though I was scared and nervous of Killian, he was hard not to admire because he was striking. And you'd know if he kissed you, it would be absolutely incredible.

My bestie, Mars, said he was cute.

But you didn't call a lion cute. Majestic. Magnificent and maybe even beautiful. But definitely not cute.

Sculpt bent and curled his fingers around my elbow to help me stand.

I stood, and my gaze locked on Killian. He was still watching me, his expression cold and unreadable.

Sculpt's hand dropped from my elbow.

Killian turned away first, and I thanked God because there was no way I was able to stop myself from peering into those eyes. And my heart wouldn't stop doing those thrills.

He is not a god, Savvy.

Just a guy with beautiful eyes who I wanted to have my first kiss with.

I cleared my throat and raised my knee to balance my bag on it while I unzipped it and quickly shoved my math textbook inside. I rezipped, lowered my leg and shut my locker.

My hand trembled as I fiddled with the padlock and I couldn't get the shackle of the lock to catch.

"I have a job for you," Sculpt said.

Damn it. I had to redo the code.

"Sorry, pardon?" I asked, then dropped my bag between my legs and spun the dial one way then the other, then back the other way.

"A job," Sculpt said. "It's fast, quick cash, and most of the time you won't have to do anything except show up."

"That doesn't sound legal." But regardless of what the job was, I was anxious to pay for dance classes, and I couldn't get a job because most places wouldn't hire me being only fifteen.

Since my dad died, money was really tight, and my mom paying for dance or even helping out was out of the question.

My lock finally latched and I spun the dial.

"Not her," Killian said.

My eyes lifted to his through a strand of my wild, red curls, and suddenly I wished I hadn't because he was watching me again, and it wasn't emotionless this time.

It was annoyed.

I didn't know why. It wasn't like I'd done anything. Maybe he was pissed Sculpt had a job for me. But what did he care?

Trapped in Killian's ice-green eyes again, I felt as if an elephant sat on my chest.

Why couldn't I look away?

I so did not want to be on his radar.

But it wasn't like I had a choice. His gaze had me locked to him, and the only way I'd be able to look away was if he allowed it.

Jesus.

"Why not?" Sculpt asked him.

Killian's jaw clamped and he jerked his eyes from mine, pushing away from the locker. "She's a damn freshman and terrified of her own fuckin' shadow. I bet she'd run out of there crying the second she saw what was happening. Not fuckin' her!" Killian repeated. Then he turned and headed down the hall.

"Shit," Sculpt mumbled. "Don't take it personally. You're one of the few he actually likes," he said, but he didn't say it like a compliment, just a fact.

That made no sense. He didn't even know me, and I wasn't sure I liked that he liked me.

Sculpt gave me a once over with his black eyes, and it was unnerving because it was like he was checking to see if I measured up to something. "You want to make quick cash, let me know."

I wanted to say yes for the fact alone that Killian said I was scared of my own shadow and would run crying out of... wherever he was talking about.

Sculpt turned and jogged down the hall after Killian before I had a chance to ask what the job actually was.

He body checked Killian and Killian punched him in the chest.

I watched them until they disappeared around the corner then flung my bag over my shoulder and ran to meet my mom outside.

An hour later, I sat on the school steps studying math because my mom hadn't shown—again. It was the third time this week. Mom was getting worse.

"You always do your homework on the steps after school?"

I gasped, twisting at the waist to see Killian standing on the top step looking like one of those Greek gods again. I wasn't an expert on gods or anything, but I'd decided that he was definitely Zeus. Powerful with a temper and if you pissed him off you were totally screwed.

I stuffed my math book into my bag. "Sometimes. When my mom is late."

"And how often is that?" he asked.

Shrugging, I said while collecting my bag and standing. "She's really busy."

He'd walked down five steps so he was beside me. He smelled fresh and clean with the lingering scent of soap, as if he'd had gym his last period and had showered.

I dragged in a deep inhale then stopped when his brows lifted as if he knew I'd been breathing in his smell.

Crap.

He continued, "Doing what?"

I hitched my bag over my shoulder. "I don't know. Stuff."

She probably took too many of those pills again and was passed out. I didn't know what they were because she'd peeled the label off.

"Come to the river with us," Killian said. "After the fight one of the guys will drive you home."

I was so not doing that.

First off, watching a fight made my stomach churn. Not because of the blood, but because I hated the idea of fighting.

The second reason, I didn't know any of 'the guys' and I wasn't getting in a car with them. I'd rather walk the *six* miles home.

"I'm okay. It's not far."

"Bullshit. I know where you live," he retorted.

He did? It was odd that Killian would know that. Why would he?

"Well, I'm used to it." And according to my mother, I needed the exercise. That was her excuse for when she forgot to pick me up. That I should walk home so I could lose a few pounds. I wasn't exactly overweight, but I was short and had bulk, but I danced, so I was toned and in shape. My body wasn't a dainty China doll like hers.

I headed down the stairs, praying I didn't trip and fall because pins and needles surged through my legs from sitting cross-legged on the stairs for so long.

I was also nervous because I couldn't figure out why Killian was talking to me again. That was twice in one day.

I hadn't done anything. I had nothing he wanted. And I certainly wasn't a threat to him or would break any of his rules.

Everyone whispered that Killian Kane only noticed the people he meant harm.

And he'd noticed me.

But Killian randomly talking to girls, and especially girls like me, didn't happen as far as I was aware. I bet his father would have a fit if he knew his son was talking to a girl in second-hand clothes who lived in a trailer.

The Kane's were wealthy, lived in the nice part of town and belonged to the exclusive country club, and supposedly, his dad had a number of horses and played polo. Rumor was his dad owned several nightclubs downtown, and that was where he made his money.

If I didn't take the shortcut home, I passed their house, and it was stunning like something out of a fairy-tale book. Manicured lawns, five-car garage, and gardens my dad would have loved.

But I didn't think it was a fairy tale inside the massive stone house because the one time I'd seen Mr. Kane, he'd looked mean. I'd never heard anything about Killian's mom or if his mom was even around.

Mr. Kane came into the school office at the beginning of the school year when I'd been filling out what supplies we needed for the infirmary.

He hadn't hesitated or knocked on the principal's door. He'd strode in, and I'd caught a glimpse of his face when he'd looked at Killian standing in front of Mr. Merck's desk.

Hatred. It was all over his face—the sneer when his lip curled, the throbbing temples and disgust in his eyes as he'd glared at his son.

The door had then slammed shut.

Then shouting had vibrated through the office before the door opened and Mr. Kane had walked out.

Killian had been behind him, his face impassive as to whatever trouble he'd been in.

Mr. Kane's piercing eyes had landed on me, probably because I'd been staring at him with a gaping mouth.

My stomach had flipped then plummeted into a cesspool of thick sludge. The hairs on the back of my neck had darted to attention and prickles of warning had tingled across my skin.

He reminded me of the devil, the monster in the closet, and the bogeyman under the bed all in one.

He was what nightmares were made of, and I'd known that because several nights after that, I woke to those hard eyes looking at Killian with such hatred.

"The job isn't for you," Killian said. "You're going to get hurt. Don't take it."

I stiffened, pursing my lips together then tilted my chin up and flung around and said, "Well, I am." I hadn't really decided yet, but now it was a definite yes. He wasn't telling me what I was scared of. He had no clue who I was. Before today he had never spoken to me.

His brow lifted with what I assumed was surprise at my firm retort, because I bet not many were stupid enough to snap at Killian.

There was a long pause, and I nearly turned and walked away thinking he wasn't going to say anything when he said, "You won't like it."

I was so taking the job just for the fact that he said that. "You don't know what I like," I said over my shoulder.

"Sure, I do. You don't like fighting, and trust me, you won't like this," he replied.

I stopped. I wasn't sure how he knew that. Maybe because I'd never been to one of his fights when most of the students had. But again, how did he know if I had or hadn't been to a fight of his.

I turned to face him. "Why do you care, anyway?"

He huffed. "You have the wrong impression. I don't give a shit about you. I give a shit about you putting the rest of us in danger."

Whoa, I knew Killian was pissed off, but he was also an ass. "Wow, you're a jerk."

He shrugged. "And a good reason for you to stay away."

I slowly turned to face him again. "From you or the job?"

"Both."

"What are you going to do? Challenge me to a fight at the river if I don't listen to you?"

"Don't be ridiculous," he barked.

I was pissed and I rarely got pissed, but he pushed my buttons. "You know what, why don't you worry about your stupid fight rather than what I do or don't do."

He stepped closer.

I backed up and my heart skipped a beat. But I raised my chin and refused to back down from him.

"Stupid fight? Do you think it's such a stupid fight when it's your mother buying drugs from him?"

I gasped.

I was aware of my mom's drug habit, but she took prescription pills, and I thought she got them from a doctor. Still, fighting didn't solve anything, and it wasn't Killian's responsibility; it was the police's.

"Fighting won't do anything."

"Sure, it does. It makes me feel better," he replied.

"When I get angry or upset I dance." I danced before classes in the gym blaring my iPod. It was my favorite time of day.

"You dance when you're mad?"

"Yeah." Dancing was my passion and the movements filtered through me like raw emotions. Sometimes, when the music played and I was lost to the sounds through my dancing, tears trickled down my cheeks.

"How long have you danced, Savvy?"

My heart skipped a beat when he said my name. His Irish accent elongated the "a" so it sounded like "ah."

"My dad signed me up for jazz class when I was five, and I've danced ever since." I loved dancing, and I think some of that was because it was all I had left of him. He used to come watch all my recitals. I'd heard him and my mom argue about him spending money on classes for me, but no matter what, he made sure I had my dance classes. Then when I was ten, he was diagnosed with cancer, and within months he was gone.

He paused a minute as if contemplating his words before he said, "Are you any good?"

I laughed. "Not really." At least that was what my mom said. She hated me dancing, and I didn't get why. But I'd never give it up because dancing lived inside me. I wasn't currently able to pay for any classes, but I still practiced every chance I got.

My dad used to say I was his little fiery sprite. I wasn't very fiery, but I had red hair. I missed my dad every single day. I think my mom did too in her own way, and that was why she started on those pills the doctor gave her after he died. She was so different, sad all the time and well, not very nice.

"Then why bother?"

I huffed. "Wow, your jerk meter is getting higher every time you open your mouth."

There was the slightest twitch at the corner of his mouth. Or maybe I imagined it because I wished he were mildly amused.

I continued, "You've obviously mastered the art of being a dick. Maybe you should learn something new like being nice."

"No, I'd suck at it." I tried to stop the smile from emerging but failed and found myself laughing. "Easier to keep doing what you're good at."

"Like fighting?"

He shrugged.

"Maybe you'd be good at doing something else with your hands other than throwing punches."

"Mmm," he drawled, and this time I was sure I saw his lips

twitch. "Please, educate me, Savvy. What do you advise I do with these *hands*?"

I stiffened, and at the same time, my belly flipped. It was like all that anger and scariness melted away with a simple lifting of the corners of his mouth and a bright spark in the depths of his green eyes.

I licked my lips then swallowed. "That's not what I meant." I may be young and a virgin, but it was pretty clear from his tone what he was making a reference to.

I should've kept my mouth shut and kept walking.

"I know. I'm attempting to keep up with your low opinion of me. Tell me, what do you have in mind for my hands?" he asked.

I tried to ignore that sexy undertone, but it was hard with that Irish lilt he had. "Well, you play the drums, right?" He nodded. "When you're angry, you could hit them instead of people. Or maybe take up boxing or something." *Or maybe get some help.* Like my mom needed, but refused to do.

He remained quiet. Expression void. Yep, void. He wasn't angry, amused, just… nothing.

"Never mind," I muttered under my breath and went to leave when he snagged my arm and stopped me. My breath hitched, and everything in my body went on high speed.

My heart pounded so hard that the sound echoed in my head.

"No fuckin' clue, orchid," he said.

Whoa. What? I didn't care what he said. It was what he called me. I stared at him like he'd grown wings, horns, and a dragon tail. Orchid? Why did he call me orchid?

Killian Kane had a nickname for me?

And it was a nice nickname. Not like Ryan from English class who called me "sniper dream." I wasn't sure if that was because I was slightly overweight or I had red hair.

He released my arm. "You need a ride. We're at the river." Then he said in a firm tone, "There is no job for you, Savvy. I've told Sculpt the same thing."

The school doors burst open and a bunch of guys barreled out, excitedly talking about the upcoming fight.

Craig, a beefy guy, jumped on another guy's back and they nearly tumbled down the stairs. I heard him say to Killian, "How did you get out of detention so fast?"

I didn't hear a response because I quickly turned and walked away as fast as my trembling legs could carry me while trying to appear as if I wasn't running away.

"What the fuck is she doing here? I told you I didn't want her here."

This was Killian, and he was not cool with me taking the job Sculpt offered. I wasn't exactly cool with taking the job Sculpt offered either because of where it was, but the money was too good to pass up. And the fact was I wanted to prove to Killian and myself that I wouldn't run away crying.

"She wanted the job and we needed someone," Sculpt said. "I told her it's only this once."

He had. Actually, he'd said no at first, but then I begged because it was a hundred bucks an hour and I could use it for dance classes.

Besides, no one my age would refuse that.

The hitch was that the job was at an underground fight. An illegal, underground fight that changed locations every week, so the police didn't catch on to its location.

I'd never done anything illegal, and my rationale was I wasn't doing anything illegal by going. It wasn't like I was fighting or anything.

According to Sculpt, all I had to do was look after a few minor injuries after the fight, and since I had my first aid certificate and volunteered at the hospital as well as with the school nurse, I was more than capable.

I asked him if I had to actually watch the fight and he'd shrugged and told me he didn't give a shit what I did as long as I was there and could do the job.

The thought of watching the fight made my stomach curdle.

Thankfully when I told Mars about the job, she totally freaked and insisted on coming with me.

Sculpt told me the location, time, and then a warning if I called the police about any of this, he'd deal with me.

I guessed what *deal* with me meant.

Killian I didn't want to mess with, but Sculpt even less because he had the mystery factor. He showed up at school on his motorcycle looking the epitome of a bad boy, stuck to himself until the cafeteria fight with Killian that day, and then hung with the most feared guy at school.

But despite Sculpt's quietness, it didn't take long for the girls to latch onto him like bees to honey because he was really good looking and had that danger aspect about him. The difference between him and Killian was that Killian didn't like the girls around him.

And even tonight, Sculpt had chicks around him and Killian didn't, although they were certainly looking.

We were in a basement of an office building for the illegal fight, and Killian wasn't paying attention to the girls staring at him. No, he was glaring at me.

Sculpt had a pretty blonde girl on his arm who I recognized from school, but didn't know her name. She also glared at me.

I certainly didn't feel welcome, but no chance in hell was I running even though my legs were already out the door.

A hundred dollars, Savvy. Dance classes.

Sculpt nudged Killian, and both guys looked to the right where a guy came out of the men's washroom a few feet away, bouncing on his toes as he made his way to the ring.

He was huge and older. Much older. Maybe twenty-five and covered in tattoos. He was also ripped. Bulging arm muscles. Legs like tree trunks. And he wore a seriously pissed-off scowl. I also noticed he didn't wear any boxing gloves, had just wrapped hands.

Holy shit, was Sculpt fighting this guy? "Umm, you don't wear boxing gloves and a helmet or something?"

Sculpt snorted with a grin while shaking his head. He eyed Killian. "You might be right."

Killian grunted.

God, what if he really got hurt and needed a doctor? I had my first aid certificate, but I wasn't prepared for serious injuries, and that guy looked like he could do serious damage.

What had I gotten myself into? What if someone died? What if he was knocked out? Or broke bones?

"Fuck," Killian muttered then grabbed my chin, thumb bruising, and forced me to meet his eyes. "Breathe."

I inhaled a ragged breath.

"I warned you not to take the fuckin' job," he said between clenched teeth. He released my chin but remained close so his heated breath wafted across my face, smelling like mint and pine.

He had. And he was right. I didn't like this. At all. But it was a hundred bucks for an hour of my life. A hundred bucks toward dance school.

"I'm fine," I replied, straightening my spine.

"You're not fuckin' fine," he growled.

"I am," I argued.

"You hold your breath when you're scared, and you get pale as fuck. You're not fuckin' fine." Killian looked at Mars. "Make sure she doesn't pass out."

Lips firm, I glared. "I'm not going to...." I stopped because he was already moving away to talk to Sculpt.

"He looks good," Killian remarked, his focus also on the tattooed monster. "Bulky."

Sculpt nodded. "Yeah. I'll drag it out. Get him moving and tired first."

They continued talking about Sculpt's opponent while I looked around. The place was packed with mostly guys, but there were some girls, and all appeared older than us. I guessed we were the youngest here.

A lot of money exchanged hands, and the noise was loud with a constant buzz of excitement. It was infectious and even though I wasn't looking forward to witnessing my first fight, I couldn't help but feel the vibe, too.

"You want to pay attention, so you don't get killed," Killian barked.

Mars tugged on my sleeve.

Killian stood in front of me again. Sculpt was gone.

"Sorry," I replied.

"Stay in this spot. Don't go wandering or talk to anyone," he ordered.

"Can we bet?" Mars blurted.

"No!" he said, but his focus was still on me. "Do you understand, Savvy?"

I nodded. "Yeah."

"You hear sirens, don't fuckin' run with the crowd. You'll get trampled." Sirens? He must have recognized my shocked expression because he said, "Fights are raided all the time. Not a big deal if you know what to do and don't panic."

Police raiding seemed like a big deal to me, but I wasn't going to tell him that. "So, where do we go?"

"You wait for me or Sculpt. We'll get you out."

"What if you can't get to us?"

"One of us will," Killian replied.

"But you might not."

He groaned. "Yeah, if you leave this fuckin' spot, we won't. So stay here and don't panic if anything happens."

I rambled when I was nervous, and I opened my mouth to do just that and go on about the possibility that he wouldn't be able to get to us if the crowd blocked him. I was also going to point out that he wasn't Superman and able to fly over everyone to get to us.

But I never said anything because Mars knew exactly what I was going to do and latched onto my arm, shaking her head.

"We got it," she said.

Killian briefly glanced at her, back at me, then nodded just as a guy announced the fighters.

Before Killian walked away, my fingers curled into the back of his T-shirt and tugged. He peered over his shoulder at me. "Are you fighting tonight, too?"

"No." He stared at me a second then added, "I don't fight for money." His shirt stretched, my fingers slow to react as he strode away toward the ring.

We were at the back wall, near a storage closet and only a few people lingered near us. Most hovered and jostled one another to get closer to the ring.

"Kite likes you." Mars bumped me with her shoulder, grinning.

"What? Are you insane?" I blurted loudly because Sculpt and the guy, appropriately called Hannibal, got in the ring and everyone cheered.

She shrugged. "Just sayin'. Sculpt doesn't look at you like Kite does with those incredible green eyes."

"He's looking at me like that because he's mad that I took the job."

"Exactly. He's worried about you."

I didn't have time to process that when I heard the first punch. The sound was like a paddle slapping the surface of the water.

My gaze shot to the ring, as did Mars's and the conversation about Killian liking me dropped as we stared transfixed on Sculpt and Hannibal.

I didn't know whether to be mortified or fascinated by the fight. My heart pounded and knees trembled as I leaned against the wall for support.

The atmosphere was electric and deafening as they went at each other. I knew nothing about fighting, but it was obvious Hannibal was getting tired as he threw punch after punch at Sculpt, who easily dodged them and threw in the odd fist to the side of the head or gut.

I winced, and the crowd hissed when Hannibal got a good shot into Sculpt's cheek and sent him back a few steps. He lifted his head and blood dripped down his cheek from the cut Hannibal just wielded.

But it wasn't the blood that had me worried; it was Sculpt squinting his eyes and staggering. The next blow Hannibal dealt to the side of his head sent Sculpt sideways, then to his knees.

"Oh noooo," I cried.

My stomach curdled, and I bit my lip so hard I tasted blood.

"Look," Mars said, "he's getting up."

I grabbed her hand and squeezed, holding my breath as Hannibal approached the downed Sculpt.

But he never got a handle on him because Sculpt swung hard and fast as he leapt to his feet and didn't stop.

Hit after hit.

I looked away, and my eyes darted to Killian instead standing next to the ring, his expression calm and focused on Sculpt.

I hadn't expected to see him calm, especially during a fight. But it was as if the crowd, the blood, the excitement, everything vanished and there was a quiet stillness in him.

And it was beautiful. He was beautiful.

I realized that the anger he carried with him ate away all his beauty. Physically he had it, but this was different. This was the beauty inside him.

I released my breath as I watched him and then as if he sensed my eyes on him, he turned.

Our eyes locked, and there was an intense craving to have him next to me. I'd never had it before, but I knew what it was.

I liked him. Shit, I liked Killian Kane.

"Police!" There was a horrendous bang as the doors of the basement burst open.

I gasped, eyes widening.

Screams wrenched the air.

My eyes shot back to Killian and he mouthed, 'Stay,' and then he headed for us. But within seconds, the crowd swarmed him as they scrambled to get out of the basement.

"Oh, my God, Sav. Shit. My parents will kill me if I'm arrested," Mars yelled. "We have to go." She yanked on my hand.

"Killian. He said to stay here," I argued, but she was already dragging me into the herd of spooked people.

"Yeah, well he doesn't know my parents."

She didn't know his. I could only imagine what Mr. Kane would do if his son was arrested for being at an illegal fight. It would be the talk of the country club.

We were caught up in the herd and shoved through the door of the stairwell. I looked over my shoulder for Killian, eyes searching.

I couldn't see him. All I saw were blue uniforms swarming the place.

We ran up the stairs to escape the building, but suddenly everyone scrambled in the opposite direction. The police were coming through the doors at the top of the stairs, too.

"Shit," Mars yelled.

Someone pushed me from behind. My knees hit the edge of the stair and I cried out in pain. People hurdled over me, and Mars blocked them from stepping on me as I tried to get up, but I kept being pushed.

A hand grabbed my elbow, and with one jerk, I was hauled to my feet.

Killian.

"I told you to fuckin' wait," he growled. His gaze went to my knees and for a moment there was a flicker of something other than anger. "There's another way out."

He locked his arm around my waist and I clutched Mars's hand as we headed back to the basement. It was easier pushing through the herd because Killian was like a bulldozer.

We veered right as soon as we were in the room where we started, and there were people lying on the ground, hands on their heads and cops handcuffing them.

Oh, my God, we were all going to be thrown in jail. I'd never even had detention before.

Panic swarmed.

Killian's palm slammed into a door that said storage and he dragged me into the darkness.

"There's a vent," he said as he led us to the back of a large room with numerous floor-to-ceiling metal shelves.

The vent cover was already on the floor. "The other fighters already went through. We always check escape routes."

"Sculpt?" I asked.

"Don't know," he said. "He was looking for you and Mars."

God, we should've stayed where we were.

Light filtered into the storage room as the door opened. We were out of sight, but footsteps headed our way.

"Go!" Killian hissed.

Mars leaped into the vent, and I went in after her, but Killian didn't follow.

I peered over my shoulder as he replaced the vent cover. "Killian!"

"Fuckin' go," he said.

"Police. Stay where you are!"

I held my breath, watching as Killian put his hands up and moved away from the vent.

No.

"On your knees. Hands behind your head," the officer said.

Killian.

I hadn't slept all weekend worrying about Killian. On Monday I didn't see him and Mars's brother said he wasn't in class.

On Tuesday, I finally saw Sculpt after English. I ran down the hallway after him and grabbed his arm, not even thinking that it may not have been smart to "grab" Sculpt.

"Killian? Where is he? Is he okay?" I asked.

He reached into his pocket and pulled out a hundred-dollar bill and put it in my hand. "Here."

"I don't want the money." I tried to give it back because I didn't do anything, but he refused.

"Take the money," he ordered.

"Where is Killian? Is he okay?"

"Don't know." Then he walked away.

I stared at him, students veering around me as fear gripped me. He didn't know? Oh, God, where was he? He was underage so he couldn't be in jail, right? It wasn't like he killed anyone.

By Friday, Killian still hadn't made an appearance at school. I sat on the steps waiting for my mom to pick me up and every time the school doors opened, I swung around hoping that it was him.

It never was.

I waited ten minutes for my mom before making the long trudge home.

I considered taking the route past Killian's house. But it wasn't as if I'd go up to the door and ask if he was alright.

But even if I did, we weren't friends. It was the opposite. He'd been pissed at me for showing up at the fight, and it was my fault he was in trouble. I did exactly what he told me not to do. Took off when the police showed up.

I was the reason he wasn't at school. I had to stop by his house. I had to know if he was okay.

Turning to take the other route, I heard the tires squeal and saw my mom's car. She did a U-turn and pulled up on the shoulder behind me at an angle.

She honked as if I hadn't seen her.

I'd have to go to Killian's tomorrow.

I walked to the car and opened the rusted door. It squeaked so loud a flock of birds lifted out of the trees nearby.

I climbed in, shut the door and did up my seatbelt. "Thanks for picking me up, Mom."

Mom huffed, shaking her head as she looked me over with a sneer.

She was beautiful with her chic-styled, walnut hair and stark, defined features. But not when she sneered.

Here we go.

"Look at you. What the hell are you wearing? You can't wear tight stuff like that."

I gritted my teeth. I wore snug jeans and V-neck white shirt. I was used to her comments, and it didn't hurt as much as it used to, but I wasn't fat. I just carried extra pounds. But I guess compared to her, I was fat.

"And that awful hair… it's a bird's nest, Savannah. The least you can do is wear a hat and hide it if you refuse to cut it off."

Her new thing was hating my bright red curls, and it was the one part of me I really liked. But I was old enough that she didn't have a say in whether I cut it.

The red hair and pale skin I got from my dad, but his hair was browner with a reddish tinge, while mine was bright red.

The car swerved on and off the shoulder as she put her foot on the accelerator.

I tensed, gripping the door handle.

God, was she on something?

I leaned forward to get a glimpse of her eyes as she stared out the front windshield.

They were glassy. Like when she took too many of those pills.

I shouldn't have gotten in the car.

My mind reeled as my mom drove too fast, then weaved on and off the road causing several car horns to honk as she narrowly missed them.

She was talking about something, but her words were mumbled and indistinguishable.

"Mom?" I said.

She went on about her job at the diner and how she needed to work extra hours this month because she was behind on our rent again. She worked nights there, so it meant I was usually alone all night.

The car hit the shoulder and skidded.

"Mom!" I shouted.

"What?" She glared at me, and I wished she hadn't because we drifted over to the wrong side of the road.

"Mom, stop the car. Please. Stop the car. I want to get out." I didn't care if she never picked me up again. I wanted out of the car.

"I came all the way to pick you up, and now you want me to pull over?"

Oh, God, please pull over. Please stop.

Bile rose in my throat. "Mom, please, I'm going to be sick. Pull over."

But it was too late.

We were going too fast.

My mom too slow to react.

Too screwed up.

Too many reasons why we never made that curve in the road. And my last thought before the deafening sound of metal crumpling was how I'd never know if Killian Kane was okay.

I sat on the damp grass cross-legged staring at the mound of dirt where my mom was buried. There was no stone yet, the funeral officiate explained to me they had to wait until the ground settled before a stone could be placed.

Everyone had left the cemetery and was at the reception. I stayed, wanting some time alone with her. Not to say anything, just to sit with her before I said goodbye. It was the last time I'd have the chance as the social worker was taking me away today.

I brushed aside the stray tears that trailed down my cheeks.

The light drizzle clung to my hair and beaded, then dripped onto my jeans leaving dark, round marks to mix with my tears.

The breeze picked up, and one of the wild pansies I'd placed on the mound of dirt blew away. I lurched forward and grabbed it, my fingers curling around the flimsy stem.

When I straightened, the hairs on the back my neck stood. I lifted my head, eyes scanning the cemetery, but I didn't see anyone.

I lay the flower back on the mound then picked up a small stone on the pathway and placed it on the stems so they wouldn't blow away.

That was when I glimpsed movement by the river, just past the sparse tree line to the west of the cemetery.

Killian.

After the accident, I'd been in the hospital for two days with a concussion and bruised ribs and chest from the seatbelt impact. When they released me to the social worker, I'd only had time to go home and change before the funeral.

I'd been immersed in my own hell, and what happened to Killian, even though it hadn't slipped my mind, had been pushed aside.

It was the wave of relief pouring over me that made me realize how worried I'd been.

He stood on the edge of the bank watching me. Well, I couldn't be sure he was watching me exactly, but he looked in my direction, and there was no one else here.

It was too far away to see his face, but there was no question it was him. Legs braced, shoulders straight and broad, and jaw tilted up.

Confident and unapologetic for staring.

He looked away and skipped a pebble across the water then kicked at something. I gasped when his fist plowed into a tree trunk nearby.

Even from so far away it was obvious he was furious, and I wondered if it was because of me. Was he mad because I was the reason he'd been arrested?

I deserved his anger. It was my fault.

Without looking in my direction, he walked away, disappearing from view, and my heart sank. I wish he'd give me a chance to apologize. It wouldn't do much good, but it was all I had.

I didn't want to leave with Killian hating me. It shouldn't matter. I'd never see him again, but it did matter—a lot.

Turning back to the grave, I ran my fingertips through the dirt. "Bye, Mom. Love you. You're with Dad now. Maybe now you can be happy."

I stood, wiping away the endless tears with the back of my hand, then weaved through the numerous stones; some extravagant and beautiful, others simple. I pushed open the small iron gate and it groaned on its hinges then clanged shut behind me.

"She doesn't deserve your tears."

My head snapped up.

Killian leaned against a willow tree ten feet away. There was no sympathy in his eyes, unlike every other person I'd seen since her death. Instead, he looked pissed off. Although, that was nothing unusual. Except for that subtle smile on the school stairs, the anger was a staple in him.

"Killian," I whispered. "Are you okay?" It was a stupid question considering he'd been arrested and probably suffered the wrath of his father. There was also a bruise on his jaw and red marks on his knuckles that looked like cuts and scabs. "Where have you been? What happened to you?"

He snorted. "You're asking about me when you were in a car that slammed into a tree going sixty kilometers an hour?" His voice rose. "Your mom could've killed you, Savvy."

True, and I was betting a lot of kids at school were thinking the same thing. It had been on the news that she was on prescription drugs and she probably would've survived the crash if she hadn't overdosed on them.

"At the fight... I'm sorry, Killian. I should've listen to you. I panicked and ran and then you had to find me and Mars, and got caught—"

"I didn't *have* to do anything."

True. "I guess, but I'm sorry anyway."

Silence.

He ran his hand through his hair, and it was odd because it was an agitated gesture and normally he was so steady. "I fight because I have to. Nothing else gets rid of the anger." He paused. "I lost my mum, too."

"You did?"

"And my father blames me."

My eyes widened and I swiftly inhaled. "Oh, God, I'm sorry, Killian."

"Why aren't you angry at your mother for nearly killing you?" he asked.

The subject about his mother and father was closed, but I suspected what he'd told me, very few people, if any, knew because that rumor had never circulated.

"She's my mom," I said while looking at the tip of my right toe poking out of my ripped running shoe.

"A *mom* doesn't drive fucked up with her kid in the car," he stated.

"She was sad all the time and had a problem, but she loved me. Maybe others can't understand but—"

"Yeah, I don't fuckin' understand," he blurted.

No, he wouldn't if he had issues with his father. And his mother, I had no idea how she died, but I was betting it had been an accident.

"Everyone has good bits, Killian. My mom had them. They were just hard to see. The drugs and her sadness smothered them. So, my tears are for those."

It was a while before he finally said, "Bullshit. Not everyone has good bits, orchid, and you're better to learn that now."

I think he was referring to his father, but then he could've been referring to himself because I didn't think he liked who he'd become.

How could he when filled with so much anger and… pain?

"Yeah, they do," I replied. "You're not so nice sometimes, but you have them, too. I think they're just buried beneath whatever eats away at you."

Our eyes locked and something happened as the green in them softened. My belly fluttered and warmth blanketed me. It was the same feeling I had when we were at the fight before the police showed up.

I was confused by it, yet it made me feel lit up inside.

"Why do you call me orchid?" I asked.

He shrugged. "It's just a stupid nickname."

It was beautiful and I liked it. But it would be the last time I'd hear him call me that.

Tears welled. There was so much hurt inside him, and I wanted to take it all away and see him smile.

It was ridiculous why I felt this way. I barely knew him, yet I would miss him.

"What happens to you now?" he asked.

I shrugged. "I don't know. A social worker is here to take me to live… well, I don't know where." I was terrified, but I didn't want to admit that. "I better go. I have the reception." His eyes narrowed and jaw tightened. "I'm really glad you're okay, Killian. Thank you for what you did for me and Mars."

I went to rush past him when he snagged my hand, and I found myself flung back and up against his chest. His heart beat steadily beneath my palm while mine pumped madly, which I was pretty sure he must have noticed.

"What are you—"

His mouth crashed into mine, and it was the very last thing I expected from Killian.

I didn't know what to do so I stood stiffly in his arms as his mouth softened on mine, arms drawing me in tighter to him, hand sliding up my back to the nape of my neck.

"Relax," he murmured against my mouth.

His lips roamed over mine, experienced, warm, soothing, and at the same time, possessive. I sagged into him and let him guide me as my mouth opened to his urging, and then his tongue was in my mouth. Tasting. Dueling with mine.

A moan escaped my throat.

He controlled everything about the kiss. A kiss that made my body tremble and awakened something strange and wonderful between my legs.

God, it was incredible. It was my first kiss, and I had nothing to compare it with. But it was life changing because every kiss from now on would be compared to Killian's.

I felt his hardness against my abdomen throbbing against his jeans and I trembled with nervousness.

He abruptly pulled back, but didn't release me. "Not everyone is good, Savvy. Remember that."

I nodded.

He frowned. "I'm serious, Savvy. You're too fuckin' trusting. You think everyone has good in them, but they don't."

"I know."

"I'm glad you're leaving town."

I stiffened raising my chin. "Why?"

"Because if you come near me again, next time I won't let you go."

He released me and I stumbled back. Our eyes locked for several seconds before I turned and ran down the driveway to the road, fighting the urge to look over my shoulder to see if he was still there.

If he still watched me.

But I didn't. I never looked back.

There was no denying anymore that I liked him. A lot.

And I was leaving.

He was right. It was probably a good thing.

I walked to Mars's house where the reception was because the trailer was too small. I fake smiled at people I barely knew who offered their condolences, while keeping the tears back.

When I should've been thinking about my mom, I thought about Killian and all the anger inside him. It invaded. And it haunted.

Maybe even hunted him.

What I hoped was that it never caught up to him. That it didn't destroy whoever he was beneath all that anger.

After the reception, the social worker drove me to the old two-bedroom trailer to pack my stuff, not that I had much.

As I approached the door, I saw a pink ceramic pot sitting on the top of the slanted rotting stair.

I crouched and picked it up.

The pot had a thin crack in it but was nice. What was in it… well, the orchid had one long crooked stem and two droopy leaves.

Nothing else. No flower.

There was a folded piece of paper stuck in the pebbles on top. I plucked it out, put the plant down and opened it.

Killian

That was it. Just his signature, written neatly and perfectly legible.

Tucking the note into my pocket, I carried the pot to the car and set it on the floor.

Then I ran back inside the trailer and packed what little clothes I had.

On the step of the trailer where the orchid had been, I placed a note to Killian. I knew he'd probably never see it and it was why I'd been able to say what I did in my reply. I put a rock on top of the paper, the white edges fluttering in the cool wind.

As we drove away, I looked over my shoulder at the rock on the steps with the white paper. A tear slipped down my cheek at the same time as the rain began to fall.

Chapter One

Present Day

Savvy

G OD, THIS WAS SUCH A BAD IDEA. BUT I WAS DESPERATE. SIX
months out of a job, reputation ruined and my savings
dwindling, my options were limited.

I clutched the phony permit Trevor, the guy across the hall,
made me to get past concert security. Ironic the last time I did something illegal was eleven years ago when I went to the underground
fight *he* had warned me not to go to. Now I was sneaking backstage
to his concert to ask him a favor.

He's only a man, I repeated for the hundredth time. He wasn't
Zeus. He was "polite." At least that was what I'd read on social media.
But most of the articles on the rock band Tear Asunder were on the
lead singer, Sculpt, and Crisis, one of the guitarists.

I approached the huge bulky guy wearing black cargo pants and
a T-shirt who stood in front of the door. His arms were crossed over
his broad chest, and his tree trunk thighs were braced, but what I
didn't like was the fierce scowl on his face.

"You have a pass?" he asked, arms dropping to his side.

I offered a shaky smile and held out my pass. "Uh, yeah." Shit, I needed to sound more confident. "First day on the job. I'm a little overwhelmed."

He examined the pass then handed it back, and I looped it over my neck. "Well, you're late. Show's almost over."

Shit. Right. "I'm cleanup crew, but I was hoping to meet the band."

He hesitated, and I wasn't sure he was going to let me in when he said, "They're good guys." He stepped aside and opened the door into a long hallway. "Go ahead."

"Thanks." I hurried inside before he changed his mind and immediately was bombarded with the sound of the music vibrating through the building. A thrill of excitement mixed with nerves filtered through me.

Music did that to me. It was as if everything else disappeared, the overdue rent, the pile of bills, the fear that I'd lost my one chance at my dream.

But that was why I was here. I wasn't giving up on dancing. It was all I had left. The one thing that stuck with me through the loss of my dad, my mom, then the four foster homes I'd been shuffled around in until I ended up with sweet Ms. Evert with her greenhouse and flowers.

The crowd roared as the song ended, and it sounded as if the roof would come down as they cheered and stomped. Tear Asunder were amazing, but it wasn't only because they had great music, but because of the charity concerts they did like this one for a children's center. I found out the center was started by Tristan Mason of Mason Enterprise. He had been one of the most eligible bachelors in Toronto along with Brett Westhill, a commercial real-estate mogul, among other things. And the other things was why I was here.

Tristan Mason was now off the bachelor list as he was with Chess, a girl who the media still hadn't managed to dig up any info on, but there were certainly rumors. One of them being Chess had been in jail for the last ten years, and that was why no one knew of her. Another being she was a mail-order bride. Of course, they were all rumors and likely lies, much like the ones about me in the dance community.

I walked down the hallway, looking at the signs on the doors as I passed. Tons of people bustled by, but no one paid attention to me. I had no clue what went on backstage of a concert, but it was chaotic, although an organized chaos as it seemed like everyone knew what they were doing.

The sound of the crowd died down, and the band was more than likely going to be coming back stage any minute.

Shit, I was hoping to find his changing room before then. But maybe he didn't have a specific room? Maybe the band shared one?

How on Earth did Trevor convince me to do this? At the time, it sounded simple. At least it did after a few drinks and seeing the unopened bills on my kitchen table. But it wasn't the sneaking into the concert part that scared me, it was facing Killian Kane.

I turned the corner and slammed into a hard, broad chest.

"Sorry," I murmured keeping my head down and shuffling past the guy.

But I only made it one step before his hand snagged my arm and brought me to a halt. Uh-oh. "Who are you?" he asked.

Shit. Shit. Shit. "Umm, I'm cleanup crew." Did they call them a crew?

I held up my fake ID while glancing at him. I immediately knew I was in trouble because I'd seen this guy in the background of pictures of the band on social media. He was security for Tear Asunder, and if he was any good at his job, which I suspected he was, he'd know I didn't belong here. He didn't even look at my ID.

"Cleanup crew? For who?" he asked.

"This place." Oh, God, that was pathetic. "For Richard."

He snorted. "The only Richard I know is the band's manager. And I know every single name who is back here tonight." His fingers tightened on my arm. "Come on. You're out of here."

He hauled me down the hallway toward the back door. Okay,

3

I'd have to go with honesty. "Please, I just need to talk to Killian Kane for a minute."

The guy stopped so fast I banged into him and stepped on his heel. But he didn't seem to notice, or if he did, he didn't care. "How do you know that name?"

His fingers dug into my arm. "Do you mind letting go of me? I won't run. Besides, you can always shoot me in the leg if I do." He snorted, but his scowl eased as he released me.

He crossed his arms over his broad chest. "I don't have a lot of time here"—he glanced at my fake ID and his brows rose—"Sara Smith."

Trevor's idea. A generic name that wouldn't draw attention. "It's not really Sara Smith."

"Figured that," he replied. "And I need an answer."

"We were kind of friends in high school." A huge exaggeration considering Killian and I only had a few conversations, most of which weren't friendly. Well, except for the kiss. That was friendly. No, that was panty melting, heated, and hot as hell.

"Name?" He lowered his voice, "Your real name?"

"Savannah Grady." There was a subtle flicker of something in his eyes as if he'd heard my name before, but that was highly unlikely considering I hadn't seen Killian since I was fifteen.

There was a loud ruckus down the hallway, and I glanced over my shoulder. That was when I saw him.

It was like being slammed in the chest with a mallet.

My breath stopped.

My heart thumped.

My belly dropped.

Killian was no longer a kid. He was a man. I mean, I knew that. I'd seen pictures of him, but nothing could've prepared me for seeing him in person twenty feet away.

A tingling of familiarity sifted through me then a warm rush of heat.

I stepped back to lean against the wall and used it for support as I stared at him chatting with the blond guitarist, Crisis.

4

There were men, and then there were *men*, and the latter were the kind who oozed sexiness. They didn't have to be attractive physically, although Killian totally was; it was how they carried themselves, how they stood, how they wore their clothes.

It was the unassailable factor. The confidence. The indifference to what others thought of them. And Killian was all of that, just like he'd been in high school, but even more so.

Yep, Killian Kane defined Greek god.

Not perfect. Not gorgeous. Not stunning.

Earthy. Raw. Strong.

Jesus, the pictures didn't do him justice. Well, they did, but in person, my body totally reacted to him as goose bumps scattered and nerves tingled.

Tattoos covered his muscled forearms and were stark against his white T-shirt. He wore snug jeans and carried his drumsticks in his right hand with a water bottle.

As if he knew I was staring at him, his gaze shifted from Crisis to me, and I was met with Killian Kane's captivating green eyes.

"You need to leave." The deep voice barreled into me, and my head snapped around to the security guy.

"But he's right—"

"Now," he interrupted. He latched onto my forearm arm and pulled me off the wall. I saw my chance slip away as he led me down the corridor away from the band and Killian.

"Luke."

My breath hitched as Killian's voice sifted through me. I'd recognize it anywhere. That Irish accent that was smooth as butter, yet had a distinct firmness.

Luke stopped, and whether I wanted to or not, I did, too. "Kite. I'm getting rid of her."

Wow, getting rid of? As if I was a piece of garbage he was taking out into the back alley. I stiffened, raising my chin and tried to jerk my arm from him, but he held tight.

Footsteps approached, and I stopped breathing as I watched Killian's long, lean legs stride toward us. God, it was the same as in high school when he walked down the hallways, that immeasurable confidence in each step.

"Let her go," he ordered.

Luke's hand dropped, and I stepped away from the scary security guy.

My eyes flicked to Sculpt, who followed Killian, and then to the other two guys in the band, Ream and Crisis, their eyes on me curiously.

Killian stopped in front of me, and any poise I may have had shot out the top of my head. I was a bowl of jelly as my knees went weak and heart slammed into my ribs.

"Killian," I managed to whisper.

Eleven years. Eleven years since I'd stood this close to him, heard his voice and breathed in his scent.

"Savvy Grady." His eyes shifted to my fake ID, and the barbell piercing in his right brow rose. "Or should I say Sara Smith?"

I felt the heat in my cheeks, and since I was fair skinned, heat meant two pink blotches high on my cheeks. Shit. "Uh, well, I didn't get tickets in time and you weren't offering backstage passes."

"So, you made your own."

It wasn't a question. "Kind of." I bit my lip as I glanced nervously at the other guys then back at Killian. "I didn't make it myself because I have no clue how, but a friend of mine does, and he makes stuff like this all the time for people, but he did it for free since I didn't have money to come to the concert anyway and…." Oh, my God. Too much information. I was rambling. "Well, I'm going to donate to the charity when I have the money."

Killian's mouth twitched and I heard a chuckle from Crisis who was behind him to the right. Ream frowned and Sculpt looked curious, but his body was a brick wall with his wide stance and crossed arms.

"Which friend?" Killian asked.

"You don't know him."

"Boyfriend?"

"No."

"Who?"

"A guy in my building." And that was all I was giving him because I didn't want Trevor to get into trouble.

His eyes narrowed and lips pursed, appearing annoyed. I had no idea what it was like to be famous, but I guessed it was irritating when random people did stuff like this, and it probably happened often enough with all their fans.

But I wasn't a fan. I was a girl he barely knew from high school, and here I was sneaking into the band's charity concert in order to ask a favor. God, that sounded stupid and crazy. But desperation made you do things you wouldn't normally do, and I was desperate.

"You have a guy in your building making fake IDs for concerts?"

Trevor did a hell of a lot more than fake IDs for concerts, but I decided it better to remain mute on the subject.

"So who are you exactly?" This was from Crisis who was now leaning up against the wall, ankles crossed and intently watching me and Killian.

"A chick from high school," Sculpt said.

"How come we don't know her?" Ream asked.

"Because she left town," Killian replied.

"So you had a phony ID made in order to get backstage to see this asshole?" Crisis said. "Might have been easier to e-mail or even send a Facebook message."

"Why would she do that? Even you don't look at that stuff. Jolie does," Ream said.

"I scroll through them," Crisis argued.

"When?" Ream was the complete opposite of Crisis in that he had dark hair and an intensity about him while Crisis was playful.

Crisis shrugged. "We've been busy with this concert and working on the album."

"I sent an e-mail." Two weeks ago to the general inquires e-mail. I hadn't been specific, only that I was an acquaintance of Kite's from high school and wanted to speak with him. It was a long shot and as I expected, I'd never heard back.

"We should give them a minute," Sculpt, who I found out, from

7

Trevor's research on the band, was really Logan, suggested. "Good to see you again, Savvy." He offered a subtle smile and a nod then headed back in the direction they'd come.

Ream nodded to me too then followed, but Crisis remained leaning against the wall grinning. Until Killian glared at him. "Fine. But I want details." He looked at me and winked. "Savvy, come back to my place for the party. It's casual and no need for a fake ID. We'll let you in."

I smiled. "Thanks." But I wasn't here to go to a party. I was here to get a recommendation for a job. One I wanted and needed.

"Come on," Killian said, and before I knew what he was doing, he slid his hand in mine and led me down the corridor to a door and tugged me inside. The door shut behind me with a solid thunk, at least it sounded like a thunk, but was probably more like a click. Regardless, my heart leaped at the sound.

And now, I was alone in a room with the guy who kissed me eleven years ago. My first kiss. A kiss I'd compared with every single kiss since.

The light flicked on, and we were in a large office with a mahogany desk, a leather chair, and a silver filing cabinet, but that was about it.

He smirked. "So Ms. Smith, what do I owe the pleasure of this covert operation?"

Killian with a sense of humor was unexpected, and it was hot. I'd only ever known him as an angry teenager with an attitude that had been really scary. He was still scary, but it had lessened somewhat, maybe because I was no longer fifteen. "You're different."

His brow rose. "Mmm, it has been eleven years. A lot has happened."

I laughed then cringed when I heard the obvious nervousness to it. "Yeah, you're a famous rock star." Who had a tongue piercing, tattoos and a hot body.

"Does that have something to do with why you're here?"

"No. But I'm happy for you and the band. You guys are really good and deserve the success."

"Thanks." He leaned up against the door, blocking any escape route. "To say I'm shocked to see you is an understatement, Savvy. And that you went to the trouble to illegally gain entry is even more of a surprise coming from you, and I don't get surprised often." His eyes narrowed. "Are you in some kind of trouble?"

"No." Not trouble in that I had drug dealers after me or the police. "I wanted to ask a favor."

"A favor?" I nodded. "Seems to be a lot of trouble for a favor. What do you need?"

"A recommendation."

His brows rose. "I haven't seen you in eleven years. I hardly think I'm the person for a recommendation. What's it for?"

"A job. I applied, but I was wondering if you could put in a good word for me. I know it's a lot to ask since you haven't seen me in… well, a long time."

"Eleven years."

"Yeah, but I'd never ask if it would look bad on you. If you could ask if he'd take a look at my résumé? Or give me an interview? I'm better in person for this sort of thing, and I understand he is a friend of yours. God, I know it's a lot to ask and I wouldn't have if it wasn't important but—"

"With who?"

"Brett Westhill."

He remained quiet a minute, eyes drilling into me. I had no idea what was going through his head as his expression was unreadable. I shifted uneasily as I waited for him to say something.

I'd done my research and found out Brett Westhill was friends with the band. According to the articles on Tear Asunder, the band got their start at the bar Avalanche, which Brett had bartended at. Not for the money obviously, as he had more than enough to retire on a hundred times over. Brett said in one article he did it because, "It grounded him."

Brett opened an exclusive nightclub in Toronto a few months ago. A club that had go-go dancers who were the best paid in the city. The problem was, it was a hot new club and getting a job as a dancer there was slim to none. Especially since my experience dancing was not in a nightclub, but teaching modern dance in a studio.

But Compass was the hottest nightclub in the city and not easy to get into especially as a dancer in one of their cages. Trevor was the one who suggested I apply as he'd heard the tips were the best in the city. I could work there while I waited for the gossip my cheating ex spread about me to die down. Eventually, I hoped to save enough money to start my own dance studio.

When I'd applied, the guy at the door took my résumé but he said I wasn't the type they were looking for. I knew I wasn't the hottest chick in the lineup and it didn't help that I refused to show more skin than clothing when I dropped off my résumé.

"You want to work for Brett?"

"Yes."

He shoved his drumsticks in his back pocket then cracked the seal of the water bottle. He offered it to me first, but I declined, shaking my head. Then I watched as he chugged it back, his Adam's apple moving up and down as he swallowed the cool liquid. How was it possible that an Adam's apple looked sexy?

I swallowed, trying not to stare, but I couldn't help it. He placed the cap back on the bottle then met my eyes again. I chewed my bottom lip nervously because despite being fairly confident, Killian had always been intimidating as hell, and as the seconds ticked by, I became more uncomfortable.

God, this was crazy. I shouldn't be here. There were other nightclubs I could apply to, but Trevor advised me not to work in those as they weren't safe and a lot of drugs flowed through them. Word was that the girls weren't treated very well either. Compass had a strict no drug rule. Anyone caught with them, patron or staff, was banned.

The door creaked as he shifted his weight, green eyes watching me and I felt as if I was back in high school unable to move.

"I'm sorry. This was a horrible idea. I shouldn't have come."

"Probably. But you're here now."

There was a low vibration coming from his pocket, likely his cell, but he ignored it. It stopped then started again. "Do you need to get that?"

"No."

Oh. I swallowed, my throat suddenly dry as hell, and I wanted to chug back the water he held in his hand, but I didn't have the nerve to ask him for a sip.

His phone rang again.

"Someone wants to talk to you pretty bad."

"Savvy, I'm talking to you at the moment. Whoever is calling can wait."

There was no quietness about him, and his deep voice sent a wave of shivers through me. I knew who I was coming to see when I'd made the decision. But there was an uncertainty with him. I had difficulty reading him. In high school it was easy because he was always angry, but now… I couldn't figure him out.

What unhinged me was that even after eleven years, I was still attracted to him. My stomach had drunk butterflies fluttering around, refusing to make a decision on whether to be turned on or frightened or feel just plain stupid for being here.

He pushed away from the door, and his grip on the water bottle must have tightened because the plastic crackled, making me jump. God, I was never this jumpy.

It took him three strides before he was right in front of me, and the smell of soap, sweat, and cologne drifted into me. It was subtle and nice. Really nice. Killian had always smelled good, so it shouldn't have surprised me. And it didn't. It was more of an awakening to emotions that were better off being buried beneath a load of cement.

"I'll talk to Brett for you."

"You will?"

He nodded. "I assume you know something about commercial real estate?"

"Well, no."

He chuckled, and I nearly fell over because I'd never heard Killian chuckle or laugh, and it was beautiful. And yes, a man's laugh

11

could be beautiful when it sounded smooth, raspy, and had a perfect rumble to it. "Savvy, I don't think my vouch for you will do anything if you don't have experience."

"I do have experience for the job I want, but it's not in his office. It's for his nightclub, Compass."

For a second he appeared startled as his brows lifted, and then he stiffened and scowled. Any amusement was quickly tucked away. Shit, he looked pissed.

"No," he said.

"But you just said—"

"You're not working at Compass."

"Why not?"

"It's a nightclub."

"Yeah, I know."

He clamped his jaw. "You're not working at a nightclub."

"I've been dancing since I was six and—"

He jerked. "Dance? You want to fuckin' dance at Compass?"

"Well, yeah. I'm a dancer. I worked for one of the best modern dancers in the industry." I'd never be famous like David, but I loved it more than anything. Modern dance was like telling a story. There were no rules to it, just movement to the emotion of the story and the music. Dancing had helped me through the difficult times in my life, and I wasn't giving up on it. I may be inexperienced at dancing in a nightclub, but I was more than capable.

"Brett isn't hiring you," Killian ground out. "And you don't fit the job description."

Wow. That made me feel like a bug he'd just stomped on. "You can just say it, Killian. I don't fit the 'standard' appearance of a dancer."

"Savvy, don't jump to conclusions. You know I'm not like that."

"Actually, I don't. I'm sorry. This was a stupid idea." I hurried past him and headed for the door.

"Savvy."

I put my hand on the doorknob to open it when his palm hit the door above my head, clicking it closed again. "Savvy, stop."

I couldn't look at him. I knew my cheeks had to be the same color as my bright red curls and I just wanted to escape before he saw how mortified I was.

"It has nothing to do with your looks," he said quietly. "The exact opposite."

Before I realized my mistake, I turned to face him. Now, I had my back against the door with his hard, broad chest in front of me and his arm over the top as he dipped his head to peer down at me. Even though there wasn't a part of him that touched me, it sure as hell felt like it.

"Savvy." The way he said my name in a low sexy growl…. "I'll help you in any way I can, but you dancing at Compass can't happen. Do you need a place to stay for a while?"

"No, I have a place." It wasn't the nicest apartment and nothing like the one I'd shared with David in Yorkville, but I had a roof over my head. Although, I wasn't sure for how much longer as I owed two months' rent.

"Money?" he asked.

I felt sick to my stomach. Literally, sick. I may be here asking him for a recommendation with the owner of the club, but I had my pride and I'd worked hard my entire life. An array of jobs to pay for dance classes while I moved from foster home to foster home for almost three years.

I didn't come to Killian because he was famous and had money.

"I don't want your money." I yanked on the door. Of course, I was upset and didn't turn the handle first so it wouldn't open, and then I panicked and yanked harder.

He sighed, his hand leaving the top of the door so it flung open and I was catapulted back into his chest. His hands instantly settled on my shoulders to steady me, and the pulse between my thighs jolted.

"Savvy, wait."

I turned to peer over my shoulder at him, and my belly nosedived as his lips were inches away from mine.

"Jesus, you don't know what you're asking of me."

13

"I'm sorry. I didn't think it was a big deal. Don't worry about it. I'll find another way to get an interview."

His eyes narrowed and jaw clenched. "Compass is off-limits." I didn't know why he was so adamant about it, but maybe he didn't like the club. "And you shouldn't have come to see me."

God, I'd never expected him to say that. I thought maybe he'd say he didn't know Brett well enough to ask him or that he didn't feel comfortable asking, but to out and out say I couldn't work there? And that I shouldn't have come here?

Well, it looked like I was either applying at other clubs or finding another way to get into Compass.

I raised my chin and met his hardened eyes. "I'm sorry I snuck into your concert. Take care, Killian." And just like that day he kissed me, I rushed off before he could say anything more. But this time, I made the mistake of glancing over my shoulder at him as I pushed on the metal bar of the fire exit door.

I shouldn't have. I should've just kept going. I knew before our gazes clashed that his eyes were on me because I had these little heated tingles.

He stood in the doorway, hands gripping the frame above his head with the familiar angry glare. But it was different now, softer. No, not softer, quieter. Controlled.

Killian Kane may fool the media into thinking he was a nice guy, but I wasn't so sure.

Chapter Two

Killian

I WATCHED SAVVY AS SHE PUSHED OPEN THE FIRE EXIT DOOR. The moonlight shimmered off her red curls hanging down the left side of her face before the door shut and she disappeared from sight.

Shit. I slammed my fist into the doorframe.

What the hell was she doing?

Christ, she wanted to dance at Compass. Savvy didn't belong in a nightclub dancing in front of a bunch of drunk assholes who were thinking about her naked.

No chance in hell was that happening. Not while air still filled my lungs.

It was completely illogical. Insane. And uncalled for, but Savvy Grady couldn't pop back into my life then expect me to help her get a job at a club dancing. Not only a club, but a club I'd invested in and half-owned. Although, she wouldn't know that. I was a silent partner for reasons that I didn't advertise. Not yet anyway.

I ran my hand back and forth over my head then down my face. Fuck, hearing her lyrical voice dripping like honey as she'd said my name was like the wall I'd put up around me splintered and lay at her feet. She barely pronounced the harsh K, so it sounded like 'Illian. Fuck, I missed that. I missed everything about her—exactly the reason I'd stayed away from her in high school until I didn't, and that led to a kiss that had screwed with my head for the last eleven years.

I'd thought the piece of Savvy I had inside me had been erased, but a girl like her you couldn't erase. Just like an addict was always an addict, she was my drug.

I'd watched her for months in high school. The girl who offered a shy smile to everyone. Who helped out the school nurse. Who volunteered at the hospital every Sunday visiting the terminal patients. I'd found out her dad had died there, but I didn't know from what. I tried to keep myself from her, but my eyes always found her in the hallways. On her walks home. I'd even gone to school early in the mornings so I could watch her through the fuckin' tiny window in the door of the gymnasium when she'd practice her dancing alone.

And she was a good dancer. Really good. It pissed me off when she'd told me she was just okay on the school steps that day, because she was better than just okay.

I was drawn to her from the beginning, partially because we were the complete opposite. I remember wanting her back then, even just to sit with her and talk, but I was too angry and fucked up to ever have her.

Then I'd kissed her at the cemetery after her mom died. A kiss that sealed her inside me.

I clenched my jaw. Damn it, I'd warned her never to come near me again.

And now she was here, walking back into my life.

Savvy.

The girl who said everyone had good bits, but it was she who carried them. She simply handed them out to everyone she encountered. Like passing out chocolates, she passed out her good bits to people when they needed it.

Even that piece-of-shit druggie Josh whom she offered a quiet smile of sympathy when I had him up against the lockers.

She'd handed me her good bits, too. There was no choice in whether to hold onto them. Once she gave them to you, they were permanent, like she was.

Her smile. Her touch. The way she cared about people.

And even me. The asshole who never smiled or gave a shit about anyone.

That was a lie. I gave a shit about Savvy, even if I'd tried not to. Her goodness was my fuckin' drug, drawing me to her.

The truth was, she never left me. I just kept myself from her because I knew exactly what would happen—this. A possessiveness I had no control over, and I controlled everything about my life. I'd never had a girlfriend. Never wanted the attachment. Never wanted something to love and lose. I'd loved and lost the most important person in my life.

It was easier being alone. It was safer.

I chugged back the rest the water then tossed it in the bin.

Jesus, was she crazy wanting to dance at a nightclub? Compass was the safest of all of them, Brett and I made certain of that, but it was still a club, and people drank and became unruly and did things they didn't normally do.

But Savvy had been stubborn. Shit, she'd come to an underground fight, something that definitely went against her principles. I knew for a fact she'd never been to one of my fights because even if I couldn't have seen her in the crowd, I'd have felt her.

"Boss?" Luke stopped in front of me. He owned Shield Security, the company we used for our rock band. He'd helped save my life six months earlier when I'd been in a car accident with him and Haven, my band mate Crisis's wife. "All good?"

Luke was quiet, calm, and vigilant about his job and had become more than just security to all of us. He was a friend.

"Yeah." And what I liked about Luke was he didn't ask questions. I was pretty sure he knew about my past in Ireland before my father moved us here, but he never mentioned anything.

But shit with my father had resurfaced after the car accident, and my dad had contacted me when it was all over the media that I was in critical condition. And it sure as hell wasn't to wish me well.

We hadn't spoken since I was sixteen and the fuckin' memories slammed into me when I'd heard his voice. I learned to live with the memories of Emmitt and my mother, because no matter how many shields I put up, they leaked through.

But him… the anger rose again like a raging bull being baited and stabbed.

"The guys are waiting for you in the limo," Luke said.

I nodded, and we walked toward the back door Savvy had vanished through a couple of minutes ago. It was the right thing to do. Let her go. She was better to escape me now because next time, I might not be so willing.

Luke opened the door, and the cool summer air wafted into me. Fuck, it smelled like Savvy. Like that sweet scent of something flowery and exotic mixed with her coconut shampoo.

"You want a man on her?"

I knew the "her" he was referring to was Savvy, and I wanted to say hell yeah, but it was better I kept myself distant from her. If I put a man on her, shit would change. I'd want to know every-fuckin'-thing about her like why the hell she was looking for a job at a night-club when the Savvy I remembered wouldn't like to be put on display like that.

"No." But just saying no was difficult.

I could ask Deck to look into her as he had more resources than Luke. Deck was a friend of mine and owned Vault's Unyielding Riot, which according to the law was a security slash investigative company, but Deck and his men dealt with the most unsavory men in the world.

Sex trade, drugs, guns, you name it, Deck and his men had seen it. Most of his guys were ex-special forces or had training like special forces. My cousin Deaglan, who was based most of the time in Ireland, had done some work for Deck. Deaglan flirted with both sides of the law, meaning he also had ties to the unsavory.

I had to let her go. Attachments like her were dangerous.

18

My father reappearing had uprooted my past and everything I'd worked hard to eradicate from my life. Now I had a chance to hurt him, I didn't want Savvy anywhere near that. Including Compass.

I stopped beside the limo, and Luke put his hand on the door before I could open it. "If she's a security risk, I need to know."

I snorted. "Savvy's not a security risk. Unless you consider a girl who thinks everyone has good bits a risk."

Luke's brows knit. "Good bits?"

"Never mind. I'm pretty sure she won't be around again." She definitely didn't like being told she couldn't work at the club. There was that little quirk in her brows just like when I told her not to take the job at Logan's fight. Stubborn yet so fuckin' sweet. Lethal combination.

I opened the door while Luke walked around the limo to get in the driver side. I slid onto the leather seat beside Logan, and he passed me a beer. We clanged bottles then Ream and Crisis raised theirs, and we did the same.

I sat back as they chatted about the concert and the money raised for the Treasured Children's Center.

These guys were my family, along with their significant others, Emily, Kat, and Haven. My uncle had been too, but he'd died a number of years ago. He was the one who got me released from juvie after the raid.

Seven days I spent there because my father refused to get me out.

I was sure he had some judge he golfed or played polo with bend the rules so I remained locked up in juvie. I sure as hell was the only one there from the raid. Although, few parents would refuse to bail their kid out for appearing at an underground fight.

Seven days.

Ten fights.

I had swollen knuckles, a bruised jaw and cracked ribs.

The wounds were from the seventeen-year-old bully I went head to head with all fuckin' week.

My first day there, he'd shoved a kid to the floor in the hallway.

I took him to the ground and warned him not to do it again, or he wouldn't like the consequences.

He didn't listen.

He also knew when and where to jump me without getting caught. The first time was at night in the washroom when I was brushing my teeth. And it turned out he was a better fighter than me.

We fought the rest of the week. Which stopped his bullying of the other kids, but it was the first time I got the shit kicked out of me.

On day seven, my uncle showed up and got me out. An uncle I'd never met as he and my dad were estranged.

And that was it. I moved in with him and never spoke to my dad again. That was until five months ago.

"So, what did the chick want? Suck your pierced cock?" Crisis asked, laughing.

I stiffened, not liking him talking about Savvy that way. Normally, it wouldn't bother me, but today it fuckin' did. "A job," I said.

Logan's brows lifted. "Doing what?"

"She wants me to put in a good word with Brett."

Ream stretched out his legs and crossed his ankles. "Secretary? Fuck, that chick just needs to show up at Brett's office, and he'll hire her."

My jaw clenched. Brett was a player and he didn't hide the fact. I'd heard he'd had a girlfriend at one time, but ever since I'd known him, he'd played the field. Sometimes a girl would last a few days, a few weeks or even a few months, but nothing permanent. "Not at his office. At Compass. Dancing."

Crisis laughed. "Fuck. She doesn't need a good word for that either. You can hire her for Compass."

They knew I'd invested in the club and they also knew why. I didn't keep much from the guys except Crisis and Ream didn't know about my kid brother, Emmitt, and all they knew about my mother was she'd died before my father and I moved to Canada when I was thirteen.

Logan pretty much knew everything.

"I'm not hiring her."

"Why not?" Crisis asked.

Typical Crisis, needing all the answers. "She's not a go-go dancer."

"It's not stripping. And Compass is high-class," Ream said.

"He doesn't like the idea of her dancing in front of leering drunk guys," Crisis said, smirking.

It took a lot, but I shrugged. "She can do whatever she wants, except work at Compass."

I met Logan's eyes as he cleared his throat and he moved the conversation on to the party at Crisis and Haven's penthouse. It was for those involved with the charity, so Tristan Mason with his girl, Chess, who had adopted a little boy from the center, would be there, as well as Deck, Georgie, and a few other friends. There'd also be the people who donated tons of money and liked to mingle with the few celebrities coming.

I wasn't a fan of parties, clubs, or big social gatherings. They weren't my thing. I'd rather go fuckin' bowling or play some pool with a few friends. Fake smiling, small talk, and mingling, I didn't do.

I chugged my beer then leaned my head back, closing my eyes. Immediately an image of Savvy slammed into me.

Sexy. Flushed. Beautiful.

Rare. That was what she was.

And what made her even more special was that she still seemed to have no clue how rare she was.

Chapter Three

Savvy

"I CAN'T BELIEVE YOU DIDN'T GET ON YOUR KNEES AND taste some of that while you had the chance," my bestie Mars said. "Oh, my God, I bet it's pierced."

It had been two days since the concert and Killian was never far from my mind. Actually, he'd infiltrated it with his Greek god powers. And Mars wasn't helping by talking about his cock. Especially as I was pretty sure she was right and it was pierced. There was a tweak in my lower belly, and I crossed my legs under the table.

We were at Compass, and I had yet to tell Mars why we were here, except for a girls' night out. But it was far more than that.

"Can we not talk about his cock?" I raised my voice so she could hear me over the loud music in the background just as a guy passed our table.

His head turned toward me and he smirked. I quickly looked away and sipped from my straw, but my drink was empty so it made a slurping sound.

She shrugged. "Hey, it's not like you don't know him, and he's

22

freakin' hot. I can't even imagine what he's like in bed. Or against the wall or on the floor. Savvy, you so need to test drive that."

"I'm not test driving anything." I'd more than likely never see him again. It wasn't like we ran in the same circles. Rock star and starving modern dance teacher with rumors like a black cloud hanging over her head didn't mix. It didn't matter that the rumors were lies my ex-boyfriend David spread when I'd caught him in our bed with one of his students. But since he was a well-known and respected dancer, his word was pretty much law over mine.

I'd worked for him in his dance studio and we'd lived together. So, walking out on him meant losing my home and my job in one day. The bastard had actually tried to get me to stay at the studio teaching, and when I refused, he started the rumor that I was difficult to work with, among other things.

"Well you need to test drive something and if it isn't Killian or another guy then definitely a new car. I was scared the other day my feet would fall through the floor."

I laughed. "It's not that bad." But it was. I just couldn't consider buying anything until I had a job. Mars had no idea how bad it was, but since I no longer had a working cell as of yesterday, she'd know soon enough.

"Fred Flinstone wouldn't even drive it."

We were giggling when Olivia arrived with three fruity drinks that had umbrellas sticking out the top. "What's so funny?" she asked.

"Savvy refused to get on her knees and suck off Kite from Tear Asunder when he asked her to," Mars blurted.

I rolled my eyes.

"Kite? You met him?" Olivia's eyes were like saucers. "And he asked you to go down on him?"

"Oh. My. God. Nooo." I glared at Mars. "Don't start rumors."

Olivia plopped the drinks on the table then slid into the booth beside Mars. She was Mars's friend from Dwight's Interiors, an interior decorating company where they worked. Olivia was married to a nice guy, lived in the suburbs and was a total sweetheart. She also had gorgeous, thick blonde hair that always looked like she'd just came from the hairdressers, and brilliant blue eyes. She carried extra weight but carried it in all the right places, and I'd seen the guys' eyes following her when we walked through the club. They watched Mars too, who was Olivia's complete opposite with dark, shoulder-length hair. And while being slim, she walked with a sexy sway to her hips. But she was conservative in that she wore nothing too revealing.

I stirred my new drink with the straw. "The first part is accurate. I met him. But the second is definitely not."

"You know he is supposedly into kink." Mars accentuated the word kink. "And he liked Savvy in high school."

Olivia's thin pink lips formed a big round O as her eyes darted from Mars to me. "Wow. You guys went to school with him?"

"Briefly," I said. "And he didn't like me." I directed that to Mars. "He was pissed at me for going to an underground fight."

"You went to an underground fight? I didn't even know those were real." Olivia's eyes were huge and moving from me to Mars and back again while she sucked on her red-and-white straw.

Mars told Olivia the story. Wide-eyed, she was captivated; Olivia had grown up in a small town in Northern Ontario and going to an illegal fight was completely out of her element.

What I'd never told anyone, even Mars, was about that kiss at the cemetery. I probably would've if I hadn't left town, but when it happened, I'd been upset about my mom, scared about what was going to happen to me, and couldn't even process what happened with Killian.

Mars and I lost touch for a few months while I was shuffled around by social services to different foster homes until I ended up with Ms. Evert. She was the one who helped nurture the orchid Killian had given me. It finally bloomed a beautiful red, and I still had it sitting on my kitchen windowsill in the same cracked pink pot. It was the only thing that I'd taken with me from home to home. Although, I wouldn't call them homes; they were more like pit stops until Ms. Evert. But she'd passed away five years ago and even though I hadn't known her long, she'd been my only family.

"Are you going to date him?" Olivia's long blonde hair slipped

24

over her shoulder and half laid on the table as she leaned forward sipping her drink.

Mars huffed. "Kite doesn't date. And I heard he makes the women he fucks sign a nondisclosure agreement. Oh, and he's never been seen with a girlfriend. Besides, Savvy would never be gagged, tied up, and spanked."

Olivia choked on her drink and spat out her straw. "He's into *that*?"

"Mars, you don't know that. The media exaggerates."

Mars shrugged. "Why would they make that up?" She put up her hands. "Just sayin'."

I'd never done anything like that, and David was pretty routine when it came to sex. Boring might be the optimal word. Looking back, the sex had become nonexistent, not because we were busy teaching at the dance studio, but because he was busy with one of the students who he was now living with.

The idea of Killian tying me up, him naked and hovering above me, those magnificent green eyes smoldering as he thrust his hips and… I sucked too hard on the straw and choked on the cool fruity liquid.

God, I had to stop thinking about him. My emotions were all over the place. Turned-on. Nervous. Excited. And a little pissed off that he wouldn't put in a good word for me with Brett Westhill.

I couldn't piece it together why he didn't want me to work at Compass. It was a classy nightclub and—

"So he flat out refused to speak to Brett about working here?" Mars asked.

I leaned back against the booth's cerulean blue backrest twirling my glass. "Yeah."

"Ass," Mars mumbled.

"Well, I had snuck into his concert, and he doesn't know how good a dancer I am. He offered me money instead."

"That was nice. Did you take it?" Olivia asked.

I huffed. "God, no. I'm not taking money from anyone. I've made it this far without help." I'd worked ever since I was sixteen.

First job was as a waitress at a diner my foster parents owned. The second I was a cashier at a clothing store, and third was at a coffee shop. Then I worked for Ms. Evert in her greenhouse looking after her flowers.

I loved that job and she paid me well, so I managed to save some money and continue dance classes. It wasn't until Ms. Evert passed away and I moved back to Toronto that I obtained my teaching certificate and met David at his studio.

Mars plopped her drink on the table. "It's not like he'd miss it."

"That's not the point and you know it. And it wasn't like we were friends or anything." He just kissed me and infused himself in me for all eternity. He probably didn't even remember. But for me, there hadn't been a guy since who measured up to that kiss.

"So what are you going to do?" Olivia asked.

I nodded to one of the cages on the pedestals that were in the four corners of the dance floor that were for the paid dancers. "Dance in one of those tonight."

Olivia gasped. "What?"

Mars laughed and slapped the table with her palm.

"If I can't get an interview, then how can they see how good I am?" My heart pattered faster and faster like someone being walked up to a sacrificial altar. I'd never done anything so daring before. But it seemed I was on a roll this week.

"Are you insane? You'll get kicked out. Banned." Olivia blurted the words so loudly that a few guys standing at the bar ten feet away stopped talking and looked over at us. And when they looked, it was with interest as they each smirked, raising their glasses.

I ignored them. Mars smiled. Olivia didn't even notice them.

"I say do it. What do you have to lose?" Mars looked at my plain black V-neck dress. "But I hope you have something else to wear."

"She can't," Olivia said, then turned to me. "You can't."

I took another sip of my drink, hoping the alcohol would settle my nerves. "Compass is the hottest club in the city and has the best dancers. Trevor says they're paid a lot of money. I could make in three nights what I made in two weeks at the studio."

"But why can't you just make them give you an interview," Olivia murmured, knowing full well that was illogical.

"Olivia," Mars said, "on paper she has the dance skills, but they don't want those skills. They want sexy-as-hell-get-men-hard and stay-all-night-buying-drinks skills." Mars stirred her drink. "But, Savvy if you're short on cash, I can help out."

Mars knew this wasn't my thing. I didn't like being the center of attention and dancing in a cage on a pedestal put me front and center.

Trying to flirt with the guys was a problem, but I was hoping my dancing skills made up for my lack of flirt ability. What I liked about Compass was the dancers were decently dressed, and the cage offered protection against any fondling or touching by any drunk patrons. I watched one of the girls hook her leg around a bar and arch over backward, her long hair touching the floor. She smiled then winked at one of the guys watching her. An inner thrum of excitement sifted through me at doing something so… well, provocative.

"Can I buy you girls a drink?"

I glanced up at the guy who had been standing at the bar with his buddies. My gaze trailed to the bar and the three friends watching. He was good looking, tall, lean, dressed in dark jeans and a navy, V-neck T-shirt that hugged his broad chest.

"Sure," Mars said at the same time I said, "No, thank you."

He glanced at Mars then back to me, his dirty-blond hair falling forward in front of his eyes. He grinned, showing off his perfect white teeth and dazzling smile. No wonder his friends had picked him to come over and ask us. He was cute, but I wasn't interested in dating or otherwise with any guy. Trusting a guy again wasn't going to be easy. For now, all I was interested in was getting my life back on track—without a guy in it.

"We're actually just going to dance," I said. It was close to eleven, and I had to change in the bathroom before I slipped inside one of the cages. Trevor told me the dancers went on a ten-minute break at the same time as the DJ at eleven-fifteen.

"Right." Mars winked at the guy. "Sorry, sexy, but we have a covert operation going down."

His brows dropped in confusion and then he shrugged. "Uh, yeah, sure. Maybe later."

"Definitely later," Mars said.

He grinned then headed back to his friends while I slipped out of the booth with my over-sized purse that held my outfit.

"I have to change. I need one of you to come get me in the bathroom when the dancers leave their cages."

Mars held up her hand. "I'm in."

Before I had the chance to rethink my decision, I darted through the crowd toward the washroom. The music pumped, the floor vibrated, and there was a lively energy in the club. An energy I'd need because my nerves were locking my limbs and I'd land flat on my face if I didn't pull my shit together.

I could do this.

I was good at this.

Well, I was good at dancing. Being sexy, not so much, but wearing a mask would help with any inhibitions. No one would know who I was. I'd become someone else just like I did when I danced. I told a story. Tonight would just be a story I'd never told before.

And it wasn't like Compass was a dive. It was a prestigious club.

I slipped into the bathroom and into a stall and quickly changed from my plain black V-neck dress to the sexy outfit I'd brought.

"Savvy," Mars called. "Come on. The girls just left the cages."

I took a deep breath, undid the latch of the stall and stepped out. The two women standing at the sink redoing lipsticks glanced at me in the reflection of the mirror.

"Holy shit, Sav, you look smokin' hot," Mars said.

"Thanks." I wore a blue sequin unitard that had a mesh mock neck and slim leg fit. I had on black strappy stiletto heels and had taken my hair tie out, so my long red ringlets hung down my back and over my shoulders. But what completed the look was the satin black cat mask I wore with tiny pearls along the outer rim.

It was the sexiest dance performance outfit I had. I normally danced in bare feet, so the heels were a challenge. But when I'd looked up images on the Internet of the dancers at Compass, they'd all been wearing heels, so I had to wear them.

Turning toward the mirror, I popped off the lid of my deep ruby-red lipstick and leaned forward, applying it over the pink gloss I'd been wearing.

"Oh, man. The guys are going to blow their loads over you," Mars said, watching me in the reflection.

Using my fingernail, I fixed the small smudge at the corner of my mouth and then stepped back. I barely recognized myself in the mirror, and I kind of liked the look. It was sexy, and I liked being sexy.

She took the lipstick from me, put the lid back on, and grabbed my purse where I'd stuffed my clothes. "Come on. Let's get you a job at Compass."

She tugged on my arm and I stumbled in the stiletto heels. Shit, I'd have to practice dancing in these if they hired me.

"You're sexy as hell and an incredible dancer," Mars said. "Just don't think about anything but the music." Her voice rose as the music blared when we came out of the washroom.

Little sparks flared across my skin. Dancing in a cage with the roar of the music and people all around had a certain thrill to it. It was nothing like in a studio with students watching or even on stage when I'd done a few minor roles in small budget plays.

Dancing to me was like jumping off a cliff and having no idea where you were going to land, but it didn't matter because you were flying and free.

It was being fearless. No problems. No restrictions. No tomorrow.

Dancing was the only place I felt as if I had no inhibitions and could just be me.

"That one." Mars pointed to one of the empty cages.

We weaved through the crowd to the cage on the white platform with five steps up. There was a red velvet rope across the stairs.

"Go," Mars hissed when I hesitated. "Security." She shoved me forward, and I stumbled up the steps and climbed over the rope. "I'll distract him."

I glanced over my shoulder to see a huge guy who looked like he could carry five two–hundred-pound men out of the club with ease. His gaze was locked on me as he shouldered his way through the crowd toward us.

Shit. I quickly opened the cage door and stood there for a second, frozen. Could I really do this? Did I want to? Did I have a choice? I could find a job in a clothing store or waitress or something, but I wanted to dance.

I couldn't imagine doing anything else. Besides, the money at Compass beat all those other jobs.

I closed my eyes, and the crowd faded out as I began to move to the music. It took a few minutes and then it happened. The world no longer existed. Nothing did except my body alive and tingling with exhilaration as I danced, letting the beat vibrate through me.

It didn't matter that I was in a club. What mattered was I was dancing and I loved it.

I heard the catcalls and cheers and inwardly smiled. And I'd never felt sexy before. Even dancing with David in the studio doing demos for students, I hadn't felt sexy. It had always been all about him, and I'd been worried about doing something wrong. He never wanted to look bad in front of his students.

I grabbed the cage bars as I shimmied down to a crouch, smiling at the men surrounding the cage who watched me. I noticed the security guy standing with Mars at the steps of the cage glaring, but he made no move to force me to leave.

I danced until my skin was damp with sweat. I wasn't tired. Actually, I was just warming up when I saw the dancers return.

I slowed my body, smiled at the guys watching me, then opened the cage door. The group of guys whistled and cheered, and two of them came over to talk to me when I walked down the steps, but the security guy blocked them.

"Nice moves," the girl, whose cage I'd hijacked said, smiling.

"Uh, thanks," I replied. "Sorry about stealing your cage. But I was hoping to gain enough attention to maybe have a chance at a job here."

"Oh, you gained attention. Talk to Frankie upstairs. She hires the dancers. Tell her Bree sent you."

My chest swelled as I pulled off my mask. "Oh, my God, thank you."

She shrugged. "No problem. Any girl who just did what you did deserves a chance." She nodded to the stairs on the right of the bar. "Frankie is in the VIP section. She and the boss saw you."

Boss? My eyes widened then darted to the VIP section. Brett Westhill was here? Had he seen me? Was that good or bad? I could only hope he'd seen me and liked my performance.

Bree opened the cage door. "Come by Wednesday afternoon at two. We go over our routines with Frankie." Bree raised her voice. "Hey, Greg. Let this girl pass on Wednesday. She needs to see Frankie."

The security guy in the black T–shirt that had Compass scrolled in white on the top right corner nodded to Bree, but he was scowling. He looked unimpressed with my little incident.

Mars passed me my purse then grabbed my hand excitedly, jumping up and down. "Oh. My. God. You were incredible. Amazing. Sexy as hell, and I swear you made a few guys come in their pants." Gross, but I smiled, acknowledging the compliment, and I loved it. "Even Greg here was drooling. Weren't you, Greg? Wasn't she amazing?"

His scowl hadn't let up, but there was a brief flicker of amusement in his eyes. "I'll have to escort you ladies out of the club." He glared at me. "No matter how good you were, you broke a club rule, and that's not tolerated."

"Yeah, okay." I was getting a chance at the job and didn't care we were being kicked out.

He ushered us off the dance floor, and a smiling Olivia met up with us, her eyes sparkling as she went on about how amazing I was.

Greg's cell vibrated as he opened the back door for us to leave. He put it to his ear. "Yeah?" He didn't say anything for a second, but his eyes darted to me. Olivia and Mars had stepped outside, but I didn't get the chance as Greg snagged my arm.

"Sure thing, Kite."

What? Kite? Did he say Kite?

He tucked his phone away in his back pocket. "Need to take you upstairs."

Oh, fuck. "Did you say Kite?" God, please say no.

Mars and Olivia turned, realizing I wasn't walking with them. "What's wrong?" Mars asked.

"Need to take her upstairs," Greg stated. "You girls can wait here." Mars and Olivia came back inside. "Give her ten minutes. You're not here when we get back, I'll put her in a cab."

"We'll be here," Mars proclaimed, and Olivia nodded.

He pulled me away from the door, but my feet weren't moving, so I stumbled. "Did you say Kite?" My voice cracked on his name.

He ushered me toward the stairs that led to the VIP section. I had to have imagined him saying Kite. What were the chances he'd be here tonight, two days after I talked to him about working here?

But if he was friends with Brett, then he could be here. He could've seen me and that was why he asked Greg to bring me upstairs.

"Listen, Greg, I…." My mind whirled for some kind of plausible excuse, but I couldn't think of anything that would prevent him from dragging me upstairs.

A girl brushed by me, clutching her stomach and running for the washroom, and I knew exactly what to do.

"I don't feel so great." I staggered, and he turned to me as I bent over, holding my stomach. "Oh, God, I think I'm going to be sick."

From the corner of my eye, I saw his face blanch. Yep, no guy wanted to see a chick throw up in the middle of a club. Especially not the guy currently responsible for me.

"Fuck," he muttered and hauled me through the crowd to the women's washroom.

I put my hand over my mouth and groaned. He slammed his palm into the washroom door. "I'll wait here for you."

I disappeared inside, and the second the door closed, I ran into a stall, took out my black V-neck dress and flats that were sticking partially out of my purse and quickly changed.

Grabbing a wad of toilet paper out of the stall, I wiped the red lipstick from my mouth then put the hair tie back in.

I came out of the stall and looked at myself in the mirror. Plain. Unsexy. Unnoticeable.

Perfect.

I hitched my purse over my shoulder and came out of the washroom keeping my head down. From the corner of my eye, I saw Greg look up, straighten then lean back against the wall when he realized it wasn't the girl with the flowing red ringlets and unitard.

I hurried through the crowd and toward the back door. Just before the hallway, I chanced a glance up at the VIP section. That was when I saw him.

Killian. Holy shit. He stood leaning his hip against the glass railing.

He was talking to a girl with jagged, short blonde hair with tattoos down one arm. She wore a tight, sequined, black, spaghetti-strapped top and looked to be in her late twenties.

Her hand rested on his arm as she said something and he laughed, his head tilting back as he did it. I was too far away to hear it, but I didn't need to. He looked good enough laughing without any sound. That was a good sign. It meant he'd probably not recognized me in the cage.

Killian's eyes shifted from the girl, into the crowd below as if he'd known I was standing there. Any remnants of a grin disappeared, and his eyes narrowed.

Shit. Shit. Shit.

I backed away then spun, banging into a guy. I muttered a fast apology and then as fast as I could, I ran for the back door.

Mars and Olivia were leaning up against the brick wall talking to one of the bouncers.

"Let's go. Now." I hurried out the back door and down the alley, not waiting to see if they followed me.

Mars jogged up beside me on one side and Olivia the other. I waved my arm out to a cab and it pulled over. Thank you, Toronto cabbies. You never had to go searching for a cab in this city.

We piled in and I gave him Mars's address as she was closest to the club.

"What's wrong?" Mars asked. "Something happen? Did you get in trouble?"

I shook my head. "No."

Mars brows furrowed with concern. "You're shaking."

Because he did that to me. I had no control over my body around him, and it was utterly ridiculous. I felt ridiculous, damn it. I'd never felt this way with David. There were butterflies in the beginning and he'd been my instructor, so I was a bit in awe of him. Plus, David Knapp was handsome and a charmer. But it had taken a year of him asking before I agreed to date him.

"Killian was there."

"Oh, shit," Olivia said. "Did he see you?"

"I'm not sure. It was far away and it was crowded, so maybe he didn't know it was me." He totally knew it was me, but there was that smidge of hope he hadn't recognized me.

"So what if he did," Mars replied. "You're out with your girls at Compass. Nothing wrong with that."

True. And I wasn't in the dance outfit. "Yeah." And if he happened to be watching while I danced, he'd have never known it was me while wearing the mask and outfit.

What worried me was that there was a part of me that hoped he'd seen me dance and that maybe Killian Kane thought I was sexy.

Because no matter how many years it had been, or what he'd said to me at the concert, my lips still burned for him.

Chapter Four

Killian

"SO, WHAT HAPPENED WITH THAT SAVVY CHICK? YOU seeing her again?" Crisis asked as he came out onto Logan and Emily's patio, holding two beers. He passed one to Ream then cracked the cap on his and the bottle hissed. "You talk to Brett about hiring her?"

He knew damn well I hadn't, but Crisis loved to press buttons, and he'd found my button—Savvy. I'd gone to Compass the other night and talked to Brett about her, but it sure as hell wasn't to hire her.

I'd arrived just as Brett was arguing with Frankie about some girl in a flashy blue outfit who had danced in one of the cages when the paid dancers went on break. Frankie wasn't happy about it, but Brett was more lenient and wanted her found so he could talk to her.

My guess he wanted to do a lot more than talk. I saw Greg escorting the girl out of the club and decided to end the argument by asking Greg to bring the girl upstairs.

But it never happened. Greg called me back and said she'd taken off. That was when I swore I saw Savvy on the dance floor. But in the crowd and dim lighting, I couldn't be sure. Before I could do any-thing, she was gone.

Crisis swigged his beer then set it on the patio table. "What's the story with her?"

"No story." But there was a story.

When I thought of Savvy, it was like peering through a stained glass window. A multitude of beautifully ornate colors that didn't al-low me to see to the other side. Nothing was clear and defined when it came to my emotions with her. But fuck, it was beautiful.

The issue was I liked clear and defined, and she fucked with that. And why it was better she stayed away from me.

"There's a story," Ream said under his breath.

"The story is we need to decide about our next tour," I said.

We were at Logan's having a band meeting. Richard was on my case about touring, and we never decided on anything until we dis-cussed it as a group.

That meant we all had to agree or it was a no go.

This royally pissed off our manager, Richard, as he thought we should do whatever *he* thought was a good idea.

"We have to decide this today," I said, looking at each of the guys. "We do another charity concert in October. We all agree on that?"

Everyone nodded, except Logan who wasn't paying attention. Instead, he stared at the surface of the pool. Tear, Emily and Logan's German shepherd, lay at his feet snoring, but one eye flicked open once and a while as if to make sure Logan was still there.

I continued, "We finish the album in the next eight months then go on tour."

"Fuck, man. I'd rather talk about that chick you're interested in," Crisis said. "And we've done enough tours for a while."

Crisis didn't want to leave Haven, especially since she was preg-nant and by the time we went on tour, she'd have had the baby. But touring after an album released was good business, and the fans liked to see us in concert.

Ream slowly turned his beer on the table. "Kat's art gallery is expanding next year. I'd like to be around to help her out, and we're trying to have a baby."

Crisis shifted his chair, and the metal scraped the patio stones. "Richard can go fuck himself. We need a break from touring."

Sitting back in my chair, leg casually resting over the other, I addressed Logan. "What do you think?"

He didn't say anything and was still staring at the pool, his brows furrowed. Logan was the band, and it meant everything to him. He was originally the one who pushed us to go on tour. The underground fighting he'd done was to make money for us to actually tour in the first place.

I may deal with the business side of the band, but Logan was the glue. He kept every single one of us on the same page.

He also had a shit past, and a dad who was a hundred times worse than mine. He'd suffered a fuck of a lot emotionally and physically to save his girl, Emily, from the bastard's sick sex trafficking ring.

There was nothing in this world Logan wouldn't do for her. There was nothing he hadn't done. And from the look of his dark, anguished eyes, whatever was bothering him had to do with Emily.

"Logan?" This was from Ream.

Logan dragged his gaze away from the pool and looked at each of us.

Fuck. It was bad. "What's up?" I asked him.

Crisis and Ream looked from me to Logan, instantly aware that this wasn't about touring.

"Eme had a miscarriage," Logan said.

"Christ," I said.

"Shit. Is she okay?" Ream asked.

Logan nodded. "It was a couple of weeks ago, but…." I stiffened, not liking he waited so long to mention it. His jaw clamped and his eyes grew dark. "It scared the shit out of me." We were silent as he leaned forward, elbows on his knees, head in his hands. "I found her in the barn on the floor and… the blood." Logan closed his eyes. "Fuck, I thought I was going to lose her."

Jesus. "What did the doctor say?"

Logan sighed. "The doctor wants to run tests, but"—he lifted his head—"I won't risk her life for a baby."

If anything happened to Emily, it would destroy him, and I suspected he'd never come back from that. Not after what they'd fought in order to be together.

There was silence for a few seconds, just the sound of Tear as he rose and walked to the pool and lapped at the water.

I pushed my beer aside. "Family first. No tour next year. We'll write songs. Record. A few local charity concerts."

Crisis nodded. "Sounds good."

"Yep," Ream said.

"Thanks, guys," Logan said. "We can talk to Matt and do a few shows at Avalanche through the year. And at Molson Amphitheatre."

Molson Amphitheatre was downtown Toronto. It was an outside venue with the cheap seats on a massive grass hill. When we were in our late teens and a struggling band, we'd been there countless times to see concerts.

"Okay," I said. "I'll tell Richard the news. Tomorrow. I don't feel like dealing with his bullshit today."

Crisis slapped his palm on the table. "So, are we going to see this concert crashing chick around?"

I stiffened, not liking him calling Savvy a chick. Fuck, she wasn't some chick.

She'd never been some chick.

"No."

"Why not?" Ream asked.

"Because I don't want her around." But it was the opposite. I did want her around, and that was fucking with my head.

"She been to your dungeon?" Crisis asked, smirking.

"No. And she won't." He was referring to my warehouse. When I moved out of the penthouse I'd shared with Crisis and Haven, I'd bought a warehouse down by the docks. Large empty space with a punching bag, set of drums, and a few essentials. It was disposable.

So was everything in it, which wasn't much. It could burn down tomorrow, and nothing would change because I had nothing to lose.

Private. Simple. Uncluttered.

There'd been so much clutter in my head growing up that it constantly felt as if it would explode, and it had. It had exploded into fighting other kids. The bullies. The kids who'd tormented others. But it was more than that. Every time I'd fought, I'd been hitting my father.

It was his blood I'd spilled.

My fuckin' dad's comments. The pictures of my brother being shoved in my face as he'd shouted at me.

The hatred blazing in his eyes.

I'd wanted to hurt. To fight and feel the pain. Because in some ways, it had been my fault.

I always watched out for him. Until I didn't.

"You seeing her again?" Logan asked.

I lifted my head. "No."

Crisis jumped on that. "Why not? You've never given a crap about a chick. What's with her? And why do you care if she dances at Compass?"

"Drop it, asshole."

He held up his hands, but his eyes were filled with mischief. "Hey, it's my turn, buddy. You were on my case about Haven."

"That's because you were texting her behind Ream's back." And payback was a bitch. "Weren't you in bed with Haven when her brother came in the room before you were together?" I turned to Ream. "He told me you sat on the bed while he was between her legs under the covers, and you never knew."

Ream's temples throbbed. "What the fuck?" He glared at Crisis who wisely pushed back his chair ready to bolt. "You were doing that shit to my fuckin' sister when I was in the room?"

"Shit, no. It wasn't like that," Crisis blurted. "You're a dick," he said to me.

"Should've left the Savvy conversation alone," I said.

"Yeah, well, game on," he said.

These guys had helped save me. The band. I sat, laughing and dicking around with them because this is what it was about. They gave me a family when I'd lost mine. When I'd been so fuckin' angry at the world, including at myself, yet they hadn't judged or questioned. Instead, they'd let me deal with whatever was fucking with me until I'd got my shit together.

Ream suddenly dove for Crisis, and beers and chairs toppled over as Crisis leaped out of his away.

The dog jumped up at the commotion, barking at Ream and Crisis.

It took two seconds before Ream tackled Crisis, mostly because Crisis was laughing so hard he couldn't run, and they both fell into the pool.

This was a regular event between them. They weren't blood brothers, but they were brothers in every other way.

They dunked one another under while the dog stood on the edge of the pool, wagging his tail watching. Then apparently having had enough of watching, it did a belly flop into the pool and tried to get in on the fun.

"She's important to you. Saw it then. See it now," Logan said.

"Yeah."

"You going to do something about it?"

"Nope. Wouldn't be good for her or me."

"You sure about that, Kite?"

I remained quiet. No, I wasn't sure. I was back then, but now....

Fuck, I couldn't stop thinking about her.

She'd been embedded in me since the first time I saw her that day in the school infirmary. I'd never looked in there. Didn't care who was in there or why.

But her long red curls had been a beacon and I'd been the lost ship looking for a way out of the angry, stormy sea of emotions.

So, I'd looked, had stopped walking and stared at her. She'd been sitting on the edge of a chair, her hands resting quietly in Daniel Hennessey's as tears streamed down his face. There'd been a tissue in his lap with blood on it and a smear still visible under his nostrils.

Savvy had spoken quietly to him, but I hadn't heard her. I hadn't needed to though. I'd seen it on her face. The compassion. Not pity. No, she didn't have the puppy-dog sad eyes. Instead, there had been determination on her face mixed with understanding.

Daniel had been new at school, like Savvy, although at the time I hadn't known her name. Daniel had a stutter as I'd heard a few kids talk about him. I'd known what was coming for Daniel as I'd known better than anyone how cruel kids could be.

As I'd watched them, she'd plucked a new tissue from the box and handed it to him. He'd wiped his tears and then she'd drawn him into her arms, and it was like all the tension drained from Daniel as he'd sagged within her cocoon of warmth and kindness.

I'd been unable to look away—from her. This girl with the red curls and warmth radiating from her.

When she'd pulled back, there hadn't been sadness in her eyes, there had been strength and she'd offered it to Daniel.

I'd noticed him struggling to get his words out, and she'd listened, nodding. No frustration. No interruption. No attempting to finish sentences for him.

She'd just listened.

My chest had swelled.

When I'd finally broken away from the scene, I didn't go to class where I'd been headed. Instead, I'd walked down to the river and skipped pebbles across the smooth surface.

I hadn't known her name. But it was the first time I'd ever wanted to know more about someone since my brother's death.

And that was when I began to watch her. It hadn't taken me long to realize her soothing quiet eased the anger in me.

As weeks turned to months, I'd liked her even more. She didn't conform to fit in with the other girls. She simply was herself. There'd been forgiveness in her. Kindness and sympathy.

She became that beautiful, coveted orchid that I could never have.

Logan slapped me on the shoulder. "Hey. If you need to fight, let me know."

He knew playing the drums helped with my anger, but even more was the punching bag or when we sparred together. The most recent being after my father had called.

I nodded. "Thanks. Might take you up on that."

Normally, I had control. Steady. Easygoing. Nothing unsettled me. But this shit with my father and now Savvy brought back everything I'd buried a long time ago.

The dog swam after Ream, paws scratching his back as he paddled away from him. "Shit. Tear. Fuckin' Kat will break my balls if she sees scratches all over my back."

Logan chuckled.

I didn't. I was thinking about the thank-you note Savvy had left on the steps for me under the rock. Some of the words had been smudged from the rain, and it was crinkled and torn, but I still had it. The only personal thing I'd kept from back then. Now, it sat in the nightstand drawer with the same rock.

Chapter Five

Savvy

"N AME?"

"Savvy. Bree, one of the dancers, told me to see Frankie, but I never told her my name."

The security guy smiled. "Right. Hijack."

"Hijack?"

"You hijacked the cage."

I offered a tentative smile. "That would be me."

"I'm Jacob." He opened the club door. "Piece of advice," he said before I disappeared inside. I turned to look at the bulky guy. He looked to be about twenty and had tattoos covering every visible inch of skin showing, except his face. "Don't let Greg see you. He's still pissed you deaked out on him Saturday night." He chuckled. "Doesn't help that we roosted him on it. Boss man wasn't too happy with him though."

I felt bad about that. I didn't want Greg to get in trouble. I'd have to apologize.

"Thanks for the advice, Jacob."

"Sure thing," he replied and shut the door behind me.

I stood in the foyer of the club, expecting it to be dirty and unattractive without the nighttime glow from all the blue lights. But the place was spotless, with clean stone floors and charcoal gray walls that had a shimmery effect on them. As I walked into the bar and dance floor area, I saw the four ornate floor-to-ceiling columns standing in a circular display around the dance floor, reminding me of a Greek arena. The cages were beside each column on pedestals and my skin heated thinking about dancing in there.

I heard voices and my gaze directed to the stairs up to the VIP section. Three women descended while chatting, and I stopped.

"Frankie, come on." It was Bree. "One Saturday. It's important."

"Everything is important to you," the woman replied. It was the gorgeous woman I'd seen talking to Killian, who I guessed was Frankie, the woman who hired the dancers. "You had last Saturday off."

"And another in May," the third girl chirped as she stepped off the last stair.

Bree sneered and shook her head, mimicking her by mouthing the words. I smiled liking Bree immediately. She reminded me a bit of Mars. She didn't look like she'd take much shit from anyone.

"God, he's going to have a shit fit," Bree muttered.

Frankie had her hand on the railing as she turned to look at Bree. "You need to dump that asshole. He's a useless piece of shit who does nothing but feed off you."

Bree's shoulders slumped. "I know. I know. But he's fun."

"He's fun because he's not stressed. Because he doesn't work and lives off his girlfriend—you"—Frankie put her hand on Bree's arm, and her face softened—"kick him to the curb, baby. Then we can go out and celebrate. Drinks will be on me."

Bree hugged Frankie. When she pulled away, she noticed me standing at the entrance. "Hijack. You showed. Come meet Frankie." She paused and said halfheartedly, "And Tabitha."

"Tab," the other girl corrected.

I walked onto the dance floor, my heels that I was forcing myself to wear every day, clicking over the polished stone floors.

All eyes were on me and my pulse raced as I felt my cheeks flush. It was unnerving to be scrutinized, and it was scrutinized because Frankie was looking me up and down probably deciding whether I looked good enough to dance, while Tab was scrutinizing, no doubt evaluating the possible competition.

"Hey." I waved when I drew closer. "I'm Savvy."

Bree skipped over and put her arm around me. "Frankie, this is the girl from Saturday night."

Frankie approached, and I was a little intimidated, okay, a lot intimidated. When she walked, it was with presence, her shoulders back, chin up, not too much, just enough to let a person know not to fuck with her. This was the kind of woman Killian would totally go for, confident and self-assured just like him.

She held out her hand. "I'm not sure if this is a pleasure or not considering you danced in one of our cages and then snuck out on Greg."

I had debated a million times over whether to come, but I had nothing to lose. At least by showing up, there was a chance I had the job. "I'm so sorry." I didn't want to lie and tell them about Killian, so I avoided. "I know I broke a club rule, but I just wanted a chance. A piece of paper doesn't show what I can do."

"Club rules aren't to be broken—ever. Got it?" Frankie said, frowning.

I swallowed, nodding.

Bree laughed. "Don't worry. You're not getting arrested or banned from the club or anything. Frankie just likes being a hard-ass. Besides, Brett wouldn't allow it. He deals with his own shit. The only time he would let the police in the club is if there was a murder, and that wouldn't happen because..." She shrugged. "Well, you just wouldn't do that shit in Compass. It's why I like working here. Safest club in the city."

"Did Mr. Westhill see me dance?" I asked tentatively.

"Call him Brett, he prefers it," Frankie said. "And yes, briefly. You're good but too technical for this place."

My heart pounded as panic set in. Shit, I couldn't lose this opportunity. I had the landlord knocking on my door this morning while I'd hid under the covers pretending I wasn't there. It was Trevor who'd saved me. I'd heard him in the hall telling the landlord I'd gone out of town for a few days.

I'd invited Trevor over for breakfast after the landlord was gone.

"I can do better. It was my first time and I was nervous."

Frankie walked toward the bar. "There is no room for nerves on the floor. And I have a thousand girls who've applied and can dance like you did."

I rushed after her. "Yes, but not a girl who wants the job as bad as me." I stopped a few feet away from her as she typed something on her laptop that sat open on the bar top. "I really want the job. I need the job. Please."

Frankie shut the lid of her laptop and swiveled around on the barstool. "Why?"

I went with complete honesty; Frankie seemed like she respected direct. "My ex cheated on me six months ago. I had to move out and quit my job because he was my boss." I heard Tab snort behind me. "He spread nasty rumors about me and now I can't get a job teaching dance. I haven't worked in months, and I need to dance. I want to dance."

She eyed me up and down, eyes curious. "You have a new boy-friend?" I had no idea why she'd ask that, but I quickly shook my head. "A guy like your ex who wouldn't want you in a nightclub dancing?"

"No." I hadn't spoken to David in months. But there was a rock star drummer who was a friend of the owners who didn't want me dancing here.

She glanced over her shoulder. "Bree, you just got your Saturday night off. Savvy will take your place for one night." She looked at me. "One night. A trial. Brett will be here. He can have the final say, but from our argument the other night, he liked you."

I wanted to jump up and down. Instead, I grinned. "Thank you. You won't regret it."

Frankie stood, and despite her five-three height, she appeared way taller. "And wear the heels 24-7. In the shower if you have to. You need to learn to dance in those. It was obvious you're not used to them."

Shit, the mask. I wanted to be able to wear the mask just in case Killian ever showed up. "So, what I was wearing the other night with the mask? Would that be okay?"

She sidled past me. "It's good. I like the mask. Mysterious. Keep it, but the blue goes. All the girls wear either black or white. Bree will find you something." She clapped her hands together. "Let's go. On the floor. Drop the bag, Savvy. You need to learn a few things before Saturday night."

I was soaking wet as I sat on the floor, knees bent, elbows perched on them, head hanging forward and water bottle between my legs.

Frankie was tough. Like tougher than Mrs. Perch, my dance instructor when I was seventeen and living in Waterloo with Ms. Evert. Mrs. Perch was called, behind her back of course, "the taskmaster." There'd always been another task to master before we were allowed to leave class.

Bree sat beside me, the girl Tammy, who I found out was always late and who carpooled with Shari—meaning they both were always late—sat on my other side. Shari was beside her, flat on her back with her arm over her eyes. They were nice, obviously good friends and were amazing dancers.

Frankie shut off the music. "Good work, ladies. Bree, go over Compass rules with Savvy?"

"Sure thing," Bree chirped.

"No hooking up with the customers," Tammy blurted. She had a high-pitched voice that squeaked a little, and massive amounts of curly blonde hair that was frizzy and stuck out in every direction. But she had cute soft features, and for some reason, the crazy hair went well with her sweet rounded face.

"Or other staff," Bree added and turned to Tab, who was ignoring all of us and putting her water and jacket in her bag.

Tab straightened and lifted her thin brows at Bree. "I can do whatever I want off the premises."

"Yeah. Sure you can. Until Frankie finds out you're fucking one of the security guys," Shari muttered without taking her hand off her face.

Bree lowered her voice, leaning into me. "Tab is sorta seeing Greg." Oh. Huh. I didn't see that coming. Greg was so direct and fierce, and I pictured him with a... well, a softer girl than Tab.

Tammy overheard and snorted. "Seeing? No, they fuck when he has nothing else to fuck."

"You're a bitch, Tammy." Tab snatched her bag off the floor and hitched it over her shoulder as she walked out.

I heard the door open and slam shut behind her.

Everyone laughed. I smiled, already feeling like I was part of the group.

"No leaving the club without an escort." Bree climbed to her feet, held out her hand, which I gratefully took, and she hauled me up beside her. "And if you have any issues, go to Greg. He'll straighten it out."

I bit my lip. "Umm, Greg is pissed at me right now."

Bree bent, picked up her bag and water. "No, he's not. He's pissed at himself for letting you get away and has a bruised ego. But Greg's ego needs a little bruising now and then. Don't worry about it." She pointed to the stairs. "Change room for dancers. First door after the bar then second door on the left. There's a ton of outfits, nothing too risqué. Brett's motto, 'class not trash.' What's your cell number?" Bree asked.

"I don't have one at the moment." If I got the job, after paying hydro and rent, I'd buy prepaid cards for my phone.

"You serious?" Her eyes widened. "You need a cell. If you're hired, which you will be, Derek will get you one. He's the manager here." Bree walked to the door and I followed. "Later, girls" She waved over her shoulder.

"Bye," I called to Tammy and Shari.

She yanked open the door, and the warm summer air billowed into me as we walked outside. "I don't need a cell."

"You will if you're hired. Compass rule. Girls text Greg when they're ready to leave the club. No exceptions. All girls. Waitresses, bartenders, dancers. He's not available, then he sends one of the other guys to escort you to a taxi, car, whatever."

"A little over the top, isn't it?"

"Told you. Safest club in the city. That's why we don't have trouble. Compass is tight, and if Greg finds out you left with no escort, he'll have your ass fired. And it won't matter how good a dancer you are."

It kind of made me feel better about leaving at two in the morning in the club district, especially Friday and Saturday nights. It was one part of the city that the mounted police often patrolled.

Jacob, who had let me into the club, was leaning up against the wall having a smoke when Bree and I came out. "You get hired, Hijack?"

I rolled my eyes at the nickname. Looks like I'd be stuck with it if I was hired. "Trial Saturday night."

He tossed his cigarette into the alley. "Good. See you then."

Bree reached into her purse as she stopped at a silver sports car. With tinted windows and sleek lines, it looked like it cost a fortune. The horn beeped as she pressed the key fob. "Need a ride?"

I was still staring at the car, trying to figure out how on Earth she could afford it. She laughed.

"Parents bought it for me. Twenty-first birthday. I couldn't re-fuse because"—she ran her hand over the lip of the roof—"well, it's sweet as hell." She slid into the leather seat and started it up. "You need a ride?"

I shook my head. "I have my car." But it was always a risk whether it would make it to its destination. "Thanks for your help. Have fun Saturday night."

"Thanks. Later," Bree called, shut her door then drove off.

I put on my sunglasses, walked to my car and climbed in when

49

a black sports car pulled into the alley and parked. I briefly glanced over and...

Holy shit. It was Killian in the driver seat.

What the hell?

I slammed my door shut and ducked down so fast I hit my head on the gearshift. I rubbed the spot as I kept tucked in next to the steering wheel. Why would he be here on a Wednesday afternoon? The club wasn't even open. But there'd been someone in the car with him, though I didn't have a chance to see who it was.

My calf leg cramped, and the car was suffocating with the windows closed from having sat in the sun for two hours. But I didn't dare pop my head up. How long had it been? Was it long enough to park and go into the club?

I peeked over the dashboard.

Shit. He stood beside his car talking on his phone, his tall, length leaning against the side of it. And Christ, he wore a pair of worn jeans, black belt, and a white dress shirt with the sleeves partially rolled up revealing his tattooed arms.

His clothes hung in crisp clean lines, defining his lean physique. Pure class.

I was having trouble breathing as the sun blazed through the windows, the vinyl also burning my ass. Shit, I was going to pass out if I didn't do something.

I kept my head down and wiggled the key out of my pocket then inserted it into the ignition and turned it once so the car didn't turn over, but the air came on. Not air conditioning, I didn't have that, but hot air.

Unfortunately, the music blasted, too.

Shit.

I scrambled for the volume knob and shut it off then peeked up over the rim of the door.

He was still on the phone but was no longer leaning against his car. He was looking my way and so was Crisis, the guitarist in the band who was by the club door talking to Jacob.

I couldn't chance staying here.

50

I had to leave before he recognized me, and the only way was to reverse all the way out of the alley because I couldn't drive past him.

I glanced up again just as he hung up and put his cell in his back pocket.

Then he headed for my car.

Crap.

Pressing the clutch, I turned the key and jammed the gear shift into reverse. I glanced back through the seats and reversed all the way out of the alley.

When I backed onto the street, I peered out my side window and saw him standing in the middle of the alley staring after my car.

Chapter Six

Past
Ireland

Killian

"EMMITT. GO. GO. GO," I SHOUTED FROM BEHIND HIM AS I blocked the opposing player from getting to him. My brother ran the length of the field, the football dribbling between his feet back and forth.

He was tall like me and athletic and could outrun most of the kids on his team and the opposing one, except me, of course.

He was also only eleven where most of the other kids were fourteen to sixteen, but Emmitt excelled at football, so my da pulled some strings, or rather donated money, to have him try out for the team I was on. As soon as they saw him with a football, they put him on the team.

I saw him hesitate and look over his shoulder for me and I weaved right then left avoiding the opposing player, and Emmitt kicked the ball to me.

It was our play. Back and to the right then I'd get in close to goal and when everyone was on me, Emmitt was open and in position.

I grinned at the asshole who tried to get the ball from me as I came in close to goal.

"You and your brother are going down," he shouted as he tried to steal the ball from me.

I laughed while kicking back with my heel then glancing up for Emmitt. My brother nodded at me, and I danced with the ball a couple of moves then shot it high at Emmitt.

He jumped up and bumped the ball with his head, and it went straight into the goal.

Our team cheered and slapped Emmitt and me on the back. I grinned at my brother and ruffled his unruly hair.

"Nice shot," I said as we jogged to center field.

"Thanks," he said under his breath while keeping his head down.

Emmitt was quiet, especially when it came to social situations. Football was one place that he could let go and be himself and not worry about his Tourette's.

In school he had a hard time with his classmates, and since I was a year ahead of him, I wasn't able to protect him all the time.

His Tourette's manifested itself in the form of involuntary eye blinking called tics, so he often kept his head down and never looked people in the eye. My da, on numerous occasions when he was younger, had locked Emmitt in his room and forced him to practice keeping the tic "under control."

But when he played football, the tic rarely happened, and I think that was partially why he loved it so much. It was the only place Emmitt felt like he was normal and didn't have to hide who he was.

"Nice goal, Emmitt," our dad shouted from the sidelines.

I didn't expect him to say anything to me, and I didn't give a shit. He'd always hated me and after twelve years of him ignoring me, I was accustomed to it.

Emmitt noticed it though and asked me once why Da never talked to me except to give me shit about something. I told him that Da and I were just different. But it was more than that.

When I'd asked my mom why Da didn't like me, she'd dropped the dish she'd been reaching for and it had shattered on the floor. As she cleaned up the shards, I saw her hands shake and there were tears in her eyes.

"I love you, Killian," she'd said. "Your da does, too. He just… has trouble showing it."

It was a lie. I'd heard the hesitation in her soft voice. But it really didn't matter anymore.

Emmitt was who mattered.

"Retard," a kid from the opposing team muttered when he banged into Emmitt with his shoulder as he ran by.

Before I had the chance to go after the kid, Emmitt grabbed my forearm and shook his head. "It only makes it worse."

I gritted my teeth. "He won't say it again if I knock his teeth out."

Emmitt jerked his chin to the sidelines where our dad stood. "Da doesn't need another reason to be mean to you."

I sighed. Emmitt had so much to be angry about, yet he wasn't. He was nice to everyone.

"I don't care about him, Emmitt. I care about you, and that kid deserves to have his ass kicked."

"Then score a goal," he said, smiling as he met my eyes.

I cuffed him on the shoulder. "Yeah. But if that kid gets near me, he is *accidentally* falling flat on his face."

It was the same story. Emmitt never wanted anyone to hurt, but he was the one who suffered all the time for something he had no control over.

"Emmitt," a kid yelled as he kicked the ball toward him.

We dove back into the game.

Chapter Seven

Savvy

SATURDAY NIGHT. TRIAL NIGHT. I ARRIVED EARLY AND WENT to try on some of the outfits, most of which were a bit snug in the hips. I had big hips. But I found a flowing white dance dress that reached my knees and flared out. It was chic. The waist was tight, but the material was stretchy so it left lots of room to dance in. It had a deep V-neckline with a scooped back and spaghetti straps.

By the time I dressed, Tammy, Shari, and Tab had arrived and were also changing. Music played and the beat vibrated through the room. I smiled. I loved loud music. The vibration filtered through me as if the instruments were being played on my body.

"You good, Hijack?" Tammy asked, leaning on the back of my chair and meeting my gaze in the mirror as I applied my red lipstick.

"Yeah, I think so."

"Okay, you're taking cage two. That's the one on the left of the stage. All new girls start there."

"Okay, sure."

"Greg will come get you when it's time for a break. It's Saturday, our busiest night, so the club is at full capacity. Do not leave the cage until one of the guys gets you. If you're tired, slow your dancing. Customers like provocative so don't worry if you can't keep up with the music. Security guys are always watching the floor so you won't have an issue getting their attention if you need it." She straightened and smiled, resting her hand on my shoulder. "Most of all have fun. Customers know if you're not having fun."

"Got it." I slipped on my mask.

There was a knock on the door and Shari skipped over. "Let's hit it, girls." She wore a ton of makeup, but it wasn't distasteful, just dramatic, almost like a mask in itself.

Greg was at the door. He wore an earpiece and was in the usual garb, black pants and T-shirt with Compass written on it. "Ladies," he said.

Shari, Tammy, and Tab shifted by him, all tapping him either on the chest or shoulder as they did.

I stood, and his eyes hit me. Greg was handsome, in a rugged sort of way. The scruff on his face, neat and sculpted, dark eyes that right now looked black, and a defined nose with a slight notch as if it had been broken a few times.

"You good?" he asked.

"Yeah."

He nodded.

I hesitantly walked toward him then stopped a foot away. "Listen, I'm sorry for the other night. That I took off. I was scared and well... I didn't mean to get you in trouble."

"No reason to ever be scared at Compass. And next time you're scared in here, you better be running to me, not away. Got it?"

I nodded.

Since he was tall, he bent at the waist to speak in my ear. "And I don't get in trouble, Hijack. I am trouble."

Jesus. His low graveled voice, words like that, he definitely was trouble. I half smiled because I thought he was teasing, but I wasn't too sure because I really didn't know him yet. But I liked that he was the one who made sure all the dancers were safe. I bet no one messed with him.

He escorted me to the cage, and I walked up the steps and into my dancing oasis for the night. Despite the platform having bars, it was at least twelve by twelve with plenty of room to move.

It was early, and the place was crowded but not yet packed. I could see the door from my vantage point, and there was a steady stream of patrons coming in.

I danced easily for the better part of the night, and Greg or Jacob came and got me every hour for a quick break. There was always cold, bottled water within reach.

It was almost one in the morning, and I was doing my last set when my heart stopped. Holy shit. That was Sculpt; I'd recognize him anywhere. He stood with his arm around a cute brown-haired girl who I recognized as his wife, Emily. He had a drink in hand and was peering over the railing at the crowd below while Emily chatted with Crisis.

Shit, Killian was there, too.

He was tilted forward, hands gripping the glass railing, and his eyes were focused on me.

I whirled around and danced holding the bars on either side. When I flicked my head back, bending over backward at the waist, my eyes went straight to him, and he was still watching me.

Shit. Could he tell it was me? No way. I looked nothing like myself and was wearing a mask. Plus it was too far away. I was being paranoid, and if I wanted this job, I was going to have to get over this fear that he'd find out. What was the worst that could happen? He'd tell Brett.

I kept my back to him as I finished my dance and the music ended.

Greg came to get me five minutes later, and I grabbed my water and… oh, shit. Upstairs. Our change room was upstairs, and I'd have to walk right by him and his friends.

I stopped.

Greg frowned, his eyes puzzling. "What's up?"

I couldn't very well try to trick him again, and there was no chance he'd fall for it, plus I had no clothes, no purse, no car keys. So I opted for the truth.

We were at the bottom of the stairs and I held the handrail, my fingers tapping the iron. "I... well, Kite is here. From Tear Asunder."

Greg frowned. "Yeah. That a problem?"

I nodded. "I'd rather not meet him looking like this."

His expression softened. "Don't worry about it. He's used to fans drooling over him."

I rolled my eyes. "I'm not going to drool all over him. Plus, he looked kind of pissed off."

"The club isn't his favorite place. He's not pissed off."

"Like fuck I'm not," Killian said, coming up behind us.

I gasped. Crap.

"Kite?" Greg questioned, his hand on the small of my back dropping away when Killian's furious glare went from me to Greg's hand on me then back to Greg's face.

There was really nothing for me to say except, "Hey, Killian."

"Hey, Killian?" His jaw clenched. "Jesus, Savvy. What the fuck? What the ever-loving fuck?"

Greg shifted closer to me because Killian was really pissed and Greg's job was to protect me, even if it was from a famous rock star. It was nice to know he had my back. I was really liking Greg.

"Is there a problem?" This was not from Greg or Kite. This was from Brett Westhill, the club owner who I now noticed stood behind Killian.

Killian's glare shifted from me to Brett. "This is Savvy Grady."

Brett's eyes widened for a second, and then he said, "Fuck. No way."

"Yeah, fuck," Killian barked, then looked back at me. "What part of our conversation did you not get? I told you, not in my fuckin' club."

I jolted. What? His club? What was he talking about? "Your club?"

I peered at Greg who looked uncomfortable as he stood stiffly beside me, uncertain as to what was going on. But Brett appeared rather amused as he crossed his arms over his broad chest and leaned his hip against the stair railing.

He was hot, a different kind of hot than Killian as they were complete opposites. Where Killian was dark and mysterious, Brett was blond and carefree, wearing his emotions on his face. I'd heard he was also a huge flirt, too, whereas I couldn't really see Killian flirting. He definitely hadn't in school.

No, he'd be the type to tell a girl to get on her knees and suck his cock, and she'd simply do it.

I swallowed then realized my eyes had shifted to Killian's crotch. Jesus. My gaze darted up to his face, and his brows were drawn over his eyes with a crease between them.

"I own half," Killian ground out.

"Why didn't you tell me?"

"Because I don't advertise it."

Oh. Okay. Well, that explains why he'd been here during the day on Wednesday. He partially owned the place, which I found odd because Greg said he wasn't even a fan of the club. Then why get into the business? It wasn't like he needed the money.

"She's not dancing here," he said to Brett.

I curled my fingers around the handrail and even though my posture was always good, I straightened more, raising my chin. "I'm already dancing here. I did."

"And you won't again."

"We'll see." The sexy mouth I'd once tasted was not looking too appealing right now as the devilish corners tipped down. Lips were pressed together as he clamped his jaw. Okay, maybe not the smartest thing to say to Killian in his current state.

He glared at Greg. "Put her in the office. *After* she gets out of those clothes." He turned to walk in the other direction.

"I'm not going to sit in an office while you make me feel like I'm in trouble."

Killian stopped. Strode back and got right in my space, the railing the only reason his chest wasn't against mine. "You don't need to feel like you're in trouble. You *are* in fuckin' trouble."

This time it was me who stepped back and found myself right against Greg. "How did you know it was me?"

Some of the tension eased from around his eyes, but not enough that I was confident there wasn't going to be some shouting in his office.

"Savvy, I know every single fuckin' way your body moves even after eleven years. So, you wearing a mask thinking I wouldn't recognize you dance... not a fuckin' chance."

My mouth gaped. He knew how my body moved? He recognized how I danced? How was that even possible? When had he ever seen me dance? "You know how my body moves?"

He didn't respond. He turned and strode through the crowd. There was no waiting for people to get out of his way; they moved. My eyes trailed after him all the way to a side door where there was an Emergency Exit sign above.

"He's leaving?" Maybe I could grab my stuff and get out of here after all. It looked like I'd need to go back to waitressing for a while.

"No. Gone outside to cool off," Brett said.

"Oh." Cool off was good. Having to go outside to cool off—not so good.

"Never seen him like that before. He's a pretty laid-back guy, but then Kite has never been interested in a chick either." Brett winked. "But he's certainly interested in you."

I wasn't sure I liked him interested, especially if I wanted a job here. "I'd like to work here."

He shrugged. "Not stepping in the middle, darlin'. This is his call."

"Boss?" Greg asked, and Brett nodded, which I found out as Greg gently took my elbow, was to do as Killian wanted, and he urged me up the steps.

When we reached the top, we had an audience—Frankie, Sculpt, Emily, and Crisis, who had his arm slung over a stunning blonde girl's shoulders.

"Nice to see you again, Savvy," Sculpt said, then cupped the back of Emily's neck. "This is my wife, Emily."

Emily smiled, brown eyes curious. "My husband told me you were at the concert last weekend. A friend from high school?"

"Kind of," I replied.

"I'm Haven," the blonde girl said, stepping forward and offering her hand. "I saw you dance. You're incredible." She reminded me of an angel with her slight frame and beautiful, flawless white skin.

"Thank you."

My gaze shifted to Frankie, who had her arms crossed over her chest, hip cocked, standing next to Sculpt who made her scariness evaporate because he was a tall, muscled guy and I knew his past and had seen him fight.

"You did great," Frankie said.

"Thanks." I did. I knew I did because I felt it.

"You have the job." My excitement lasted about the same time as a flash of lightning. "If Kite says yes and by the looks of whatever was said downstairs, that probably isn't going to happen."

And defeat. My shoulders slumped, and I saw everything slowly slipping through my fingers. Losing my apartment, my car, any hope of ever owning my own dance studio. It didn't depend on this job, but it sure felt like it because the last six months had been shit, and everything was piling up.

"Don't you dare," Frankie said, her tone gruff and hard. "You fought for this job. You wanted it, and you showed me you wanted it. Now, show him." I heard Sculpt clear his throat, and Frankie rolled her eyes at him. "I know there's history, but I don't give a shit. Kite's being a dick."

Sculpt replied, "Maybe, but he owns half this club and that history you don't understand."

"It's Brett's too, and they are my girls. Compass is known for the best club dancers for a reason. He needs to get over whatever is fucking with his brain and see her as a dancer. A great dancer."

"Oh, he sees her alright," Crisis said, grinning.

Frankie looked back at me. "Fight for it."

Sculpt shook his head. "Frankie, you don't know what you're

messing with. I've never seen Kite like this." And that was the second time someone said that.

She shrugged. "I have a feeling Savvy can handle herself." Then Frankie reached out and lightly squeezed my hand before she walked down the stairs.

Greg put his hand on the small of my back and urged me forward as I said, "Nice to meet you, Emily and Haven."

"You, too. I expect we'll see you again soon," Emily replied.

Greg waited outside the dressing room while I changed into my jeans and T-shirt. He then escorted me down the hall into an office.

The walls were gray like the club, but the floors were a distressed hardwood. There was a desk with iron legs, a shiny metal surface, and two mahogany drawers on one side. Two chairs sat in front of the desk and a floor-to-ceiling wood cabinet on the opposite side of the room with hardcover books and a couple of plaques. There was a small window to the right and another the length of the room, which overlooked the dance floor. Since I'd been on the dance floor, I knew you couldn't see into the office from the other side.

"Sit. Not sure how long he'll be."

I didn't.

It was obvious why Greg stayed in the room with me. He didn't trust me when there was a window. Although, I don't know what he expected me to do considering we were on the second floor.

"Maybe I can come back tomorrow and talk to him?" My hopeful tone drifted off when Greg chuckled midsentence as he stood beside the door, arms crossed, stance wide.

Okay, I wasn't getting out of this, so I had to man up and do what Frankie said. Killian was just a man. He wasn't a freakin' god.

I amended that thought when the door clicked open, and my heart shot off into a pattering of rapid beats as Killian's presence filled the room. Maybe I should sit? No, I had more power standing. Power? Against Killian? The thought was laughable.

"Thanks, Greg," he said, but his eyes were on me.

"Sure thing," Greg replied. "Be right outside." He looked at me, so I think the comment was for my benefit.

The door clicked closed. Twice now I'd been with Killian in an office. Alone.

Killian had yet to move. It was unsettling, especially since he didn't look angry anymore. He looked pensive as if he was deciding what to do.

He took a deep breath, ran his hand through his hair, and bowed his head. "Don't know what to do here, orchid."

I gasped, hearing the nickname he'd given me in high school.

If he heard me, he didn't give me any indication he did as he continued, "You're good. Fuck, you owned that cage tonight… mesmerizing." He paused then slowly raised his head and locked eyes with me. "To me and a hundred other guys."

"Uh, thanks?" I kept my tone quiet because maybe, just maybe, it would help my case.

"But like I said before, you can't work here."

I gritted my teeth. "Why are you being this way? It's just a job."

He stiffened. "You don't belong in a nightclub, Savvy."

I hadn't seen him in eleven years. He had no idea where I did or didn't belong. "Whether I do or don't, that's my choice, Killian." I hardened my tone. "I like it here. And I like the other girls."

"I'm glad. But it's still no."

Shit. I was nervous about working at the other clubs. I didn't know the owners or the rules, and the club district wasn't the safest. But I might not have a choice. "I didn't realize you had such a strong dislike for me, Killian." I started for the door. "I'll find another club."

"You're not working in another club either."

I froze.

He strode toward me, and I inched back until my heels banged into the wall. When he was a foot away, he stopped, but it was close enough that his scent drifted into me and my belly whooshed.

I hadn't had many people in my life tell me what I could and couldn't do. And Killian saying I couldn't work at *any* nightclub… that pissed me off. "If I can't work here, I am."

"Like hell."

His expression was angry again, eyes dark, jaw clamped and even though he was scary looking, he was still sexy, and that softened the scariness—mildly.

"You don't have a say."

"You're not dancing in a nightclub, orchid."

I stiffened as a red flare went off inside me. "Don't call me that."

"You're orchid to me. Always have been. That shit doesn't change."

"Well, I want it known that I don't like the name."

He had the nerve to grin. *Grin.* The heart-melting grin that turned me into a puddle of goo. "I know you liked it then and you like it now. You're flustered and have that pink glow to your cheeks. It makes your freckles stick out."

I did, and it infuriated me that I loved that he had a nickname for me that no one else called me. But no way was I admitting that. Killian had enough confidence to scale Mount Everest without knowing I liked his nickname.

He stepped closer, and I held my breath knowing if I inhaled, my breasts would brush against his chest.

From the twitch of his lips, the spark in his eyes, he knew exactly what I felt when my breasts brushed his. If he tilted his head down, he'd see my erect nipples pressed into my tight black sparkled top. He'd also see the goose bumps that had popped up on every inch of my body.

I was praying he couldn't hear my heart thumping like crazy or see my pulse throbbing in my neck.

He did. "You okay, Savvy? You look a little... rattled."

There was the urge to tell him to go fuck himself, but it wouldn't help my case at all, and I rarely said anything so mean. "I'm fine. But I've been sweating for the last four hours. Need a shower and would like to go home." I paused then added, "With a job."

He growled low in his throat, the amused grin fading. "You know I can't do that."

I crossed my arms so at least his chest hit them instead of my breasts. "I don't know. All I've heard is no without reason. You even said I looked good out there. Why won't you let me dance here?"

"Jesus," he muttered as he turned away, took two steps and then came back. This time he didn't stop a foot away. This time he kept coming until he pressed against me. Until I had every inch of his delicious rock-hard body against mine and his hand fisted in my hair at the back of my neck.

Oh, God.

"This is why, orchid," he said, just before his mouth slammed onto mine. My head would've hit the wall with the force of his kiss if he hadn't been holding my head.

Any thought of resisting eradicated as his mouth claimed mine, roaming, searching and reigniting something that had been sampled but not fully discovered eleven years ago.

His grip on my hair tightened almost painfully, and I moaned into his mouth. Not because I didn't like it, but because I did.

Killian's solid thigh gently eased mine apart, and he pressed it against my sex.

Holy shit.

This wasn't a boy kissing me for the first time. He was all man, and there was no question he controlled everything about it.

Come to think of it, he had then too, but back then I had nothing to compare his kiss to. Now I did, and no man had ever kissed me like this.

I sagged into him, hands on his chest, fingers curling into his tailored shirt. His hand slid down my side, one rib at a time until it settled on my waist, fingers tight as if to let me know that I wasn't moving until he said so.

His swollen cock pushed up against my belly, and a parade of heated sparks danced across my skin.

Oh, God, I wanted him inside me.

I wanted to feel every inch of him.

Have him call me orchid as he thrust into me again and again and then watch his face as he came. And then I wanted to memorize every inch of his body. Trace his tattoos with the tips of my fingers. Put my mouth around his cock and…

Christ. What was I thinking?

He was distracting me from what I really needed, and that was a job dancing. A job I was desperate for as I really didn't want to wait tables for shitty tips at an all-night diner like my mom.

But it was Killian who ended the kiss first.

"That's why," he stated, then spun on his heel, walked to the door and opened it. But it wasn't Greg standing there; it was Luke, the guy who almost threw me out of the concert. "Luke," Killian nodded. "Everyone still here?"

"In the lounge."

"Do you mind taking Miss Grady home?"

"Wait. What?" I stammered, still flustered from the kiss and trying to wrap my head around the fact that Killian just kissed me. "We haven't discussed this."

"We just did." He nodded to Luke who looked at me, eyes flicking to my mouth that was no doubt red and swollen.

"We didn't," I shot back. "You said no then kissed me."

Luke cleared his throat but didn't say anything.

"Yeah. We did," Killian repeated.

"Well, kissing isn't a discussion."

"It's mine." He glanced over his shoulder at me. "And now you're going home."

"Fine, but I'm going home with a job."

"Jesus, you're stubborn. No fuckin' way. Get it through your head. I don't want you dancing here, and since it's partially my place, I don't need a reason, although I just gave you one. You need money. I'll help, but working here or any other club is off limits."

"The media said you were nice." My lips still tingled and my body still swam in heated desire.

"I was never nice, Savvy."

He nodded to Luke, who stepped into the room, but he made no move toward me. "A word, boss."

"You can say what you need to in front of her, Luke."

66

His brows lifted as if surprised. "She wants to work here?"

"Yes," both Killian and me said at the same time.

"Better here than in *his* clubs. And Brett runs a tight ship."

Killian's jaw clenched and his hands curled into fists.

"His?" I asked.

Silence. Who were they talking about? Maybe Trevor knew who owned the other nightclubs.

I waited, heart still pounding, the scent of Killian still in the air around me, the taste of him still on my lips.

"Give us a minute?" Killian finally said to Luke.

Luke nodded and left, quietly shutting the door behind him.

"Who were you referring to?" I asked.

"Seamus Kane." *Oh, shit. His father.* "He owns the competition. Two nightclubs."

Right. I recalled hearing in school Kite's dad owned nightclubs. "Does he know you part-own Compass?"

"No. But if he looks hard enough, he will find out. Not that I give a shit." He walked over to the desk and leaned his butt against it while crossing his arms. "Sit, Savvy."

Since my knees were about to give out from the mixture of dancing for the last five hours and his kiss, I sat on one of the chairs in front of him. It was obvious Killian and his dad were not on good terms, which wasn't surprising.

"What happened?" he asked.

"Meaning?"

"Something happened. I may not have seen you in years, Savvy, but you're the same core person. I see it in your eyes, and I felt it in your kiss. You've been involved in two incidents within a week, one being illegal. Maybe I'm wrong, but that's not you. Something's happened."

He read me right. That wasn't me, but life had a way of throwing hardballs, and I was still learning how to swing the bat. "Why do you want to know? Will it make a difference on whether I get the job or not?"

"Maybe."

I swallowed. "Okay. I was involved with my dance instructor who later became my boss when he hired me, and I taught dance at his studio. Fast forward two years and he cheated on me with one of his students. I moved out of his place and quit my job."

He frowned, jaw ticking. "So, why a nightclub? Why not work at another dance studio? His can't be the only one."

"He didn't like that I quit and moved out." He snorted. "So, he spread word in the industry how difficult I was to work with." Among other things. "No one would hire me."

"And he thought you'd have no choice but to come back to him?" I nodded. "Fuck," Killian muttered under his breath. "How long has it been?"

"Six months."

He nodded, head bowed, eyes on the floor as if he were contemplating something. I was about to get up when he looked at me.

"I have a proposition for you."

"Does it involve getting the job?"

"Yes. But with one condition."

I nervously laughed. "What? Personal lap dances?"

A mild smirk emerged. "Would you like that, Savvy?"

"Of course not." But the image barreled into me of sitting on Killian's lap, his mouth on my nipples while I rode him. "So, what's the condition?"

"You'll date me for a month."

Whoa. Of all things for him to say, that was the furthest from my mind. "Excuse me?"

"You heard me."

"You're kidding, right?"

"No. I'd pay you, of course. Just name your price."

I stood. "That's the most ridiculous thing I've ever heard. You're a rock star and can date any girl you want. Why would you pay me to date you? God, that's crazy. I'd be your what... call girl?"

He shook his head. "The dating would be for appearances only, Savvy. And the reasoning is simple. I can't stop you from dancing in another nightclub, so I give you the job here, but everyone knows you're dating me and off limits. You won't take my money to help you out, so this way you can work for it."

"By dating you?"

"I didn't say it would be easy."

I found that hard to believe. "What about the club rule?" And the fact that he just kissed me and I had a hard time resisting him. "And the fact that you don't date."

He frowned. "Club rule?"

"No fraternizing with the other staff."

He grinned. "Do I look like staff?"

No. He looked like a sexy, hot, pierced rock star who I'd had a crush on since I was fifteen. And he wanted me to date him, but not really date him. This was insane. "And what about the *Kite* who doesn't date?"

He shrugged. "My publicist will be happy I'm dating as it will be good for my reputation. The added bonus is you know me. You know my past. Not many do. It makes things easier."

I can't believe I was even having this discussion and actually contemplating it. "I'm not fake dating you."

"Orchid."

God, he purposely used my nickname, and like the flower, I bloomed a little inside every time he called me that. "I dated my boss already and look what happened."

"We're not really dating. There's a difference. And I'm a silent partner at the club."

"No. Thanks, but I'll find something else." I stood and headed for the door.

Dating him was dangerous, but with each step, the weight grew heavier. Could I really walk away from this? Could I afford to? Did I want to waitress? Would I end up like my mom?

Now knowing Killian's father owned the other two clubs that had go-go dancers, there was no chance I was working there, despite what I'd said to Killian.

I stopped, my hand on the door handle. I then released it

and turned to face him. He remained leaning up against the desk, looking totally delectable.

"Why me, Killian?"

He casually strode toward me. Predatory. A lion stalking his prey and I wanted to run, but instead, like I'd done as a teenager, I froze. He stopped an inch away, towering over me and I stopped breathing.

His finger came under my chin, and he tilted my head up so our eyes met and held. "Breathe."

It was said quietly, a graveled whisper that caused a tightness in my lower belly.

"I'm protective of those I care about, Savvy. And you had an impact on me in high school. This helps us both."

Oh, God. I exhaled and my heart slammed into my chest. Killian cared about me? I impacted him? How was that even possible? He didn't even know me. Not really. But I found myself saying, "What does fake dating you involve?"

"Being seen with me." He paused. "And obviously no dating other men."

"Would that go both ways?"

His hand slipped away from my chin and he grinned. "Savvy, I don't date, so it isn't an issue for me."

"But you... uh, sleep with women."

"That wouldn't happen."

"How much?"

"What do you think is fair, Savvy?"

"One month dating you?"

He nodded.

"Six thousand." I smiled, knowing it was far too much for a few dates.

"How about twelve. And you make yourself available to me seven days a week."

Holy shit. Twelve thousand. For appearing in public with a hot guy like Killian?

I bit my lower lip as my mind whirled. Date Killian Kane.

Okay, it was fake dating, and I'd be able to get my dance studio sooner rather than later with the extra money. And dating him might help repair the reputation that David smeared.

God, I might be able to lease space next month and start taking students while I continued working here.

"Would I be able to still work here after the month is up?"

His jaw ticked and he hesitated. "No. But you will have enough money not to have to."

Fair enough. It wasn't as if I'd be sleeping with him. And I had no interest in real dating anyway after David, so I wasn't missing out on meeting someone else.

"Can I think about it?"

He chuckled. "No."

"Why not?"

"Because I let you think about it, you'll come up with a million excuses not to take it."

"And for good reason."

"No. Excuses are never for good reasons. They're excuses." When I opened my mouth to refute the point, his thumb grazed over my lower lip. "Besides, you already know the answer."

It pissed me off that he was right. I did know. I pulled back as his hand fell to his side. "No kissing. Or touching."

He shook his head. "We're dating. Touching is mandatory."

"Okay, but not like that."

The corners of his mouth twitched. "Like what?"

I frowned. "Like that. Touching my lip like that."

"Does that bother you, Savvy?"

"Yes." It made my knees weak and was way too intimate.

He laughed and the rumble sank deep inside me like an anchor. And damn it, it was good hearing Killian laugh. "Okay. No thumb grazing across your lips."

"And I want three nights a week at the club dancing."

"Two," he said. "I'll give you half the money now and half at the end of the month."

"Three," I pushed.

"Fine. Three. But Saturday nights are mine."

He brushed by me and opened the door. Luke stood there, and I wondered if he heard the conversation. But his face was stoic and I couldn't tell.

"I want word spread she's with me."

Luke gave an abrupt nod.

"Make sure she gets home safe." Killian turned to me. "Do we need paperwork on this?"

I shook my head.

"Good. I'll be in touch." And then he walked out.

I had no time to process everything that just happened as Luke said, "The car is in the back alley. I'll drive you home."

The car? I had my own car and could get home fine, but Luke was already gone and walking down the hall.

I hurried after him, noticing the club was slowly dying down as people filtered out since drinks were no longer served after two. The music played, but it was softer.

Luke waited for me at the bottom of the stairs then kept close to me as we merged with the patrons, his body a barrier from anyone banging into me. Greg appeared and nodded to Luke and me, then came with us to the side door where I'd snuck out the other night.

"You convince him, Hijack?" Greg asked.

I wouldn't call it convince, but I had the job. "Yeah."

He winked at me. I offered a hesitant smile because I wasn't too sure yet if I was crazy for agreeing to date Killian. But a month wasn't a long time. And it was twelve grand. I'd be stupid not to take the offer, although I was still leery on his reasoning.

Luke opened the door to a black limo. "Actually, I have my own car. It's in the parking lot across the road."

"Give your keys to Greg. He'll follow in it."

"Why?"

Luke's brows knit together. "So, you have it for tomorrow."

"No, I mean why don't I just drive my own car home, since it's here and it's my car."

"Kite wants to make sure you're home safe."

"And he gets what he wants?"

Luke's lip twitched, but he didn't say anything.

Hmm, well, I could suck it up, get in the car and be taken home in style. Or I could fight it and lose the battle. And by the look of Greg and Luke, I'd definitely lose, and be tossed in the car and be taken home in the limo anyway.

I shrugged. "Fine."

"Your address?" Luke asked.

I smiled. "You're his security. I have a feeling you already know."

He snorted, and by the pull at the corners of his mouth, it looked like he was trying not to laugh. But I did hear him mutter "smartass" under his breath. I didn't give him my address, and he didn't ask again.

Greg held out his hand for my keys. I dug into my purse and pulled them out. I took off my house key and handed the car key over. "She's the rusty brown one. Be careful with her. You treat her rough, she might fall apart."

He laughed. "Women fall apart in my hands all the time. Rough or not."

I rolled my eyes, and Luke's hand came down on Greg's shoulder drawing him back. I didn't know what Luke said to him, but Greg's smile vanished then he jogged off to get my car.

I slid onto the posh leather seat and Luke strode back, shut my door then drove me home. When he opened the door for me and I got out, he didn't look pleased. Actually, he shook his head with a scowl.

"This is where you live?"

"Yeah. You obviously knew that."

"I knew the address. Not the shape it was in." He walked me up to my apartment door, and I pressed in the code. The front door buzzed as it unlocked. "Thanks for the ride."

But Luke came inside the building with me and headed for the elevator. "No. The elevator doesn't work. But I'm only on the third floor."

We walked up the stairs in silence. It was only after I put my key in the lock that Luke spoke. "Kite's a good guy."

"I know." I'd always seen the good in Kite when he was younger, but I did wonder how much he saw in himself.

"Those he lets in, he's protective of. He let you in." Luke didn't wait for a response, not that I had one, as he headed down the stairs. "Lock your door," he called over his shoulder.

Chapter Eight

Savvy

I HAD A TASTE OF KILLIAN'S PROTECTIVENESS WHEN I WOKE THE next morning to knocking on my door. Actually, Actually, it was more an abrupt thumping.

I'd had a hard time falling asleep last night because I'd been thinking about Killian and concerned about Greg not showing up with my car.

It took me a few seconds to register that the thumping was a fist on my door and not the construction outside my window.

Wearing my pink boxer shorts with bunny rabbits and a white spaghetti strap tank top, I stumbled out of bed and into the living room. I swung open the door to see Luke standing there looking suave in a light blue T-shirt and a pair of black cargo pants.

"Is Greg okay? Did my car not start last night?" It was unreliable, and I was concerned about the colder weather coming and my car not starting.

"Use the peephole before you open the door. That's what it's there for. And I didn't hear a chain."

I held my tongue because he was a security guy and he was right. But usually it was Trevor or Mars at my door.

Luke held out a cell phone.

"What's that for?" I asked.

"Your cell," he said and when I hesitated to take it, he continued, "Killian wants you to have it." When I still didn't take it, he said, "He told me about your arrangement and he needs to be able to get a hold of you."

I took the phone.

"There's a contact list programmed in," he said.

I tapped the screen.

Killian cell.

Killian home.

Compass.

Luke.

Greg.

I pressed Killian cell and put the phone to my ear. Luke crossed his arms over his chest and waited.

"Savvy," Killian drawled. "You received the phone."

Did he have to sound so damn good at seven thirty in the morning? The deep burr caused butterflies to do the jig, and I rethought my decision to call him. "Where's my car? Greg was supposed to bring it back last night, and now Luke shows up with a cell phone instead."

"You need a phone for safety and for me to be able to reach you."

"Okay, but where's my car?"

"Where it should've been ten years ago." His tone sounded slightly amused, and it took everything I had not to hang up on him.

"What are you talking about? Where is it?"

"The wrecking yard."

I gasped. "Killian!"

"Mmm?"

"You can't do that. It's my car."

"I *can* do that because it's already done."

Screw missing his laugh. I liked it better when he was mad. At least then I didn't get weak in the knees and would do anything to hear it again.

76

"Tell Greg to bring it back."

"Was the car safe to drive?"

"What does that have to do with it?"

"It has everything to do with it, Savvy. Was it safe?"

My hand clutched the cell. "Not really, but—"

"Sentimental value?"

"God, no, but—"

"Did it cost you a lot in gas because it was a piece of shit?"

Hell yeah. It drank gasoline like a camel before a long journey except the journeys were never journeys, they were jaunts. I didn't respond.

"Savvy?"

"Fine. Yeah, but it was mine, and you had no right to decide her fate. Technically, it's stealing."

That got an out and out laugh, and my belly flipped. I knew it must have taken a lot for him to get to a place where he could laugh again, and it warmed me that I got the chance to see that.

"Savvy, the car was dangerous. Greg knew it, called me and I went out to see it. I can't have you drive that piece of crap and risk your life every time you get in it. What if it broke down on your way home from the club one night?"

My eyes shifted to Luke as I now realized what he'd been warning me about. Killian's protectiveness. I was getting a taste.

"You had no right, Killian." Even I noticed my tone sounded deflated and if I noticed, he certainly did.

"I was just hopping out of the shower, Savvy. I'll call you back." Before I had a chance to say anything, he hung up.

An image of Killian dripping wet with a towel slung low on his hips slammed into me. Jesus. I needed a long cold shower, and I had a feeling I'd need a lot of them. I tossed the cell onto the couch and looked at Luke. He held a key in his hand.

A car key. But it wasn't my car key. This had one of those trunk buttons, lock, unlock buttons and a panic button.

"Savvy. Just take it. I'm not allowed to leave until you do."

I walked over to the window and in my parking spot was a red car. Not shit brown. Not rusted and with a dent in the right side where some jerk hit me because he was texting on his phone.

"It's not a big deal." He tossed the key on the couch.

I spun, stomped as best I could in my bare feet, picked the key up and threw it back at him. The key landed on the floor in the hallway, because Luke was gone and his footsteps were on the stairs.

"Luke!" I leaned over the railing.

He glanced up, brows lifted. "Don't throw them. I won't pick them up and then you can explain to Kite why someone in your building is driving the car he gave you."

"That's the thing," I yelled. "It's not my goddamn car."

He disappeared from view and I heard the front door open.

"Shit." What had I gotten myself into?

I spun around to go back in my apartment when I saw Trevor leaning against the doorframe of his apartment. His arms were crossed, and his dark auburn hair was up in a bun. He wore a pair of jeans with a hole in the right knee, and the top button was undone as if he'd quickly yanked them on.

Shirtless, his six-pack and rock-hard chest were visible. No tattoos that I'd ever seen or piercings like Killian.

He smirked. "That bad that you have them running for their lives in the morning. Need some pointers, sweet cakes?"

"Very funny." I rolled my eyes. He was clearly amused that I was in my pajamas out in the hallway shouting at some guy who was making his escape.

Trevor was a player. He had different chicks in and out of his place all the time, and he made no qualms about it being known he was a player. He was twenty-four, and his aspirations in life were getting laid, video games, and partying so he could find a girl to get laid. He didn't need to find them though; they found him.

Despite his douchebagness, he was a good guy—as long as you weren't sleeping with him, which I wasn't and wouldn't.

"Maybe I can help." He pushed off the doorframe, left his door open and strode toward me. "Coffee made?" Then he added with a devilish grin, "How about breakfast? I'll cook."

"You always cook."

He strolled into my apartment. "Because you suck at it."

I sighed, shutting the door. He wanted breakfast because he was escaping his apartment. "Seriously, Trevor. Why do you bring them home? Why not go to their place?"

I had no attraction to him, but I appreciated his hotness like any girl with a libido would. He'd moved into the building on the same day as me six months ago. We met when I'd been carrying the tenth box up the stairs with red-rimmed eyes after the David fiasco and violently cursing the out of order elevator.

He'd been coming out of his apartment and saw me struggling. While a player, Trevor was also a gentleman and had jogged down the stairs, took the box from me and then insisted on getting the other five boxes from my car.

We'd been friends ever since. And not once did he try to hit on me even though he playfully flirted. It came out one day when we were on my couch watching a movie that he didn't screw around with girls who lived in his backyard.

Made sense. He didn't want to have to bump into them after he fucked them.

He also said, if I didn't live here, he'd ask me out. And I told him it's a good thing I lived here then because he'd face rejection otherwise. I didn't date or sleep with a guy who couldn't keep it in his pants for one weekend.

So, we were apartment friends and he'd helped me look for a job, hence the idea of working at Compass. He'd met a dancer from the club, meaning he'd slept with her, and she'd told him about the great money she made there.

Trevor didn't work, at least according to the government. He was a hacker and was probably pretty good at it considering all the people he had in and out of his apartment constantly. He also made fake IDs on occasion like the one he made me to get into the concert.

Trevor went straight to the kitchen, opened the drawer under the oven and took out a frying pan, setting it on the stove. He opened the fridge. "You have eggs?" I couldn't afford eggs.

"No." I shut my door and followed him into the kitchen.

"Bacon?"

If I couldn't afford eggs, bacon was a hell no. "Nope."

"Pancakes it is." He reached up into the cupboard and took down an orange plastic bowl, then the "just add water" pancake batter, a banana sitting on the counter, and went to work on making banana pancakes.

"So who's the guy running from you at seven-thirty in the morning? New boyfriend?" He peeled the banana, took a bite and said with his mouth full, "If you want, I can check him out. Make sure he doesn't have a record or anything."

I poured water into the top of the coffee maker. "Is that what you do for people?"

He smirked over his shoulder at me. "Babe, I do lots of things for people if the money is right. I'm a genius on the computer."

I laughed. "A genius who is going to land himself in jail."

He shrugged. "Life is too short to worry about the what ifs." The fork hit the sides of the plastic bowl as he leaned his butt against the stove, bowl perched in his hand and against his naked chest while he stirred the batter.

"The guy's security," I said.

"For?" He stopped stirring, eyes widening. "Fuck. Strip club security?"

"No." He chuckled, and I realized he'd been teasing. I put the carafe under the spout and flicked the on switch. "I got the job at Compass."

His brows lifted and he started stirring again. "Wait a sec. You told me Kite wasn't going to put in a good word for you."

"He didn't. I hijacked one of the cages the other night and got an interview. They hired me." It was a little more than that, but I wasn't sure whether to tell Trevor about the other half of the job. It was probably better I didn't, at least until I talked to Killian about the rules. But Mars had to know the truth; that was non-negotiable.

"No shit." He laughed. "Didn't know you had it in you, sweet cakes."

The percolator hissed and bubbled and then the sweet aroma of coffee drifted into the air. There was nothing better than the scent of fresh coffee in the morning.

Except maybe Killian. God, why did I even think that? *Because you had him locked to your lips last night.*

"So, the guy isn't a boyfriend. But you're in the hallway yelling at him in your pajamas, and he's running for his life out of the building." He dropped sliced pieces of banana into the mixture. "Fuck me. You had a one-night stand."

"He's security for the band Tear Asunder."

He snorted. "You're screwing the security guy with the band?"

"God, no. I didn't sleep with him."

"Dating then, which leads to sex, hopefully."

I sighed. "I'm not dating him either, and I'm not going to be sleeping with anyone. He was dropping off keys. He kind of had my car. Well, the guy, Greg, at the club had my car, and the guy who was here drove me home last night in the band's limo. Greg was supposed to drop off my car, but he took it to the wrecking yard instead." Trevor wasn't pouring the batter into the frying pan that sizzled with butter. Instead his eyes were on me with rapt interest in my story. "This morning security guy Luke brought me my keys. But they weren't my keys. They were new keys. To a new car."

"He gave you a new car?"

"No. Well, yes, but not Luke. Killian."

"Killian?"

Right. Most people only knew Killian as Kite. "Kite. The drummer in Tear Asunder."

"Fuck, sweet cakes." He shook his head. "When you go for a guy, you go big."

I scowled. "I'm not going for any guy." I took two mugs out of the cupboard and poured the coffee.

Trevor was quiet and he rarely had nothing to say, so I looked up, and he was smirking annoyingly.

I set the coffee pot back. "What?"

"Let me lay it out for you. The drummer from the rock band

buys you a new car because yours is crap." Opening my mouth to refute, he lowered his voice. "And it was crap. It needed to be set on fire years ago." He flipped a pancake. "The guy has money, sure, but I doubt he buys new cars for random people. So, what's the deal?"

Trevor may be a douche, but he was smart as hell and supposedly had two degrees. Computer science and engineering. He also read people well, so I was going to have a hard time convincing him that my dating Killian was real, especially since he knew about the situation with David and I'd told him I didn't plan on dating again for a long time.

"We're dating. Well, plan to. We talked about it. Going on a date. Probably for coffee or something."

He gestured to my new cell sitting on the couch. "And the phone is from him, too?"

I nodded. "It's a Compass rule. For safety."

He flipped the pancakes again then placed them on the plates.

"I like him already."

"You do?"

"Well, yeah. You shouldn't be driving around in that car, and no chick should be without a cell phone. He just handed you those things. So, yeah, I like him."

I put the mugs on the table and sat, my mind reeling.

Killian hadn't given me any money, but he hadn't needed to because he did it in a way so I couldn't take a check and rip it up. I had to have a cell, club rule, and he dumped my car so I needed another one.

The job I'd fought for. He hadn't wanted to give me that, but he did and more.

Shit.

We sat and ate banana pancakes, and Trevor let the subject of Killian go. We chatted about movies or rather debated as I liked old classics and he was into anything sci-fi.

After we finished the pancakes, my cell vibrated on the couch.

I ignored it because it was likely Killian calling back and I didn't want to talk to him in front of Trevor.

82

Trevor had other ideas as he dove for the couch and snatched it up and pressed Accept.

"Trevor. No."

He turned his back to me as he said, "Yeah?"

Scrambling from my chair, I grabbed his arm, but he merely walked away with me hanging off him like a puppy. "Trevor," I growled beneath my breath.

"Yeah. She's here. Who's this?" Pause. "Yeah, I saw the name on the screen, but I'm asking anyway." Another pause, longer this time. "Live across the hall."

Oh, my God. I darted around Trevor and gave him my most doleful eyes while mouthing "please."

"Nope, not her fuck buddy either. Savvy never brings guys home. I hear you asked her out."

Oh, God. I slapped my hand on my forehead and slumped my shoulders.

"Don't hurt her." There was another pause before he said, "Yeah, she's here."

He passed me the phone, and I mouthed "asshole" to which Trevor winked then strolled back to the table to clear the plates.

Putting the phone to my ear, I plopped down on the couch. "Trevor is my neighbor."

"He said," Killian replied. "I assume the one who made you the fake ID?"

I didn't say anything.

"Luke said you didn't like the car."

"He's right."

"It's not a new car, Savvy. It's been sitting in my garage. It needs to be used and you need a car. When you buy a car, I'll take it back."

"But I had a car."

He sighed. "Can we not argue this anymore? Christ, your car didn't even have airbags."

Of course it didn't. Airbags weren't around when my car was built. "Do you give cars to all the girls you date?"

"No." There was no hesitation. "And you're the first girl I've dated."

"Fake dated," I corrected in a whisper so Trevor wouldn't hear. There was no response. "I don't want people to know you gave me a car. It looks… well, bad."

Trevor snorted as he picked up the maple syrup off the table.

"The only people who will know are the ones you tell."

"Killian—"

"Jesus, Savvy. I'm not asking for your soul here." It sure as hell felt like it because Killian always had a part of me. "I'm making sure you're safe, and it starts with a cell and a car."

"Your safe is overwhelming," I grumbled.

"Yes."

I was surprised he admitted to that, but then I was discovering Killian had no qualms about telling me exactly what he thought. "Why are you calling?"

Trevor snorted. I guess that didn't sound appropriate to a guy I was supposedly dating.

"Were you wet last night when I kissed you, orchid?"

Jesus. "That's why you're calling?" I felt the heat in my cheeks and that familiar ache between my legs.

"Answer the question."

"No."

"Bullshit. But I'll let you have that until my fingers are inside you, then I'll ask you again."

I sharply inhaled. "That isn't going to happen." I lowered my voice. "It isn't part of the arrangement."

"Then you won't have to worry about having to tell me the truth."

"When did you get this way?"

"What way, orchid?"

Infuriating. Sexy. Dirty talking. Hot as hell. Panty melting. "I have to go."

"I'll pick you up at ten for our date. Dress casual." Before I could respond, he was gone.

I pulled the phone from my ear and tossed it on the couch before turning for the kitchen. Trevor had his hands in the sink filled with sudsy water and was looking at me, laughing.

"What?" I picked up our mugs and brought them over to the sink then plopped them into the water.

"You'll be fucking him by the end of the week. And, babe, I'm being generous. I think it will be by the end of the day because you have a history with him. Plus, I spoke to him, and he doesn't seem like a guy who gives in if he wants something. And he wants you."

"Well, I'm not sleeping with him."

"Want to bet on it?"

"Oh, my God, I'm not betting on when I'm having sex with a guy."

"So, you are going to have sex with him? You just don't know when?" he teased.

I groaned. "No. God, no. I don't want to have sex with him."

"Then why bother dating him?" Trevor asked, grinning.

I slapped his shoulder shaking my head, and he flicked soapy water at me.

"Trevor?" It was a girl's voice out in the hallway.

I lifted my brows and he cursed under his breath. "Breakfast for a week," he said.

I shook my head. "No. I'm not doing it again. It's mean, and you were an ass for picking up my phone."

"I'll owe you," he said. "You can call it in at any time. And by the sounds of it, you're going to need it."

"So like what?"

"Anything."

"Anything?"

He grinned. "Yep. Even sex."

"Gross," I muttered because Trevor was like a brother to me.

"Trevor?" the girl called again.

I sighed. "God, fine. But I'm holding you to the anything."

He smirked and grabbed the flowered dishtowel off the hook beside the fridge and picked up a plate to dry it.

I walked to the door and opened it to see a gorgeous, curvy blonde standing in the hallway looking over the railing. There was a purpose to Trevor leaving his door open when he came into my place. He hoped the girl would just leave. This one was hanging onto the idea that he'd be back for her. He wouldn't.

"Trevor left," I said.

She wore his Toronto Raptors jersey that hung to midthigh. Trevor wouldn't be impressed she was wearing his favorite basketball team's shirt.

"But his door was open," she said with confusion.

God, I hated this and I was enabling him in his slutty ways. Trevor had to get his shit together.

"Yeah." I shook my head sighing and pursed my lips. It wasn't my best performance, but she wasn't even looking at me as she examined her leg for some reason. "I heard him on the phone as he ran out. Something about his mom being in the hospital." Trevor's mother lived in California on the beach with her latest squeeze.

Her eyes widened. "Oh. Hmm, okay. Do you think he'll be back soon?"

I just told her his mom was in the hospital. But only twenty percent of the girls I told this story to ever asked if his mom was okay. Those were the ones I felt bad for. "His mother lives in California."

"Oh. Do you have his cell number? I'll call him later." Trevor's other rule, never ever give out his cell number to the girls he brings home.

"No, I don't. But I'd be happy to give him yours and tell him you dropped by." I played it like I had no clue she'd stayed the night.

She flicked her hair over her shoulder, but it was too short to be flicked, so it swung back in exactly the same place. "No. I'll leave him a note under his pillow."

"Good idea," I offered, smiling. A guy like Trevor *loves* a girl leaving her number under his pillow.

I shut my apartment door.

Trevor lounged on the couch, bare feet on the coffee table, ankles crossed while he flicked channels on the TV.

"You know, one day the lies are going to slap you in the face, and when it does, I hope it knocks you off your feet."

"Babe, I'm clear with them before I fuck them. Not my issue if they think I'm so good they want second and thirds. And my mom does live in California."

I put my hands on my hips. "Yeah, but she's not sick. And you're eating pancakes and watching TV across the hall. I'm not doing it again."

He patted the back of the couch with his hand. "Sit. This shit with the rock star is fucking with your head. The chick will clear out in ten and I'll get out of your hair."

I walked over and sat, curling my legs beneath me. "Seriously, Trevor. I'm not covering for you anymore."

"Okay."

"Okay?"

"Yeah. But I still want to come over and have breakfast."

"Fine, but you need to learn to make eggs benedict."

Chapter Nine

Past Ireland

Killian

"LOOK AT HIM."

I squeezed my eyes shut, turning my head. I didn't want to. I hated looking at the pictures.

Da twisted my arm behind my back, his fingers digging into my skin. I sucked in air at the pain then fell to my knees.

"Look, damn it."

I did. I looked at the picture laying on the floor in the bedroom. My brother's bedroom.

Empty. No sound of his laughter. No train running on its tracks. No superheroes flying through the air as he ran around the room making a zoom sound.

God, he'd wanted to be a superhero. To fly away whenever he wanted. To punch through steel. To be invisible.

And now I knew why. So people wouldn't look at him with pity and kids wouldn't make fun of him.

"This is your fault. They killed him, and where were you? Where the hell were you? Kissing some fuckin' girl." My da threw my arm away and kicked me in the back so I landed on my stomach, inches away from the picture of my brother's smiling face as he sat on his brand new red bike.

"Tear it up."

It was stupid to fight the inevitable. He'd make me, and if I fought, he'd make it harder on me.

"Pick it up, Kill," he ordered. He loved calling me that. Ironic, he said.

I stared at Emmitt's smiling face, and a tear slipped from my eye and landed on the picture. He'd only been eleven.

I didn't protect him. I was too busy talking to Keeva Campbell in the science room.

Emmitt. I'm sorry.

"If you don't do as I say, it will be longer this time. Do you want that? Do you want to hurt your mum like that?"

No. I didn't. I hated my mum crying all the time. Begging my da to let me out of my room. He never did. He couldn't stand looking at me. But it had always been that way. He hated me from the day I was born. Emmitt was his only son, according to him. And now he was gone.

Hatred blazed in his eyes as he spat, "It should've been you. He had a chance at making it big in football. You took that from him."

I didn't care what he said to me anymore. But what I hated the most was the locked door. Closed in. The anger building each day.

"Rip it up," he barked.

I reached out and picked up the picture, holding it between my trembling hands.

I closed my eyes and tore the picture in half. But I knew that wouldn't be enough for him. He wanted it in shreds.

I tore it again and again until the tiny pieces lay in my palm. Then I closed my fist around them.

My mum's footsteps hurried up the stairs and then she appeared in the doorway, a choked sob emerging when she saw me on my knees.

But it was nothing new. This was his mantra.

It had been eight weeks since Emmitt died and his room remained untouched. Mine, however, was empty.

My da had taken everything away after the funeral. It was like he wanted to erase everything to do with me.

We'd gone in my room, and he'd forced me to break, ruin, destroy every single thing I was able to, and what I couldn't, he did. He said if Emmitt wasn't here to enjoy his stuff, then I wouldn't either.

Then he took everything out of my room except my bed and that was only because of my mum. He'd have preferred if I slept on the floor with nothing.

"Go to your room," my da said when my mum approached.

I was getting off easy tonight.

I climbed to my feet and brushed past him. My mum had her hand on my da's arm, and tears stained her cheeks. But it was rare they didn't. She was always crying.

And she never ate anymore.

"He's only twelve." I heard her say as I walked down the hallway. She no longer said it wasn't my fault.

"Don't start with me, Cora. He doesn't deserve to be here. It should be Emmitt. He was my fuckin' son and was going to be something."

I didn't hear her response, if there was one, as I went into my room and shut the door. A minute later I heard the lock click, and I opened my palm and let the pieces of the photo flutter to the floor with the rest of them. Hundreds of shredded photos all over my floor like a carpet of memories. A carpet of Emmitt.

I hated my da more than anything for what he made me do, but he was right.

I should've saved Emmitt. I should've walked home with him after school.

Sitting on the floor, I leaned against the wall and stared out the window and watched the sun slowly sink, leaving me in total darkness.

Only then did I get up and start training like I did every night.

When my da finally let me return to school, I'd find my brother's tormentors.

And I'd make them pay for what they did.

Chapter Ten

Savvy

I SHOWERED AFTER TREVOR LEFT AND WAS PUTTING ON MY BRA when there was a knock at the door. Shit, was it ten already? I slipped on my panties, and a pale pink T-shirt then tugged on my snug three-quarter-length jeans.

Another knock. Patient, but loud.

"One sec," I called as I walked to the door.

I flung it open and my heart sailed. No, it didn't sail. It flew out of my chest. Did Killian ever not look sexy? It was ten on a Sunday morning and we'd been at the club until two. He had on designer jeans that hugged his muscular thighs, a pair of black motorcycle boots, and a dark green T-shirt that appeared custom fit.

"This is a shit building," he said. My eyes snapped from admiring his chest, to his face. "And you didn't use the peephole."

Did he have X-ray vision? "You told me you were coming by at ten. It's ten. I didn't need the peephole." Well, that was a guess because I hadn't checked the time.

"I could've been some drunk idiot coming home after an all-night party. Or a *customer*, and I use that term loosely, of your hacker friend across the hall."

How did he know Trevor was a hacker? "But you're not." Not even close. He was my delicious smelling high-school crush, who I was *dating*.

"Are you going to invite me in?"

I hesitated, glancing over my shoulder. I was a pretty neat person, but I didn't need him to see a pair of panties on the floor. Deciding it was safe, I stepped aside, and he came in, took two steps and I saw his back tense as he took in my apartment.

Peeling wallpaper. Old, worn wood floors. A crack running the length of the ceiling in the living room that concerned me, but not the superintendent. I had minimal furniture because most of it had been David's when we'd lived together. I did manage to take the television though because we'd bought that together. The only reason he'd allowed me to take it was because Mars was with me and she was bitching at him, and I think he just wanted us gone.

"How did you get in the building?" I asked.

"One of your *friendly* neighbors." Killian had grown up wealthy and was now a rock star, so I was pretty sure money had never been an issue for him, so seeing my apartment was probably a shock.

Well, there wasn't much I could do about where I lived. Besides, this was not bad compared to the trailer my mom and I had lived in and Killian had seen that, too. At least the outside of it when he left me the orchid.

"So have you changed your mind about dating yet?"

"I don't make decisions where I need to change my mind, Savvy. And we're going to Logan and Emily's farm for brunch."

Yeah, he'd contemplate everything first before he did it. "We are?" He nodded. "Isn't it kind of early in the fake dating to be meeting your friends? They don't even know we're dating. And since you don't normally date, it would look odd showing up at their place with me in tow. Maybe we should do a coffee date in public first." The truth was, I was nervous meeting his friends again. Logan especially, because Killian and he had been friends in high school, and I was pretty sure he'd know the second he saw us together that it was a ruse.

He snorted. "Coffee date?"

I shrugged. "It's a standard first date. An easy way out if you don't like the person and you can end the date after a coffee, but if you do, then you can extend it. Better than dinner or going to a friend's place where you're stuck with the person for maybe hours."

He chuckled. "Firstly, there is no way out. Secondly, you like me and we do connect, and thirdly, our dates will always be hours, Savvy."

I swallowed, pulse racing and mind whirling because he was right. I felt the connection, and I did like him, and there was definitely no way out. At least if I wanted to keep my job.

He continued, "Savvy, there is nothing about us that compares to a first date. And you've already kissed me twice. And the first one was your first kiss."

My eyes widened. "How do you know that?"

He moved in on me, and I backed up until my spine hit the wall. His arm bridged over my head, palm on the wall above me. "You were nervous as hell. And had no idea how to kiss me."

I scrunched my nose and frowned. "Well, I was fifteen. Lots of girls haven't kissed a guy at fifteen."

"Mmm." He lowered his head, and I thought he was going to kiss me, but instead, he said in a low tone, "I'm glad I was your first kiss, Savvy Grady." He pushed off the wall and strode into the kitchen. "Coffee?"

I watched him as he moved around my kitchen. My eyes dragging up his thick muscled thighs to his tight ass, and as he turned, to his chest and the hawk tattoo peeking out of his shirt on his corded neck.

My gaze skidded to his face where he was grinning like a Cheshire cat because he caught me checking him out.

Shit. I inwardly moaned.

"I liked when you did it then… but now I can do something about it, so I like it a hell of a lot more."

"What do you mean?" I had no idea what he was talking about, but maybe if my brain wasn't muddled with what was tucked inside those jeans, I'd have had a clue.

"You were scared of me, but you checked me out." I opened my mouth to deny it but clamped it shut because there was no refuting it. I was surprised he'd noticed any girl checking him out though. It never appeared as if he noticed, but more than likely he hadn't cared.

He reached in the cupboard for a travel mug then poured coffee into it. "You want milk or sugar?"

"Neither. But—"

The lid snapped closed. "Ready?"

No. Spending several hours with Killian was a horrible idea and I hadn't considered hanging out with his friends. I'd thought a few public dinners, maybe a party or two. But going for Sunday brunch at his best friend's place, not on that list.

"No kissing," I reiterated the rule.

He picked up the travel mug and prowled in my direction. And it was a prowl because I felt like the hunted. I felt like that rabbit quivering in the hole as the wolf approached. The difference was, there was a part of me that wanted to get caught.

I raised my chin and crossed my arms over my chest.

He stopped in front of me and held out the mug. "Coffee."

I took it. "Thanks." I thought he'd walk away; instead, he cupped my chin between his thumb and finger. The tips of his fingers weren't soft, they were rough and firm, but his touch was gentle. "I'll follow your rule, Savvy, but just so you know, I'm good with you kissing me."

I snorted.

He smirked and his hand fell away. "Let's go." He strode out into the hallway.

There was a brief moment when I considered slamming the door and locking it, but slamming a door in Killian Kane's face would lose me a job, and I no longer even had a car to live out of if I couldn't pay my rent next month.

"What the hell am I doing?" I muttered under my breath as I grabbed my purse off the kitchen counter and noticed the slip of paper sticking out. I took it out and glanced at it.

It was a check. Half the money up front. I hadn't seen him put it in there.

"Savvy?" Killian called.

"Yeah." I shoved it back down inside, grabbed my cell and keys, and met him out in the hall.

We drove to Logan and Emily's farm, which was in King City, about a half-hour drive from the city, and Killian kept the conversation revolved around me. He asked questions about the foster homes where I'd lived, jobs I'd done, dance classes I took. I noticed David's name never crossed his lips as he skirted around the subject. I told him about Ms. Evert and her greenhouse and learning about flowers, but I failed to mention the orchid, and he never brought it up.

He was a perfect gentleman, keeping his hands to himself and I even found myself laughing as he talked about Emily taking him and his bandmates horseback riding and how Crisis fell off four times on the trail.

But by the time we arrived, I was on edge, probably because I'd been breathing in his deliciousness for the past half hour and my body was reacting to it.

He drove through massive iron gates, up a winding driveway, and then stopped in front of a stable. The house was off to the left, so I wasn't sure why we were parking here.

But what I did know was that I needed out of the car so I could finally inhale a breath of non-Killian air.

As if he knew exactly what I was doing as I scrambled out, he smirked while walking around the front of the car. "Problem?"

"No. My legs were cramped." I nodded to the stable. "The word farm gives an impression of manure, rusty hinges, and a crappy wood barn. This is like a five-star hotel for horses."

He grinned. "Emily loves her horses."

We walked side by side toward the large double doors with iron hinges. "Are we having brunch in the stable?"

"No. But I thought you'd like to see the horses. Plus, I wanted to check up on one in particular."

"Oh, I never saw you as a horse person."

"My father had a number of horses growing up, still does. I never rode, but I heard a lot about them when he was bitching about losing a polo match." His jaw clenched and back stiffened. "He wasn't nice to his horses, and he isn't now."

He also hadn't been nice to Killian. "Do you... talk to him?"

There was a tick in his jaw as he nodded. "Yes, but only recently. I didn't for eleven years." I decided to not ask anything more because his father had always been an issue, and a touchy subject.

We walked the rest of the way in silence, but it wasn't uncomfortable; instead it was... nice, our breaths synchronized, our hands occasionally brushing against one another.

A small side door of the stable opened. "I thought I heard voices."

I recognized Emily from Compass, and I'd seen pictures on the Internet of her, with Logan, of course. There were also numerous videos of her working with some dangerous horses. I'd only watched one, but it was really impressive. The horse had reared up right in front of her, yet she had been so calm about it. She had a quiet strength about her, and I imagined she needed that strength with Logan. He was intense and a famous lead singer in a rock band with tons of fans. Mostly girls.

"Savvy, nice to see you again. It's so great you and Kite have reconnected."

"How is Lucifer?" Killian changed the subject.

"As well as can be expected." Her smile faded. "It will take time before he'll trust anyone again. What he did to him...." She glanced at me.

"She's welcome to hear anything you have to say," Killian said. "She knows Seamus is an ass."

Seamus Kane wasn't a father of the year, and he was the first person I'd considered may not have any good bits, and that was only from a brief encounter.

Her eyes curiously landed on me then shifted back to Killian.

"Seamus put some severe wounds on him. They'll heal, but his spirit… I don't know, Kite. It will take a lot of time." She lightly touched his arm. "At least he has that chance now. You've given him that."

Killian nodded.

Sounded like Emily had an abused horse, and Killian's father was responsible. What I didn't know was how the horse came to be in Emily's care.

Killian's hand slid down my back as his eyes shifted to me. "Savvy, why don't you go in the stable and visit the horses."

"Only Lucifer is inside. He'd love a visit," Emily said. "Apples are in a bin across from his stall."

"Yeah, sure, of course."

I walked toward the stable doors and just before I went inside, I glanced over my shoulder at Killian and paused. His face was void of expression.

Nothingness. No inhales or exhales. No swallowing. No stiffening of the spine or jaw or fist clenching.

Stillness. Complete and utter stillness.

Was this what he did with the anger? Put it behind a wall of numbness? He had to be furious at his father for abusing a horse.

Killian had been a fighter, but he protected the kids who needed it, and now being older, I wondered if there'd been a reason for his vigilance to protect those who were weaker. What drove him to do that? Why was he so angry?

My eyes adjusted from the sunlight to the shaded barn. I took in the wide cobblestone aisle, which was cleaner than my kitchen floor, and high ceilings that had skylights throughout. The stalls were large and currently empty of horses. When I inhaled, it was to the scent of shavings and freshly cut hay.

As I strolled down the aisle, I noticed all the stalls had half doors at the back of them as well as the front and it offered a heavenly cross breeze.

I stopped when I saw the horse in one of the stalls.

"You must be Lucifer," I cooed.

Smiling, I approached his stall, but the minute I saw his body, my heart dropped. There was an extensive bandage-like cast on his front legs and welts on his rump and side so deep, they cut into his skin.

His head hung low and he didn't even acknowledge me.

"Hey, boy." I leaned over the half door as I wasn't brave enough to actually go in the stall with him.

His body quivered once and he bobbed his head, eyes flicking to me for a brief second. They were wonky and lazy, so I guessed he was on some kind of painkiller.

His lower lip was so relaxed it flopped when he'd bobbed his head.

I reached my hand out so he could smell it. I was uncertain the protocol of approaching horses, but it was what I did with dogs.

He didn't object, so I stroked his velvet muzzle then up to the white star on his forehead, tracing the swirl with my finger. His head lowered farther, and I continued to softly talk to him as I patted his face.

"You'll be okay. I know you will. Emily will take care of you." Tears welled in my eyes at this magnificent horse so broken and beaten. "You're a good boy. You know that?" I said.

"He knows," Killian said, coming up behind me.

I hadn't heard him, too absorbed by the horse.

Lucifer's lip made a popping sound as he attempted to shut his mouth a few times before giving up and letting it dangle loosely again.

Killian moved in beside me and reached over the stall door to stroke Lucifer's neck.

His thigh brushed against mine and goose bumps rose on my arms. "Why doesn't he have a mane?"

"They shave polo ponies' manes and forelocks. It can get tangled in the reins and mallets. It's called roaching. They also tie up the tails during a match."

"It looks funny. Horses are meant to have long flowing manes."

He chuckled. "Don't let Lucifer hear you say that. He's pretty particular with how he looks." It was nice to see Killian teasing and relaxed, almost as if seeing Lucifer did that to him.

"You like him, don't you?" I said, half turning and tilting my head up so I could see his face.

He nodded, his eyes on Lucifer as he ran his hand up the length of his neck and down again. "Yes. I was fourteen when my father bought him. I normally didn't pay attention to the horses, but I'd been suspended from school for fighting, so he had me work at the stable for a week mucking out the stalls. Lucifer arrived that week."

"So he's old?"

"About fifteen now. But he hasn't had it easy right from the beginning."

"What happened to him?"

"Not everyone is gentle starting horses. Breaking a horse is a term that shouldn't be used, and Lucifer experienced the word to its full capacity."

Tears filled the lower lids of my eyes as I thought of anyone hurting this magnificent horse.

"As a two-year-old, he already had scars from the unbreakable nylon rope they more than likely tied him up with. The horse breaks before the rope is a motto used."

My breath hitched. I'd seen the few white hairs across the bridge of his nose, but I hadn't known it was from scarring. I couldn't imagine anyone being so cruel to an animal.

"When my father bought him… I remember the look in Lucifer's eyes. Dead. The fight, spirit, it was gone. I never paid attention to the horses. I was too angry dealing with my own shit to care about them." He stopped talking while he stroked his hand down Lucifer's face. "I saw in him what I was afraid one day would happen to me."

Oh, God. A tear escaped and trailed down my cheek. I had the urge to curl my arms around him, but I couldn't. We had to maintain some sort of distance, but Killian was making it really hard when he shared personal stuff, because I was betting he didn't share a lot of himself.

"Did you buy him from your dad? Is that why he's here?"

He turned toward me, his hip against the stall door, hand absently stroking Lucifer's muzzle. "I'm paying a kid at my father's stable to give me proof of any abuse. He gave me something on Lucifer and the authorities went in and removed him. He's been charged, but it's only a fine. The charges for animal abuse are unfortunately minimal, and for a man with money, it's a slap on the wrist. Emily is friends with animal services and had Lucifer brought here."

"He won't go back to him?"

Killian snorted. "Fuck no. I'd never allow it. And my father won't fight for him either. Not now."

"Why not now?"

Killian put his hand on the small of my back. "Emily wants you to meet Clyde and Dale before brunch."

There was no fooling myself. I liked his hand on me. I liked being here with him and hearing him talk. He was much more relaxed than he'd been at Compass and the concert as if he let down his wall a little. The good bits of Killian were visible and raw. But he'd avoided the question and that bothered me.

His hand dropped away, and despite my "no touch" rule, I was disappointed. God, that was so wrong. There were so many reasons being with Killian couldn't work. I'd hooked up with my boss, and it left me without a job, money, or a place to live.

Killian was overbearing and demanding and way too overprotective, which I'd had a taste of already. And I was completely attracted to him. While that was a good thing, it was also bad because I was afraid of losing myself to him in the next month.

I inhaled a deep breath. How was I going to do this? It was day one of our first date.

"You good?" he asked as we walked out to the paddock.

"Yeah. It was nice to meet Lucifer." *And see you like this.* "I love the horses, but the closest I've been to one is on a calendar. They're kind of huge."

He chuckled. "Wait until you meet Clyde and Dale."

The horses were out grazing in enormous fields as far as the eyes could see. We strolled out to where they were munching on the grass, and the horses came over and nudged us for treats. Killian put a handful of jelly beans in the palm of my hand.

"Jelly beans?"

He grinned. "Less slobbery than apples." He uncurled my fingers.

"Keep your hand flat." I nodded, and a gray horse gently nibbled the candies out of my palm. I laughed, his muzzle tickling.

He fed another horse a few. "Me, Logan, Emily, Kat, Crisis and Ream lived on a farm together. Kat and Ream own it now, but this horse was one of Emily's first rescues." He patted the neck of the stunning white horse I'd been feeding. "His name is Havoc. And jelly beans are his favorite treats."

I hadn't realized the band was that close and that they'd lived together. It was like… a family. It warmed me to hear that he had that and obviously still did.

More horses wandered over and ate the candy, some bobbing their heads as they chewed the sugary treats. I fed the last of them to a compact bay horse, laughing when he spat out the black one.

Killian slid his arm around my waist and with one tug, I was up against him. "What are you doing?"

"Touching you." His fingers brushed my bare skin between my T-shirt and my jeans sending heated shivers across my skin. His other hand cupped my chin, thumb stroking back and forth. But I noticed he was careful not to touch my lip.

The sun beamed down on us as the horses grazed nearby, while I stood in Killian's arms. Any resistance was left back in the car or maybe even farther back at my apartment.

I melted. My body sagged into his while he held me.

Oh, God, I was in trouble.

Killian did it for me. He was confident, always had been, and maybe that was what attracted me to him in the first place. He took risks and didn't give a shit what others thought of him. You either liked him or didn't. And when he spoke to you, his attention was solely focused on you.

I hadn't known him to laugh before, but I did now, and it was real. There was no pretense; it came from deep within him, and it set off sparks of colors inside me.

And finally, when Killian kissed me, it was all those things combined. Risky, confident, owning.

It was all consuming.

I thought he was going to kiss me now, but he didn't.

"Emily is coming," he murmured and tucked a strand of hair behind my ear.

My heart dropped. That was why he was holding me. So, Emily would see us.

"Logan has been calling your cell. He's in the house." Emily came up beside us, and Killian slowly released me, but his finger lightly hooked my belt loop, keeping me from moving too far away.

"I left my cell in the car," he said. He leaned in and kissed the side of my neck. "I'll leave you with Emily. You good?"

No. I wasn't good. I was confused and turned on and I wanted him to grab me, pull me into his arms and do a hell of a lot more than kiss me.

Emily smiled and walked away to pat Havoc.

"Yeah. Good."

He tugged on my belt loop, so my back landed up against his chest and then his hands slid down my sides to my hips and tightened.

My breath stalled. My heart raced. My body quivered.

"You're going to kiss me, Savvy. And when you do, there'll be no going back." His warm breath grazed my neck as he whispered, "Breathe, orchid."

He released me and I spun around, stepping away from him.

He winked at me then walked away.

As I stood and watched him, his words drummed into me. He was right. There'd be no going back and that was what scared me.

"Ready to meet Clyde and Dale?"

I turned to Emily and smiled. "Can't wait."

But what I really wanted to do was run after Killian, leap into his arms, and kiss him.

Chapter Eleven

Past Ireland

Killian

I WALKED DOWN THE SCHOOL HALLWAY, MY LIPS STILL TINGLING from kissing Keeva Campbell in the Science lab when our hands bumped as we both reached for our books on the desk we shared in class. We were the last ones to leave the classroom as it was our day for cleanup, meaning making sure everything was put away.

I'd taken the opportunity and leaned in and kissed her. It was more like my mouth pressed against hers for a brief few seconds, but it was my first time kissing a girl, and I really didn't know what to do once I got there.

A few of the older guys on the football team talked about kissing girls, but most didn't.

My brother, Emmitt, being one of them, but he was a year and a half younger, so he wasn't interested in girls. He thought they were disgusting.

I couldn't wait to get home and tell him about it. He'd no doubt make a gagging sound and then want to know every detail.

I pushed open the school doors, and the damp, cool air hit me. I glanced up at the dark clouds and figured I had about five minutes to get home before it poured rain. It was a fifteen-minute walk, but I'd take the shortcut through Mr. McCurdy's sheep field and across the bridge.

Hitching my rucksack over my shoulder, I jogged across the parking lot and climbed the stone fence. I ran across the field, hoping to make it home before I got soaked.

Rain drops fell, and I figured I was going to get wet no matter what so I slowed my pace. Da was going to be furious my new shoes were covered in sheep dung.

That was if he even looked at me.

I didn't care. Not anymore.

And nothing could take away the excitement that I'd kissed a girl. The prettiest girl in school who said she liked me.

Reaching the other side of the field, I jumped the stone fence and headed for the bridge across the stream where Emmitt and I often went and skipped pebbles whenever Mum and Da were fighting. And they fought a lot.

The wet wooden panels on the bridge clunked as I crossed. I stopped in the center where Emmitt and I often grabbed either side of the railings and tried to make the bridge swing. It never did, but it was fun anyway.

The rain fell harder, and I peered over the side of the bridge to look at the stream below where we skipped stones. We had a competition as to who could skip the most and Emmitt was winning with six skips.

That was when I saw it.

The familiar red coat snagged on the rocks.

My heart stopped.

My stomach lurched.

My mind spun.

The water rushed around the red material making a V as if... as if something was blocking its path.

Then I knew. I knew what was obstructing its path.

"Emmitt," I shouted.

Chapter Twelve

Savvy

I GLANCED AT MY PHONE AND THE THIRD TEXT FROM KILLIAN. IT had been two days since the visit to Emily and Logan's farm, and I hadn't spoken to him.

After Emily had shown me the two massive Clydesdale horses that she'd rescued from the horse auction, we had brunch with them on their deck, and it was nice. Really nice because Logan and Emily were amazing and Killian was relaxed and attentive.

He usually had some part of him touching me, whether his thigh under the table or his hand on the small of my back or the light touches like pushing a curl behind my ear. By the time he drove me home, my panties were soaked, and I was contemplating either forgetting the entire arrangement or jumping him right there in the car.

Savvy. Pick up your phone, please.

I wasn't ready to talk to him. My mind hadn't stopped spinning with thoughts of Killian, and I wasn't sure what to do about it yet.

Hence why Mars and I were out for dinner and drinks. She

insisted on it being her treat as an early birthday present, saying I needed this now, not in two months when it was my actual birthday.

"Is it him again?" Mars asked.

"Yeah." I shut off my phone and placed it in my purse. I'd talk to him tomorrow when I was sober. Drunk texting was a bad idea. I'd probably end up inviting him over and sleeping with him.

We were on the patio of an Italian restaurant on King Street where we'd had dinner and shared a couple bottles of wine while I'd told Mars everything about the arrangement with Killian. Of course, she had to swear on her life not to tell anyone about the fake dating.

And at first I thought it was a great idea to go out and have a few drinks. Now that I was tipsy, I wasn't so sure. I had no willpower to block him out.

I was thinking of when he held my hand as we walked back to his car after saying goodbye to Emily and Logan. And even though I knew it was for show, it felt right.

How he was so relaxed with them and how he and Logan were pumped about the new album they were working on. His intense side had always attracted me to him, but seeing him so easygoing, that was on another level and I didn't know if I could resist him.

"Oh, just fuck him and get it out of your system already," Mars blurted.

My sex tweaked at the thought. God, I wanted to fuck him. There'd never been any question I did. I wanted to feel his hands all over me, to taste every inch of his body, have him sink inside me.

I sipped my wine shaking my head. "No. I can't."

"Why not?" Mars wore that tiny mischievous smile where the right side of her mouth twitched.

"He's paying me to date him, that's why." Although, I had yet to cash the check. I didn't know why, but it was still shoved in the bottom of my purse.

"Did you ever think about why he's paying you to date him? I mean he doesn't need to pay a girl. They'd pay him to date them."

True, but Killian didn't date. "He doesn't want the hassle of dating."

"But he's never dated. Why now?"

I shrugged. "He said it's good for his reputation."

Mars laughed. "Savvy, that man doesn't give a shit about what other people say about him. No, I think he just wants to date you, and this way you can't say no. The guy liked you in high school, and he likes you now."

"That's ridiculous," I muttered.

"He wants you, so just fuck him and have fun for the month. And, babe, if you ever date him for real, he is nothing like the douche David."

No, he was nothing like David. Killian turned my body into a puddle of melted butter. David never did that. "He'd never do what David did. That's beneath him."

"So call him. Tell him to come over and fuck you. And then tell me if he has a cock piercing."

"Oh, my God. I'm not telling you that."

"But you are thinking about it."

"No." I changed the subject because her idea was sounding better and better. At least my body sure as hell thought so. "What about that guy you met at the gym?"

"Matt?"

"Yeah."

She shrugged. "Nope. Do you know he told me my outfit was too revealing and gave guys the wrong impression?" She shook her head. "I'm working out. What does he expect me to wear? A snowsuit?"

We both giggled, and she flagged the bartender and ordered another bottle of wine, which we consumed while laughing over the silliest things like how her boss Dwight walked like he'd been spanked the night before.

It was nearly midnight by the time we stumbled out, still giggling and I'd thankfully wiped Killian from my mind with the blissful numbness of alcohol.

The cab dropped me first, and I stumbled out, nearly falling when my foot didn't lift high enough to step onto the curb. Mars laughed her ass off, and I gave her the finger. The cabbie waited until I was in the front door of my building then drove away.

I looked up at the three flights of stairs I had to climb. Shit.

I gripped the railing with both hands. "Damn, this sucks," I mumbled as I started, slowly, up each step that appeared as if it was swaying or was it me swaying?

"What the fuck?"

Hmm, that sounded like Killian's raspy voice. Was he so ingrained in me that I was hearing him everywhere I went?

I was concentrating on the next step and not the footsteps coming down the stairs toward me or the curses that accompanied the footsteps.

"Jesus." Then he said, "She's here. And by the looks of it smashed."

"Damn. I've never seen her smashed."

Was that Trevor?

I looked up and a blurred vision of Killian stood on the step above me. I rocked backward because he was really tall and I had to crank my neck far to see his face.

His arm shot out to hook my waist and stopped me from tumbling down the steps.

"Ya're... here?" I slurred.

Killian was here. In my building. How was he in my building? Why was he in my building in the middle of the night?

"Mmm," he murmured.

He bent and scooped me up in his arms. My arms hooked his neck, and my head lolled to the side to rest against his chest.

I closed my eyes and sighed. It felt good in his arms. Safe. Warm. Protected.

I'd never felt protected. I'd always had to rely on myself, but with Killian... it felt as if I wasn't alone. But what scared me more was that it felt like I'd come home.

A home I'd never had before. At least, not one I could remember before my dad died.

"I'm home," I whispered.

"Yeah."

But that wasn't what I was talking about.

Killian carried me to my bedroom then lowered me to the bed. "Let go, baby."

Baby? Did he just call me baby? Oh, God, he couldn't say things like that.

I uncoiled my arms from his neck and leaned back on the pillow, closing my eyes. "Thank you."

"You won't thank me in the morning," he said.

"Why not?"

His hands were on my right foot, and my heel slipped off and clunked on the floor. "We're not talking about it while you're piss drunk."

"I'm... not... pissss drunk."

"You are." His fingers encircled my ankle as he raised my left foot and tugged off the other high heel.

"Mmm, maybe. A little," I murmured, closing my eyes and snuggling my cheek into the plush pillow.

"Lift your butt."

His hands were on either side of my waist, and I sighed when the tip of his finger brushed my bare skin.

He grunted.

I kept my eyes closed, imagining him climbing onto the bed and straddling me. Then the feel of his hard body on top of mine, his hips grinding into me.

"Jesus Christ. Stop," he barked.

My eyes flew open, and I groaned as the room spun. "Stop what?"

"The sighing and moaning. Butt." I lifted, and he yanked off my skirt. "Where are your pajamas?"

I watched as he folded my skirt and placed it on the bench at the bottom of my bed. God, he looked incredible standing in my bedroom. Biceps bulging, tattoos vibrant and his towering frame standing next to my bed.

"Do you have a cock piercing?"

His head jerked up and eyes snapped to mine. I expected him to either not answer or change the subject because he was scowling at me and didn't look pleased with the question.

"Yes," he replied. My eyes widened and my sex tweaked, despite the amount of alcohol I'd drank. He walked back to the head of the bed where his fingers undid the tiny buttons on my top.

My breath hitched as his knuckles grazed my breast. "Killian." It totally was the alcohol talking, inhibitions slandered by red wine. "I don't like drunk butterflies. You do that to me."

It was as if I hadn't said anything as he undid the last button. Then he put his hand on my shoulder and eased me up while he pulled my top over my head.

"Under the covers." He yanked them down from beneath me then drew them back up to my chin.

"She okay?"

"Trevor?" I mumbled.

"Yeah. Came to check on you," he replied.

I tried to sit up, but Killian put his hand on my shoulder. "Lie down."

"Okay." I closed my eyes and my head stopped spinning. I heard low talking but couldn't decipher what Trevor and Killian were saying. "You have good bits, Killian Kane. Lots of them."

I heard a grunt followed by footsteps before the light flicked out.

I then passed out.

"Oh, God." I sat up holding my head, the pounding like shards of glass piercing my skull. I rarely drank like that. Actually, I couldn't remember the last time I had.

I glanced over at my clock. Eight. I plopped back down and put the pillow over my head, groaning. How the hell did I get home last night?

The last thing I remembered was crawling into a cab with Mars at the restaurant.

I rolled onto my side and reached for the bottled water I kept there. That was when I saw the two pills beside it.

Did I put those there last night knowing I'd feel like a truck had run me over then backed up and did it again? I must have.

I grabbed the two pills, put them in my mouth, then cracked the seal on the bottle. Tossing the lid on the nightstand, I then swallowed the pills while chugging the water.

I put the half-empty bottle back on my nightstand and lay back again. "God, never again."

That was when I heard voices in the kitchen. What the hell?

I darted upright, which was a bad idea because the shards turned to a sledgehammer.

Oh, my God, tell me I didn't bring a guy home with me last night. I'd never done that in my life, but there were a lot of things I'd been doing lately that I'd never done in my life.

I threw back the covers and realized I was in my panties and bra. Did I undress last night? I looked on the floor for my clothes, but they weren't there. No chance was I in good enough shape to put them away. Then I noticed them folded neatly on the bench at the foot of my bed.

I never put my clothes there.

My heart pounded as my mind spun with possibilities. There was a flicker of a memory of Killian, but then I'd been thinking of him a lot, so that wasn't unusual.

Jesus, what did I do last night?

I got up and went to my dresser, pulled out black yoga pants and a white V-neck T-shirt. After putting them on, I crept to my bedroom door.

"I have someone looking into it." Holy shit, that was Killian. What the hell was he doing in my apartment at eight in the morning?

I opened the door, and both heads turned to me.

My mouth dropped open at the sight. Trevor stood at the stove cooking what smelled like bacon, and Killian leaned against the counter, a steaming mug in his hand.

"What are you guys doing here?" I held the doorframe to keep myself steady because my balance was a little off.

Killian set his coffee down and strode toward me. Even with a head that felt as if it had a ticking time bomb inside ready to explode at any moment, Killian had my girly parts tingling.

"Umm, what are you doing here?" I asked, softer this time because he was closer.

His brows lifted with that sexy piercing. "You don't remember?"

"Remember?" My heart thumped faster. Ah, shit. I'd slept with him. Mars and I had been talking about me sleeping with him and... oh, my God. Did I call him last night?

I may have woken in my bra and panties, but I didn't feel like I'd had sex. I mean, I'd feel it even if I didn't remember. Right? My cheeks felt on fire, and I wanted to dive back into my room and under the covers and do my wake up all over again.

"Nothing happened," Killian said.

"But you were here last night?"

"Mmm."

"How did you get in?"

"That would be me," Trevor called.

I frowned. He winked then turned back to the sizzling bacon.

I peered at Killian. "Why are you here now?"

"I haven't left."

My eyes widened and I quickly took in his rumpled T-shirt and hair. "Oh."

With his hand on the small of my back, he guided me to the table and urged me to sit. I didn't need much urging because my legs were quivering. Whether it was hangover quivers or quivers from Killian, I wasn't sure yet.

"You didn't answer your cell last night." Killian had it in his hand and slid it toward me.

I glanced at the screen. Five text messages. Twelve missed calls.

All Killian. "Why would you call me that many times? I was out with Mars."

Killian didn't sit; instead, he leaned against the table, brows low and the amusing grin gone.

Trevor took the pan off the burner. "I forgot the eggs. Be back."

I glared at him as he passed, but he kept his head low as he brushed past me. Traitor. I was so letting any girls who knocked on his door into his apartment.

The door opened and shut.

I started to stand. "I need—"

"Sit."

Not a good tone. I sat.

This was his play. Silence. He was annoyingly patient and of course it made me uneasy, on edge, and probably exactly what he wanted.

"I texted and called you, Savvy."

My head swam in sludge, and I was slow on the uptake this morning, so I remained quiet.

I heard a clank and Killian set a coffee in front of me. He nodded to my cell phone on the table. "You need to answer that."

"I didn't answer because I turned it off."

He gave me a "no shit" look, which meant brows raised.

"I didn't feel like talking to you."

"Why?"

Why? Hmm, because every time I hear your voice, I get all weak and pathetic and think about you kissing me again. "I was out with Mars."

"And you couldn't pick up your phone or check your messages. Send me a text?"

Of course I could've, but I was trying to numb Killian out, and hearing his sexy voice on the phone when drunk wouldn't have been a good idea. "Where did Trevor go? I'm starving."

"He won't be back."

Double traitor.

He stepped closer to me, so his thighs were an inch away from mine. Then he reached forward and with the tip of his finger, he slid it ever so slowly across my collarbone. My heart shot off as goose bumps rose and my sluggish aching head was having a hard time keeping up with my body's reaction.

"Why did you shut off your phone?" His tone softened and sounded sexy as hell.

His hand moved up to cup my chin and tilt my head so I was forced to meet his eyes.

Shit. I really loved his eyes.

"Why did you shut off your phone, Savvy?"

"Because I didn't want to talk to you."

"Why?"

"Because of this."

"What is this?"

"I don't like it. What you do to me. I feel… helpless."

He sighed. "You'll never be helpless, Savvy. You're the least helpless woman I know."

I shoved back my chair and stood, which thankfully dislodged his hand. "Thank you for last night, but you better go. I volunteer at the hospital on Wednesdays and need to get ready."

I took a wide berth around him, went behind the counter, feeling a little more secure having something between us and grabbed a piece of overcooked bacon. Trevor always made it so crunchy it broke apart in your mouth.

But my security didn't last long because he came around the counter and trapped me, arms locking me in so my abdomen pressed into the lip of the counter, his hands resting on either side of me with his chest to my back.

"Orchid." His whispered word wafted across the back of my neck, and I shivered. "I need you to answer your phone when I call or text, please. I was worried. You live in a shit neighborhood and an unsafe building." Okay, that was kind of nice that he was worried, but he wasn't my boyfriend or anything.

He moved in closer, so his hard body was pressed into mine. My pulse spiked. "Looks like the same pot I gave you."

I stiffened, eyes darting to the orchid in the cracked pink pot sitting on the windowsill. Of course he'd notice.

"That my pot, Savvy?" he asked.

There was no denying it. "Yes."

"My orchid?"

"Yes."

His warm breath was against my ear as he whispered, "Exotic. Graceful. Beautiful and strong. And one of the most coveted plants." He lowered his voice even further, so his words were barely audible. "That's why I nicknamed you orchid. You are all those things."

My body sank into a pool of heated bliss. "We're fake dating." I said it to remind myself that Killian and I weren't real.

"You can call it whatever you want. But you know exactly what this is."

The second the warmth of his body left mine, I wanted it back again. God, I wanted Killian back. Not that I'd ever had him, but a taste of him.

"What do you mean?"

He strode to the front door. "I'll see you at Compass."

"What? You're going?"

"Savvy. You're dancing at my club. Do you really think the guy you're dating wouldn't be there? Answer your phone when I call. Unless of course you enjoy me showing up and undressing you." He offered a crooked grin. "Nice panties by the way. I love black lace."

I gaped. He opened the door and was gone.

Chapter Thirteen

Killian

I HATED THE CLUB.

I wanted to be punching my bag in my warehouse rather than sitting here with a drink while Savvy danced in a fuckin' cage with guys looking at her.

Watching her lasted a total of five seconds before I had to walk away; otherwise, I'd have dragged her out of the cage and the club.

How the hell did this happen?

Fuck. The instinct to protect her was so strong it ate at my control. A control I'd built up since I'd stopped fighting.

The need to protect those I cared about was embedded in me. I lived with losing Emmitt every fuckin' day. I relived the image of him cold and lifeless in the stream. Cradling him to my chest while the rain pounded down on us and the river soaked me as I sat in the water with him on my lap. It was hours before someone found us. I didn't even know who it was. I just remember fighting them when they tried to take Emmitt away from me.

Emmitt lay dead in a cold stream, and I'd been kissing Keeva Campbell.

I'd done everything I could to change who I'd become after his death. The fighting. The anger. The volatile emotions like lightning strikes going off at any given moment.

But Savvy... Savvy had always had something in her that tamed the lightning ever since the first time I saw her. She believed in people. She was stubborn and determined to get what she wanted, yet giving and accepting of others at the same time.

Fuck, she still volunteered at the hospital. But that shouldn't surprise me. That was who she was. She obviously had no money from the state of her car and her apartment. That fuckin' ex-boyfriend screwed her over and instead of being bitter, angry and complaining about it, she was trying to get her life back together while still taking the time to help others.

Emmitt would've gotten along with her. They were similar in that they both had kindness running through their veins. Forgiveness.

I didn't forgive so easily.

I knew Savvy's attraction to me was just as strong as mine. She tried to hide it. Fight it. But you couldn't hide goose bumps. Shivers. The way her breath hitched and her heart pounded.

One month. I had one month to convince her to be with me for real.

A shadow hovered over me, and I glanced up to see Luke. His gaze shifted to my untouched scotch.

I couldn't drink. Not tonight. Not when I was feeling volatile. "Did you find him?"

"Yeah." He paused, then, "He's a scumbag."

I snorted. "Yeah." I'd asked Luke to locate David so I could have a chat with him. I'd already known he was scum since he'd cheated on Savvy. Not only did he cheat, but he cheated on someone as fuckin' rare as Savvy which made him a scumbag and a bastard.

Luke frowned. "Jolie won't like it if you confront this guy."

Jolie was the band's publicist and she most definitely wouldn't be happy about me going to my "girlfriend's" ex-boyfriend's place to beat the shit out of him. But I didn't do that anymore. I was going to have a conversation.

"The faster I deal with this, the faster I can get her out of here," I said. Because I wasn't sure how long I'd be able to handle her dancing at the club.

"I'm not letting you go without me," Luke said.

I grinned. "I know."

Luke nodded to the dance floor. "She's on break." Then he walked away.

Savvy. I wanted to see her. I always wanted to see her. Be near her. Fuck, what the hell was I going to do if at the end of the month she wouldn't be with me?

That couldn't happen. Keeping away from her was impossible now.

I pulled out my phone and texted. She'd have her phone as all the girls did when they were on the floor in case they needed security. No drugs and every precaution for safety were nonnegotiable when Brett and I discussed opening Compass.

I want to see you.

With Savvy, it was better to be direct. As direct as I could be without scaring her off.

I'm going to refresh in the change room for ten minutes.

You can refresh with me. I'm upstairs.

There was no response and my hand tightened on my phone, but it was the movement by the stairs that caught my attention and had my heart slamming into my chest like some fuckin' teenager seeing the hot girl walking down the school hallway.

Fuck.

I'd always thought I never dated because of what happened when I'd kissed Keeva Campbell. I'd let Emmitt walk home by himself when I knew the kids teased him. But at the time, kissing a girl became more important.

As Savvy walked toward me, I realized it wasn't that. It was because I never wanted to date anyone else.

Just her.

But I kept myself from her. The one girl who made it okay to forgive myself for what happened to my brother.

Her skin was flushed, the blue lights in the club bouncing off the glistening of sweat on her bare neck. A neck I couldn't wait to taste and nip and run my tongue across.

I tossed my phone on the glass table in front of me and sat back on the leather couch, the material scrunching.

Then I watched as she walked toward me. Seductive. Slow and sexy as hell, yet completely unaware of it. Her hair was loose, just the way I liked it. It hung over her right shoulder and breast.

She approached me and her chest rose and fell with quickened breath.

My cock was rock-hard, and it took a fuck of a lot to stay where I was and not grab her and take her into the office so I could tear off her clothes and fuck her on the desk.

She frowned as she stopped in front of me. "Are you okay?"

Fuck no. I was sitting in a club I'd bought in order to hurt my father's business with a girl I wanted, but couldn't have. At least not yet.

"Come here, orchid." I held out my hand.

She hesitated, before placing her warm hand in mine. I tugged her forward until she stood between my legs. "I don't have long."

"Then we better make the best of it. Would you like some water?"

"No. Thanks."

I took another second to admire her standing between my legs before I urged her down to straddle me.

"What are you doing?" she asked, stiff and uncertain as I positioned her, so her thighs were on either side of me.

"Being with my girl on her break," I replied.

Her chest rose and fell erratically. "Here? Now?"

I smirked. "Where else? Would you prefer somewhere more public than this?" I sure as hell didn't. I wanted her in my bed without anyone knowing my fuckin' business.

"No, it's just...."

It was cute she didn't know where to put her hands, so I took them and placed them on my chest. Maybe not the smartest idea considering my cock hurt like hell, and all I could think about was kissing her slightly parted lips.

I raised my brows. "Just?"

"Unprofessional."

I chuckled. "This is a club. It's midnight and you're dating me."

"I already have a bad rep, Killian."

And I was going to do something about that. "No one will talk bad about you dating me, Savvy. Fuck, I'd never allow it." And the media treated me with respect because I did them. And if anyone treated Savvy with anything but respect, they wouldn't like what happened.

"Relax, baby," I whispered as she sat tensely on top of me. I released her wrists and settled my hands on her thighs that were covered in tight black pants. Her top was white, beaded with spaghetti straps and a snug bodice. Classy and sexy as hell.

I slowly slid my hands down her thighs to her knees and back again. Her fingers curled into my dress shirt, and I inwardly smiled.

"How do you expect me to relax when you touch me like that?" she whispered.

At least she was admitting my touch did something to her. I just needed her to admit she wanted me.

"You piece of shit!"

My hands stilled on Savvy's thighs, and I stiffened at the familiar voice behind me. Savvy looked over her shoulder, and her hands released my shirt as she scrambled off my lap.

"Seamus. Now, this is a surprise," I managed to ground out.

"Kite," Luke said, coming up behind my father. He was letting me know, he'd escort him out with one word from me.

But this conversation was bound to happen. I just didn't like it being done in front of Savvy. I didn't want her tainted by his cruelty.

He glanced at Savvy, his eyes trailing down the front of her. I clenched my jaw, standing to block his view of her. "Fucking the lowlife dancers, Kill?"

I heard Savvy's sharp inhale and Luke's grunt as he stepped toward my father. I shook my head at him.

I had the urge to smash my fist into his arrogant face, but I refused to give him the satisfaction. "Club business not doing well, Seamus?" I asked politely.

His eyes narrowed, and I remembered that look. The hatred blazing as he towered over me while calling me a bastard and a useless piece of shit. The sound of the door slamming shut as he locked me in my empty bedroom. "You can't get away with this. I have friends, powerful friends, and the second this club fails one inspection or has one incident, it's over."

He did have powerful friends, but then, I did too.

I glanced over at Luke. "Take Savvy out of here."

He nodded and Savvy moved from the couch as Luke stepped forward to use his body to protect her from my father's view, but it wasn't enough. The bastard had to open his fuckin' mouth.

"I'll double your pay if you come dance at my club," he offered Savvy.

My temple throbbed, but I refused to say anything. Not yet. No matter how hard it was, Savvy was more than capable of answering him herself.

She did better than that. Savvy shrugged out of Luke's hold and walked up to him. "I'd have to be dead before I worked for you."

"You're going to end up dead if you hang out with him."

Fuck.

Savvy didn't even flinch, but then she had no idea he was referring to Emmitt and my mother.

This was the side of Savvy I'd seen on the steps outside of school. Defiant, determined, and beautiful as a raging river glistening in the morning sunrise.

"Better to die happy with him than alone and never knowing what an amazing man he is."

My father's mouth opened in shock and before he could mention Emmitt or my mother, I stepped in and hooked my arm around Savvy's waist. "Go with Luke, baby," I whispered.

She did, but several times she looked over her shoulder at me, as if making sure I was okay before she disappeared downstairs.

Then I turned my attention to my father. "You're not welcome here. I expect you to leave quietly and never show your face here again."

"You think because you're in a famous band now that you can do whatever you want? You'll never escape who you are." He looked me up and down with a sneer. "Look at you. Tattooed. Pierced. You don't deserve to have the Kane name."

I stared at the man who made my life hell for years. I didn't give a shit how he treated me before Emmitt died as long as he'd treated my brother okay. But I didn't need to take his shit anymore.

"Are you done?"

He pursed his lips together. "I can have it shut down." He had a few judges in his pocket, but I had Deck, and Deck had a number of friends in the police department.

It was probably why for years my father had the club district. He had others who tried to open clubs shut down before they even had a chance.

He got right in my face, his finger pointing at my chest. "This is far from over."

"Nice to see you again, Seamus," I said, then nodded at Luke who was back without Savvy.

"Mr. Kane. If you'll follow me," Luke urged. He took his cues from me, and I knew he'd do it politely unless my father objected, then all niceties were thrown out the door along with my father.

I picked up my Scotch and chugged it back in one shot. Then I called Logan.

"You okay?" Logan asked since I rarely called him after midnight.

"You up for sparring? My place."

"Meet you in thirty," Logan said without hesitation. There were no questions as to why I needed to fight at midnight. It was my way to get rid of the anger, and he knew that.

"Give me an hour?" I asked. There was no way in hell I was leaving Savvy here alone.

"Sure," he replied.

I hung up then walked to the railing to make sure Savvy was okay. She danced in the cage, looking fuckin' stunning and sexy and everything inside me wanted to run down the stairs and kiss her.

I turned away, leaning against the railing, arms crossed and body tense.

It was the longest fuckin' hour of my life.

As soon as Savvy was finished for the night, I made sure Luke stayed with her then escaped the club through the back door and went to the warehouse where I met Logan. We fought until neither of us could lift our arms anymore.

Chapter Fourteen

Savvy

"K ITE," THE MAÎTRE D' SAID WITH A BROAD SMILE AS WE walked into the restaurant. "It's been too long."

It was Saturday night and I hadn't seen Killian all week. I wasn't sure if it had something to do with his father showing up at Compass or not. He'd texted me though and called a few times just to talk, which was nice and unexpected from him considering it wasn't like he had to or anything since the dating wasn't real.

And I liked that. God, I liked it a lot.

I worked again Thursday and Friday night, but Killian hadn't been there, although Luke was always within eyesight.

"Good to see you, François," Killian replied and shook his hand. "How have you been?"

"The building has not been the same."

Killian chuckled. "Meaning it's quiet."

François smiled. He looked about fifty and had strong, defined features, dark bushy brows with a speckling of silver that matched his thick head of hair. Attractive.

"Quieter, yes," François said with a broad grin.

"This is Savvy. Savvy. François," Killian said.

François took my hand and kissed the back of it. "Lovely to meet a friend of Kite's."

Killian put his hand on the back of my neck and squeezed, then slid it down my bare back.

I shivered as the callouses on his palm lightly scratched my skin, leaving behind a lingering path of heat. I'd been a yo-yo of emotions ever since I opened my apartment door to see Killian dressed in suit pants and a white dress shirt.

He was perfection. Dark gray slacks fitted low on his hips with no creases, the material falling in all the right places. The top two buttons on the white dress shirt were undone, and his tattoos were barely visible under the luxurious material.

But the tattoo of the bird of prey on his neck was vibrant against the stark white shirt.

There was no tie and it was too hot for a suit jacket, but he looked classy, even with tattoos and a piercing in his brow.

There was no question that anyone who saw him knew he had money. Not just because of his clothes, but because he owned who he was.

Not showy, but with a quiet confidence.

The first words out of Killian's mouth when I opened the door tonight were, "So, beautiful."

"It fits perfectly. Thank you." A package had arrived in the afternoon and in it was a note that read, 'Please accept this gift. I'll pick you up at seven. Killian.' It was a sweet gesture and my heart raced and hands had trembled when I opened it. Not so much that it was a gift, but the fact that Killian had been thinking about me.

The black dress was stunning and fit perfectly, the shoes gorgeous and they should be because I'd seen the label and knew they had to be at least five hundred dollars. I'd never worn anything so expensive in my life.

"My pleasure." His finger had slid over my bare shoulder to the spaghetti strap where he'd traced the length of the strap. A bundle of nerves swarmed into a tight knot in my core. "You have an incredible body, Savvy."

Heat burned in my cheeks under his intense gaze, and since the dress clung to every inch of my body, it felt as if he were looking at me naked.

"Inside and out you're beautiful."

"Thank you. You look really good, too, Killian."

He'd grinned, then slid his hand into mine. That's when I felt the scab on his knuckle and when I looked there was bruising too.

Now, we were being led to a table in a fancy restaurant by François. Killian thought it was a good spot for a more public appearance of us dating.

He stayed close to me, his hand on my back as we weaved through the tables. Several people, mostly women, admired him as we passed. But I noticed men looked at me, too.

"Sexy as hell," he whispered, leaning into me. "You have every man's attention in this fuckin' place. I may have to start fighting again."

"You see guys watching me dance at Compass."

"No. I don't watch you. Luke does." No wonder I never felt his eyes on me when I was dancing. "When I watch you dance, Savvy, it will be for my eyes only."

Oh. Wow.

François sat us at a corner table where the lights were dim, and no other tables were within five feet. On the center of the table was a silver oblong bowl with several candles floating in cerulean blue water with white rose petals. There was a hint of their fragrance drifting in the air that mixed with the sensual scents of spices from food at nearby tables.

Killian pulled out the chair for me. "Thanks, François," he said. "Appreciate the table."

"Always a pleasure, Kite. Mademoiselle Savvy." He bowed his head to me, backed a couple of steps and then turned and hurried away.

Killian didn't sit across from me. He sat in the chair next to me, so we were close and intimate.

126

I placed the napkin on my lap. "You know one another?"

"When I lived with Crisis and Haven, we had a place around the corner. I came here for lunch sometimes. But I got to know François from our building. He had the other penthouse." He continued, "He owns the restaurant."

"Oh. I thought he was the maître d'."

Killian sat back in his chair and straightened his legs under the table so they brushed up against mine and stayed there.

I swallowed, wanting to shift my legs away and yet unable to move because I really liked the sweet torture of having his leg against mine.

"He's here every lunch and dinner looking after his guests and refuses to hire anyone else to do the job. He says this is how he gets to know his customers, and they him. This place is his pride and joy."

"I can tell," I said.

I'd noticed François nod and smile at patrons on the way to our table.

The place was classy with expensive chandeliers and intricately carved woodwork on the chairs and bar, but it had a personal feel to it. As if we were all guests in François' home.

He opened the folder and scanned the contents. "Red or white?"

"Red, please," I answered.

The waiter arrived, and Killian ordered wine and sparkling water. We then chatted about the band and the tours. I wanted to ask him about his father, but it wasn't the place, and Killian seemed so relaxed, I didn't want to ruin that.

I did notice his knuckles had cuts on them and wondered if he had fought his dad after I left.

He asked me about Mars, what movies I liked and the plays I'd been in. I talked and he quietly listened.

And when Killian listened, he did it completely. He never appeared bored and his eyes never wandered. He focused on me and nothing else.

It was unnerving to have someone's attention like that, yet it made me feel as if every word out of my mouth was important, and he wanted to know more about me and what I'd done for the last eleven years. I had to keep reminding myself that this wasn't real. But God, it felt real.

We hadn't even opened the menus when the waiter asked what we'd like. Killian looked at me. "Is there anything you don't like?"

"Oysters. But that's about it." David had liked them and ordered them all the time when we'd gone out. I'd tried one of his once, but the texture bothered me.

He nodded and turned back to the waiter. "Tell Chef Fredrick it's Kite, and we'll have whatever he suggests, except oysters."

"Of course, sir." The waiter nodded. "He will be pleased to hear that." The waiter hurried away.

"You know the chef, too?"

"François and Fredrick are a couple." He reached for the bottle and poured me more red wine and he refilled his sparkling water.

We ate and chatted about everything except his father and what happened at the club. There was something there though. I'd tasted the animosity in the air and it was obvious Killian owning the club wasn't just an investment opportunity. Then there was the issue of him paying someone in his dad's stable to get proof of the abuse to the horses.

After we finished, Killian asked the waiter to bring Chef Fredrick's best dessert to share.

"Oh, my God, I don't have any room for dessert," I said, laughing.

"He'd be offended if we didn't," he replied, then leaned back in his chair. "And I'm not ready to stop watching you lick your lips," he drawled.

I resisted the urge to lick my lips as my core heated and tightened, and tingles sprinkled everywhere.

A shadow cast over our table. "I'm so sorry, but can I get your autograph? I'm a huge fan of Tear Asunder."

I lifted my eyes to the twenty-something girl standing beside Killian, a cocktail napkin and pen in hand.

My gaze shifted to Killian who wasn't looking at the girl but at me. Bold, intense green eyes observing, no doubt for my reaction because a girl stood beside our table in a fancy restaurant asking for Killian's autograph.

I smiled, brows lifting. It was kind of cute, especially since he wasn't the type to bask in the attention of fans.

Killian politely took the napkin and pen from the girl and placed it on the table. He glanced up at her. "What's your name?"

"Veronica, but just Vee is good," she replied, her hands clasped together in front of her, expression awestruck.

She briefly met my eyes, and I smiled because her voice quaked and hands shook. She was really nervous.

He scribbled something on the napkin and passed it back. "All the best, Veronica."

"Thank you so much. I can't wait for your new album." She pranced away, her eyes glued to the napkin, and since she wasn't looking where she was going, she ran into a waiter who nearly dumped his tray of drinks on the elderly man and woman.

"Does this happen often?" I asked.

He shrugged. "For Logan it does. For me, not as much."

The waiter arrived with the dessert, a crème brûlée with raspberries and blueberries.

He set it between us with two spoons. "Coffee, sir?"

Killian raised his brows to me, and I shook my head. He looked back at the waiter. "No, thank you. Please tell Chef Fredrick everything was outstanding."

He moved off, and I picked up a spoon, cracked the brown sugar topping with the tip then scooped out a spoonful of sweet whipped deliciousness.

Casually lifting my chin and tilting my head, the spoon midway to my mouth, I said, "So, I guess word will spread that you were having dinner with a redhead?"

Killian grinned. "Yes. It was probably on social media the second we walked in." His grin faded and in its place was a smoldering, heated intensity in his eyes as he watched me slide the silver spoon into my mouth.

The thin sweet crunch mixing with the light, airy cream tickled my tongue.

Indulging was rare. Indulging in something like crème brûlée was heaven on a spoon.

But what made it even more like heaven was that Killian watched me with desire blazing in his eyes.

I swallowed, then with the tip of my tongue, I slid it over my lower lip, licking the remnants of cream.

"Fuck," he growled.

I secretly smiled, heart pumping wildly.

I'd never been sexy or tried to be sexy, but I wanted to be with Killian. He made it easy for me to be brave.

Lights dim, candles flickering, the soft jazz music in the background, skin tingling from the sexy-as-hell man next to me, yeah, I was brave.

I dipped the spoon in again, but Killian's fingers spanned my wrist, stopping me.

I met his eyes and without a word, but knowing exactly what he wanted by the silent exchange of his steady expression, I released the spoon to him.

His attention went to the dessert where he tapped the light thin sugar shell before breaking through and sinking into the airy lightness.

He lifted the overfilled spoon at the same time as his eyes.

I thought he was going to take a bite himself, but he held the spoon out to me. "Open."

I nervously laughed, thinking he was kidding; it was a huge mouthful. "It's too much."

"I know. Open, Savvy," he said.

Oh, God, my belly dropped and my sex clenched. I swallowed, licking my lips again.

"No," he said with a firm voice. "I didn't ask you to lick your lips. Although that is fuckin' delectable as hell." His tone lowered further. "I asked you to open your mouth."

My eyes widened. Holy. Fuck. That was hot. Demanding and a

little scary because him using that voice I'd pretty much do anything he asked.

I opened, and he slid the dessert into my mouth, and since there was so much, it hit the roof, sides, and back of my throat. He didn't remove the spoon right away and watched as I struggled not to pull away.

When I was just about to say screw it, he said, "My cock will fill your mouth a hell of a lot more than this."

I nearly choked. And I would've if he didn't slowly remove the spoon, my lips dragging over the cool, smooth surface of the spoon to make certain I took the entire dessert.

His elbow rested on the table, spoon in his hand, eyes on mine as I swallowed little by little until it was gone. The entire time I thought about his cock.

Was it possible to have an orgasm with no touching? Because if it was, I was going to come right here at the table with people all around and Killian watching.

God, why did I find this so hot?

Okay, I'd never had a man speak to me like Killian.

But it was more. He was polite and casual yet intense and demanding. He also obviously liked to get his own way.

"Open," he said.

I did, and he fed me another mouthful watching my every movement.

After the third spoonful, he dropped the spoon on the dish, and it made a loud clatter. My breath hitched and heart jumped at the sound.

He'd done it on purpose. It was as if he wanted that reaction. A contrast from the slow and gentle to the loud and abrupt noise.

"Good, orchid?"

"Yes," I whispered. "Thank you. Aren't you having any?"

"No. Watching you was my dessert," he drawled before catching the eye of the waiter and offering a nod. "Are you ready to go?"

"I uh, just have to go to the ladies' room first." Because I was flushed and my panties were wet, and I so needed a minute to collect myself before I sat in the car with him.

His brows lifted as if he knew exactly why I needed an escape. "To the right of the bar." He gestured with a nod.

The escape to the ladies' room was a relief to be out from under Killian's attentiveness.

There was no question he desired me and giddiness filled me to know the confident, sexy, smoking-hot Killian was interested.

But that giddiness also had a layer of uncertainty. There was something dangerous about him. Not fighting dangerous. That had been tamed. Maybe it had shifted to something different.

Something that demanded.

Something that controlled.

Owned.

That was what it was—owning.

The signals indicated that Killian got whatever he desired. And tonight, it was me.

I leaned over the counter as the thought slammed into me and my face heated and sex clenched.

God, what was I thinking? But from my body's reaction, I knew exactly what I was thinking.

Sex with Killian. Rough, demanding sex that owned a woman's body. Protected. Coveted.

I turned on the taps, cupped my hands under the steady stream and brought the cool water to my face.

Was I strong enough to have sex with him and keep my heart? My heart had already been broken once. I'd trusted David, and he'd taken advantage of that trust. He'd made promises and broke them. Maybe I was blinded by those promises of a family and a home, but it had still hurt like hell.

Except this was about sex. Sex with Killian, not a relationship. He wasn't making promises.

But there'd be no question experiencing Killian would leave bits of myself behind just like it had with my first kiss.

And then there was the issue of him paying me to date him. If I slept with him, what would that make me?

"Are you dating Kite?"

I darted upright at the woman's voice, having not heard the door open.

Water dripped down my cheeks, and I quickly reached for the paper towels and dried my face before the water stained my dress.

I looked at her in the reflection of the mirror. She was about twenty or so, with long brown hair and light amber streaks. It reached past her shoulders, and there were some layers at the front that framed her soft, pretty face. Well, it would be soft if it weren't for the harsh eyeliner and bright blue eye shadow.

"Uh, yes."

"I saw you go into the washroom and well, I didn't want to come to your table because I heard he likes his privacy, but I really, really like him." She inhaled then trudged on. "I like his playing. On the drums, I mean. I've seen Tear Asunder in concert four times, and Kite is so calm and easygoing when he plays. He's mesmerizing." Another deep inhale. "I love Ream, too. He's intense and God, he's so sweet and protective with Kat. Well, all the guys are from what I've read and seen. Emily is a sweetheart and rescues horses, and Sculpt isn't into them, but I've seen pictures of him at her horse whispering clinics supporting her. Oh, and Haven is like an angel and helps kids on the street." Another breath. "They are the coolest band around. Sometimes they do surprise gigs at Avalanche where they first started playing. It's so cool of them."

When she paused to take another breath, I quickly interrupted, "Would you like his autograph?"

"Oh, my God, would I? Yes. Yes. I was going to ask if you could maybe ask him."

I smiled. "I'll ask. But I'm sure he'll be fine with it." It was weird because to me, Kite was just Killian. But these girls saw him as a god. An idol.

I laughed to myself as I led the girl back to our table because I'd compared him to Zeus that day on the school steps.

Killian stood beside the table talking to François when I approached with the girl trailing behind.

"Thank you, François," I said. He took my hand and kissed the back of it. "The meal was amazing." Everything had been perfect, including Killian.

"Mademoiselle, it was our pleasure, and when we are not so busy, you must meet my other half."

"I'd like that," I replied, but that was unlikely to happen since our arrangement was over in a month.

He nodded to Killian and then weaved through the tables.

"Killia—" I stopped myself, remembering the fans called him Kite. "Kite, this is..."

"Jenny," the girl offered, stepping from behind me.

"Jenny," I continued. "Do you think you could give her your autograph?" I tried not to laugh because it was odd seeing him as a celebrity.

Of course, Killian saw me biting my lip to stop myself from laughing and rolled his eyes.

Then he shifted his attention to the girl. "Of course," he replied.

The girl took over from there and repeated pretty much what she'd told me in the washroom, except this time at warp speed.

Killian politely listened.

I tilted my chin down to hide my smile.

If only these girls knew what Killian was like before. They wouldn't even consider walking up to him and asking for his autograph.

The girl finally bounced away with Killian's name scrolled across a cocktail napkin. I thought of that day I found the orchid on my trailer steps.

The note where he'd signed his name. It read Killian though, not Kite. I still had it tucked away in a book that sat beside the orchid.

"Ready?" he asked.

"Yes. Thank you for dinner." His gaze flicked to my mouth, and his eyes smoldered. "I was thinking maybe... well, you have fans here and they're watching so maybe I should kiss you? For the publicity, I mean."

He didn't grin. Didn't respond. Didn't do anything for a

moment and I wasn't sure if I said something wrong until his hand slid into mine and our fingers interlocked. He briefly squeezed.

I thought he might kiss me when he moved in closer, but instead, his mouth hovered close to my ear as he whispered in the sexiest voice ever, "No, orchid. I'm not sharing the first time you give in and kiss me with anyone."

Chapter Fifteen

Killian

I HATED DROPPING HER OFF AT THIS FUCKIN' PLACE. IT MADE ME uneasy that there was no security in the building, not even cameras. Then there was the smell of marijuana in the stairwell. A stairwell she had to take because the fuckin' elevator didn't work. My only consolation was as of three days ago, I had Roman—part of Luke's security team—keeping an eye on the place in the evenings.

Bottom line was I had to get her out of here. I just didn't know how to do that yet without pissing her off. Savvy may be kindhearted and sweet and thought everyone had good bits, but insisting she move could shatter anything I'd built so far.

Yet leaving her here didn't sit well. My instinct was to protect. To make sure those I cared for weren't threatened in any way. Fuck, Logan and I had put all the money we had into buying a farm for Emily so she'd feel safe after what happened to her.

"I don't like you living here."

She half laughed as she turned the key in the lock. "Well, this is where I live."

"Savvy, it's a dump." And she deserved better than this.

She smiled, leaning back against the door, her hand behind her on the doorknob. "So what, are you going to burn it down so I have to move?"

I shrugged. "If I have to."

She snorted, and it was so damn cute it took everything I had not to kiss her.

"It's unsafe."

"I've been here for months, and there hasn't been one incident."

"It only takes one," I replied.

"Trevor's across the hall."

"The hacker," I said. "Who makes fake concert passes and whatever else. And therefore has God knows who knocking at his door." Trevor wasn't the problem. I had Luke look into him. The guy was a genius and had graduated with two degrees. What I didn't like was who came to his door for his illegal hacking services.

"Are you embarrassed to *date* a girl who lives here?"

I jolted, scowling. "Fuck, Savvy. No. You know I don't give a shit what people say. I've never been like that."

"But you're dating me for your reputation. Isn't that a little contradictory."

I put my hand on her hip and nearly groaned out loud when I felt her shiver in response. "I think you know this has nothing to do with my reputation."

She tensed. Then within a breath, she relaxed again. "Thank you for tonight."

She stood on her tiptoes, and before I knew what she was doing, she kissed me. It was brief, but the touch of velvet plush lips against mine was irresistible. And when she pulled back, our lips clung for a second as if not wanting to let go.

Fuck. "Savvy," I murmured, fingers tightening on her hip and dragging her into me.

My cock jerked, and it took all my control to not scoop her up into my arms, kick open her door and carry her to bed. But this was about her, not me.

And this was far more than fucking her one night. This was

letting her in and having all of her. If I fucked her while I was paying her to date me... she'd regret it. I couldn't have that.

The creak of the door handle turned and then her door was opening, and she disappeared inside, quietly shutting the door behind her.

I stood in the hallway for a minute staring at the door and listening to her heels click on the hardwood floors inside.

"Don't hurt her."

I stiffened, slowly turning to see Trevor leaning against the doorframe, arms crossed. "I don't plan on it."

"Yeah, well, you're a rock star with a shit track record. Actually, no track record because you don't date. Except suddenly you're dating Savvy and giving her a new car and telling her she can't live here."

"You heard."

Trevor knocked on the wall. "Like you said, a dump. Thin walls."

"Babe, are you coming back to bed?" a female voice called from inside his place.

Trevor ignored her. "I like you because I think you care about her. And you rock on the drums." Trevor pushed off the doorframe. "But this bogus dating thing is bad news."

"She told you?" Fuck, the fewer people who knew about our arrangement, the better. I didn't want Savvy to get hurt by it because the media might not be so kind if they found out, even if the truth was I wasn't fake dating at all.

He shook his head. "No. She didn't have to. Savvy gets a job at Compass, new car, cell phone, and is going on dates with you. She'd never take that shit from you if there wasn't something else going on."

"She didn't willingly take it. And I'd never hurt her."

He shrugged. "Just sayin'. I saw the way she looked at you the other night. She was drunk maybe, but the truth is often revealed when you're drunk. There was nothing bogus about that." He turned, went inside his place and closed the door.

The only way I got her to take the car, money and the cell phone was because of the arrangement we had.

I understood it. She'd worked for everything she'd ever wanted and had grown up with a mother who hadn't given a shit about her. To only then be thrown into the foster care system. But she continued to dance. She took that with her and I wanted her to have that.

But not at a nightclub.

As I walked into my warehouse a half hour later, I tried to picture Savvy here, in this empty, desolate space with no memories, no attachments, nothing except brick walls and the necessities.

She'd want memories. Pictures on the walls and knickknacks on the shelves. The question was if I could give it to her or was I delusional in thinking this could work.

Tonight had tested my control, watching her eat dessert. The way the cream clung to her lips. How she held it in her mouth, her cheeks flushed.

My dick was so fuckin' hard. It took everything I had not to follow her into the restrooms at the restaurant and fuck her up against the wall. But the first time wouldn't be a quick fuck against a wall. The thought of slipping my cock into her... I didn't know how long I'd last, but I wanted to savor that moment, a moment I'd never experienced before. A moment that would change everything.

I unbuttoned my dress shirt on the way to the bathroom, peeled it off and tossed it on the bed. I finished stripping in the bathroom, my cock jutting out.

I turned on the shower, the rainfall teeming down from the sprayer on the ceiling.

Stepping into the tiled oasis, I stood under the waterfall, tilting my head back, running my hand through my hair then down my chest to my abdomen, then to my cock.

It jerked the second I touched it. *Christ.*

It wouldn't take long tonight. I'd been hard for the last five fuckin' hours.

Closing my eyes, the heated water drizzled over my skin and my hand tightened around my cock as I pictured Savvy.

Her hips swaying seductively in that dress as she walked. A sway she had no idea she had, so completely unaware of her beauty.

I grunted and gripped harder, slowly moving my hand up and down.

Her on her knees in front of me. Still wearing that dress as the water soaked into the material. Her mouth inches from my cock, her hand around it and those doe eyes asking me.

Asking me if she could suck me.

I groaned, my head back, hand moving faster. Tightness clenching.

No. Not yet. Not fuckin' yet.

I slowed. I wanted her mouth first.

Her mouth full of me like the crème brûlée.

She opened her mouth and took all of it. All of me.

I'd purposely given her more than her mouth could comfortably take, wanting to see her reaction.

And I nearly came in my pants like a fuckin' teenager when she did it.

God, she was fuckin' perfect.

I groaned louder as I jerked my cock harder.

Faster.

I leaned against the wall, legs braced, picturing Savvy between my legs sucking me off. My fingers fisted in her red wet curls as I pushed deeper. And deeper. A little choking sound and then she sucked harder.

Her slight gasp.

"Fuuuuckkkk." I groaned as my balls tightened then jolts shot through me again and again as I came.

My cock still in my hand, water drizzling down my wet skin, heart thumping, I bowed my head. "Jesus."

Three more weeks and then this bullshit with the dating would end, and I'd be able to have her.

And when that happened, Savvy Grady was going to place her good bits in my hand, and when she did, I'd close my fist and never let them go.

Chapter Sixteen

Savvy

THE ONLY WAY I COULD DESCRIBE DATING KILLIAN KANE WAS frustrating. I'd never wanted a man as much as I did him, and he didn't make it easy on me. In the last week, we appeared in public places, restaurants, the club, the boardwalk, and the Science Center because there was an exhibit on Wild Weather he wanted to see.

But what really did me in was showing up at my door looking smokin' hot with coffee and croissants for the last five mornings. Sometimes he didn't stay as he had to go to Logan's to work on the album, but other times he did, and we'd sat at my kitchen table and talked while eating the delicious pastries and the best coffee I'd ever had.

One morning Trevor even joined us. It said a lot about Killian as, despite his overprotectiveness and how he reacted to me dancing at the club, he was okay with Trevor being around.

We also went and visited Lucifer again where I broached the subject of his dad. All he told me was he and Emily were attempting to get the horses away from him, but the law wasn't on their side.

Killian was pissed about it, too. I had the feeling he'd drive over there and steal the horses if he could.

I liked him. I mean, I had before, but I really did now.

I knew he wanted more, but there was so much of Killian he kept hidden, and that scared me. I'd trusted David and maybe that was partially my fault, but I wasn't making the same mistake. I didn't even know where Killian lived.

It was nine on Sunday morning and I was getting dressed when there was a knock on the door. I caught myself smiling because I knew it was Killian with coffee. He'd told me last night that he'd pick me up at ten to go for brunch. It was early, but I'd discovered Killian was usually early and never late.

But when I opened the door, it wasn't him.

It was David.

I believed in the good in people. I gave them the benefit of the doubt. I forgave them. But David hurt me. No, it was more than that. He destroyed my willingness to trust.

He stuck out his foot when I tried to slam the door. "Savannah, baby, please. Give me five minutes." He hated my nickname Savvy, said it sounded childish, so he always called me Savannah. I'd never minded until now. I loved how Killian pronounced Savvy with the "a" elongated to "ah."

"No," I retorted and tried to shut the door again, but he pushed inside, and I was forced to back up.

He clicked it closed behind him.

"Get out, David."

David wasn't bulky big, but he was tall, agile, and strong. After all, he did lift dancers above his head. He was good-looking, kind of a pretty boy look with short dark blond hair, a square jaw, and baby blue eyes. He also had a panty-melting grin and was armed with a wink that had all the girls in dance class swooning. And probably why one of them ended up in his bed.

"I want you to come back," he said as he walked toward me. I backed up until my calves hit the coffee table. "I made a huge mistake. It was stupid. You're the best thing that ever happened to me."

"You should've thought of that before you shoved your dick into another girl's pussy." I rarely used language like that, but I was mad that he was here, bringing up all the hurt and emotions that came with him. *God, I can't believe I fell for him.* "You purposely ruined my reputation, David. You sent out an e-mail!"

He bowed his head and ran his hands back and forth over the top. "I know. I know. I was desperate and mad and wanted you back."

"So, you spread rumors that I was difficult to work with and slept with one of my students when it was you who had. I couldn't get a job. No one would hire me. You hurt me, David. What makes you think I'd ever come back to you?"

He was inches away from me now, and my stomach curdled. Slimy. That was what he was. I'd been blinded by him and knew now it was because he'd fit into my dream. What I'd been working for since I was a kid. I loved working at the dance studio. He'd told me he wanted a family. *A family, damn it.* I'd never had a family. God, he'd said he wanted kids.

"I fucked up." He reached for my hand and linked our fingers together. I jerked back and tried to brush past him, but he hooked my waist from behind and pulled me into him. "I love you, Savannah. Please, give me a second chance. You believe everyone deserves one, so why not me?"

I shoved at his arm. "Because you're undeserving. A real man is one who protects those he cares about, not destroys them." I realized after I said it that I'd been referring to Killian.

He stiffened. "You're going to throw us away for a piece-of-shit rock star."

I froze, then violently shoved his arm off me and stepped back swinging around. "Is that why you're here? You saw I was dating him and decided you better get me back?" I pointed at the door. "I won't ask again. Get. Out."

He hesitated a second and then headed for the door. "If you ever want to work in the industry again, I'd think about what you're doing, Savannah. It's not me ruining your rep anymore. Being a club-whore dancer for a rock star is."

I gasped. God, what happened to him? David wasn't at all like this when I'd met him. Or maybe he was, but there'd been no reason for this side of him to come out.

He jerked the door open, and a bulky guy I didn't recognize stood there wearing a black T-shirt and cargo pants, and he had his phone to his ear.

"She's here…. No. She looks fine. Got it." He nodded to me. "I'm Roman, work for Luke. Kite's calling you." His eyes shifted to David. "I'll escort you from the premises."

"I don't need a fuckin' escort, asshole." David shoved past him, but I didn't see what happened because my cell rang on the kitchen counter and I went to answer it.

I glanced at the screen. Killian. "Hey."

"Savvy. You good?" Worry edged his words.

I hadn't realized I was shaking until I heard his voice and suddenly everything hit me. I hadn't seen David in six months, and the confrontation was overdue, but his words had shaken me. I knew he said them to hurt me, and it worked. They had.

"Yeah."

"Is he gone?"

"Yeah." I sat at the kitchen table, head resting in my hands.

"Deep breaths, orchid."

Tears welled. He cared. Killian may be closed off, overprotective, and have underlying issues with anger, but he cared. About me.

"It wasn't a coincidence that Roman was here, was it?"

"No."

At least he was honest about having Roman here. But there was more to this. More to why Killian was so protective of me. "I want to see where you live."

"Okay."

"Okay?"

"I have no problem with you seeing where I live, Savvy. We can go anytime you'd like."

I inhaled a shaky breath. "The fake dating… I don't want to do it anymore." I'd find another way. I still had the check in my purse, and I couldn't cash it because the truth was, none of this was fake. I wanted to date Killian.

I'd made a couple grand at the club and paid two months' rent and my hydro bill so it may take longer to get my dance studio, but I'd get there.

"I'll be there in five."

"Killian…." The phone went dead and I sighed, tossing it on the table.

It was less than five minutes before there was a knock on my door as I was opening the fridge for the orange juice.

The door opened, as I hadn't locked it after David and Roman left, and Killian strode in, coming straight for me. His captivating green eyes read complete possession.

I stood frozen in the open fridge doorway.

He reached me and without hesitation, his hand cupped the back of my neck, and his other gripped my hip then slid upward to my waist under my shirt.

He tilted my head back. "You're dating me. For real."

Then his mouth slammed down on mine.

There was nothing polite about it.

Nothing. Not one thing.

We banged into the fridge and something crashed to the floor.

I was so shocked that it took a second before my mouth eased under his. And then my hands were in his hair, and I was dragging him in closer. But he was already as close as he could get.

His fingers tightened painfully in my hair, and his thumb stroked back and forth under my bra strap.

"Savvy," he murmured against my mouth, and the vibration sent a flare off inside me. "Christ, baby."

His tongue swept inside my mouth, and I felt his tantalizing piercing. If it felt amazing in my mouth, I could only imagine what it would feel like between my legs.

His kiss devoured. Demanded. And everything in me became his. I was tired of fighting it. I wanted Killian. I wanted to feel him inside me.

He broke away and my face burned from his scruff. But I wanted more. Needed more.

"No more bullshit dating, Savvy," he reiterated.

"The check… I can't take the money."

"You did the work."

I smiled. "It's never been work dating you, Killian." But it kind of was. "It was work resisting you."

He groaned, eyes flicking to my lips and then slowly back up to meet my eyes. "I want you. All of you."

My breath hitched. I wasn't sure exactly what he meant, but it didn't matter. I wanted Killian inside me, and I was going to get that. "Yes."

His hands were on my hips as he lifted me up and I wrapped my legs around his waist. He carried me into my bedroom and tossed me on the bed.

The mattress sagged under his weight as he kneeled on it then straddled me.

He hovered over the top, the long strands of his hair hanging over his right eye. His arms bulged with the black ink, and my eyes shifted to the scales of a dragon that breathed fire into a river with pebbles skipping over the surface.

I ran my hands up his arms then down again.

Our eyes remained locked, and it was timeless. There was nothing else but us. No past. No tomorrow. No hurt nor pain. No defining what we were doing.

Just this.

He bent and nibbled on my lower lip while his hand slid up my inner thigh then stopped, his little finger resting in the curve of my thigh and pelvis.

My sex ached for him to touch me. To be rid of the material between us. But he kept his hand there while his mouth roamed lazily over mine.

His kiss slid to my neck, beneath my ear, nibbled on the lobe and then across my collarbone. And not once did his hand move, driving me crazy as I arched my back to feel his touch harder.

He stopped kissing me and sat up. Then his hands went to his belt and he unbuckled it. Pulling it through the loops before he tossed it beside me. He then reached for my shirt and yanked it over my head.

Within seconds he had my bra off and then his shirt before he undid the buttons on his jeans. I was having a hard time breathing as I watched him.

Every movement poetic—muscles flexing, valleys and hills that ached to be touched and discovered by my fingertips.

My eyes hit the nipple piercing, and I reached up to touch the silver loop. He sucked in his breath, and I smiled, loving that I could do that to him.

I went farther, caressing his chest, the ink that covered almost every inch of him all in black. My mind was unable to take in all the images as they merged over his skin.

He didn't move as I trailed the tips of my fingers down farther to his abdomen. "You're striking."

Cupping my chin, he tilted my head so our eyes met. "You were always meant to be mine, Savvy."

My breath hitched and my heart skipped a beat.

His mouth came down on mine again. Consuming. Powerful. Intense.

It was Killian, and the man he was and who he'd become.

The storm that had raged inside him, I tasted it in his kiss. The fury and the calm clashing together. But it wasn't chaos. It was as if each knew the direction it had to go. And within that was the tranquil beauty of who Killian was.

"Savvy." He pulled back and picked up his belt.

My sex throbbed and ached for him. For more. But the belt I wasn't so sure about. Mars was right. The gossip was true. Killian was into kinky. I just didn't know how far he was into it.

"Give me your wrists," he said gently.

I did as he asked, and he was slow and deliberate as he wrapped his belt around them, snug but not painful. He raised my arms above my head and pressed them into the mattress. "Don't move."

My chest rose and fell as he slid his hands down my sides, goose bumps rising behind his touch. When he reached my jeans, he undid them and tugged them off, my panties going with them so I lay naked.

He traced his finger over the subtle red line the rim of my panties had left across my pelvis. "Never wanted anything so fuckin' bad, orchid."

My thighs quivered. My breath locked in my chest as my pulse raced.

I gasped as his finger slid lower to my sex where he slowly slipped his finger into my folds. "So wet."

I'd been wet since I saw him again.

He crawled down the bed and positioned himself between my legs. Then he lowered his head and his mouth was on me. Tongue flicking and his piercing... oh, my God, his piercing grazing my clit sent jolts through me.

"Killian. I can't... last." Like a lit dynamite wick, I sparked and burned as I drew closer and closer to detonating. My fingers curled into the pillow as I fought against the constraint of the belt.

"I knew you'd taste fuckin' amazing."

I panted, my body arching as his tongue brushed over my clit several times before circling. My thighs shook, and he opened my legs wider.

"Oh, God. Killian," I screamed, closing my eyes as every muscle jerked and tensed. I sucked in air. "Oh, God. Oh, God." My womb tightened. Tantalizing heat soared. My body rode the tidal wave as I slipped into the abyss of Killian.

I collapsed, sagging into the mattress, my body clenching with aftershocks.

The weight shifted on the bed, and I opened my eyes as Killian sidled up beside me. His mouth took mine, and I tasted myself as he leisurely kissed me. Mouth roaming over mine as he pinched my nipples.

"Never thought I'd hear you scream my name like that, Savvy." He lowered his head and his mouth replaced his fingers on my nipple. When his teeth grazed the sensitive surface, I sucked in air.

"I think you were pretty confident I'd end up in your bed." I moaned when he moved to the other nipple.

He lifted his head. "We're in your bed. And I'm confident about most things, but having you, that was always something out of my reach."

He shifted off the bed and dragged down his jeans. His boxer briefs went with them. Shameless, he stood in front of me naked. His thick swollen cock with a small silver stud pierced through the ridge on display.

I stared at it for several seconds, wondering what it would feel like inside me. Because his tongue piercing sure as hell felt amazing.

"A dydoe piercing," he said.

"Yeah, uh, that's hot."

He chuckled. "Glad you think so because it's going inside you in about twenty seconds."

My belly flipped. "Do you have a condom?"

He picked up his jeans, took out his wallet and pulled out a condom. He ripped it open with his teeth and I watched as he rolled it on.

"Can you untie me now? I want to touch you." Being restrained with the belt was an adrenaline rush and feeling I couldn't escape him was... sexually arousing as hell and I realized I trusted Killian enough to do that.

He knelt on the bed straddling me, undid the belt, then trailed kisses down my arm to my neck. I weaved my hand into his hair, and my other slid down between us to the sparse hairs.

The tip of his cock brushed my knuckles, and I heard his soft inhale. I smiled, loving that sound coming from Killian and that I was the cause of it.

"Open your legs for me, Savvy. I'm going to fuck that pussy until I hear you scream my name again."

Chapter Seventeen

Killian

S HE OPENED HER LEGS, BENDING HER KNEES AND I SETTLED between them, my throbbing cock nestling against her. I stayed still for a minute, absorbing that this was going to happen. I was going to sink inside her for the first time. The girl who ruined me for all others.

I wrapped my fingers around her ankle and caressed up her calf before raising her leg and putting it on my shoulder.

My thumb teased her nipple back and forth, then I pinched it, and she sucked in air. That sound coming from Savvy's throat was like fuckin' honey, and I wanted to bottle it up so I could hear it whenever I wanted.

Jesus, if she only knew what she did to me. If she knew the truth—a truth about how much this girl affected me…

"Kiss me, Killian. I want you to kiss me."

I squeezed her nipple hard at the same time as I claimed her mouth. Her gasp vibrated against my lips.

Control was a device. It was regulated and right now that regulator was spinning at its limit as I kissed Savvy.

Eleven years. Eleven fuckin' years I waited for her to come back. I may not have known I was waiting, but I knew it now. She was the one I'd been waiting for. Why I was never with anyone else.

And now that I had her, I was never letting go.

I devoured her, and she surrendered to my hands, my mouth, my body.

Without lifting my lips from hers, I grabbed my cock and slid it up and down her wetness. "This pussy is mine," I murmured against her mouth. More than she fuckin' knew.

I kissed down the column of her throat then bit the tender skin at the base. She whimpered, arching her back.

She made a low, frustrated moan as I continued to tease her with my cock and hands and mouth while she writhed underneath me.

And when she was panting, and her skin was red and heated, body writhing, I slipped my hand underneath her ass, fingertips curling into the crevice as I squeezed.

She moaned and lifted her ass into my grip.

Fuck. Her ass was made for spanking. But not yet. All I wanted was to sink inside her. Feel what it was like with her around me. "Orchid. Look at me."

She opened her eyes, and I just about came when I saw the desire swimming in their depths. Jesus, this woman was made for me.

I tilted my hips and agonizingly slow, sunk my cock into her wet pussy. "Christ," I growled.

Cathartic. That was what it was. And I needed to savor this moment even if it killed me.

"Killian," she murmured, eyes closing.

I stopped halfway into her tight blanket of warmth. "Open your eyes. Watch me fuck you, Savvy."

She licked her lips, the surface glistening and inviting as she looked at me again. Only then did I push my cock all the way in. A half moan, half sigh escaped her lips, and she arched her neck.

Like a fuckin' rare flower blossoming for the first time. And I would protect it. Nurture it. Nurture her.

I waited for a second for her body to adjust to me.

But not long. I had control, but not much when it came to Savvy Grady.

She swung her other leg up around my hip and I sank deeper. *Holy fuck.* Who knew how goddamn amazing it would feel.

"Killian," she cried out, fingernails digging into my shoulders.

A gruff groan emerged, and I pulled back then thrust into her. Once. Twice.

Our eyes locked as our bodies became one, moving together in perfect harmony. It was slow at first, and then when her thigh tightened around my hip, and her hand ran down my back to my ass, that was it... the regulator busted.

I thrust faster. Harder. My mouth crashing into hers, fingers fisting a handful of hair.

She panted beneath me.

Rough.

Raw.

Raging.

As if neither of us could get enough of one another. We both lost control and grabbed at one another in a frenzy of need. Mouths and hands everywhere.

Starved. That was what I'd been for years.

I'd been denied. No, I'd denied myself. I hadn't thought this was possible. I'd been too fucked up and angry and had never wanted that attachment. To risk losing again.

But whatever happened, I'd always protect her.

Her sex clenched around my cock. Muscle spasms then short gasps before she screamed, "Killian. Yes!"

I thrust faster several more times before my cock jerked and I joined her. "Fuck," I growled, coming like I never had before. "Jesus. Christ."

It was several minutes before either of us moved. My forehead rested on her shoulder, her hand in my hair as we lay quiet except for our panting and the sound of the sheets crinkling as our chests rose heavily.

Finally, I raised my head.

She opened her eyes. They were gentle and lazy, and her lips were swollen from my kisses. With a red chin from my stubble, she looked completely sated.

I ran my hand down her side to her thigh and lowered it off my shoulder, and her other leg slipped off my hip. My cock remained nestled inside her where it was meant to be. Where it was always meant to be.

I lowered my head and kissed her, taking my time.

Savoring. Tasting. Enjoying the laziness about it. I'd never kissed a woman like that before. I rarely kissed a woman period. It didn't do anything for me.

It was her. Kissing Savvy for the first time at the cemetery... innocent and sweet, and her mouth easily melding to mine, nothing compared to that kiss.

And now... fuckin' now it was as if for years my lips had been cold and lifeless, and now they'd woke the fuck up and were alive with her kisses.

I lifted and stared down at her flushed face and glazed eyes.

This. Right fuckin' here. I'd never had it. But I wanted all of it.

With her.

But I wasn't going to define this. Not to her anyway. I had my issues and she'd had a taste of them, and I knew I'd have to give her more of me. The parts of me I kept hidden. Emmitt. She needed to know about Emmitt.

My fuckin' father was something I didn't want to share with her, only because I didn't want her touched by it, but Savvy with me was going to be thrown in the path. She'd had a taste of that at Compass.

I'd protect her from him. And soon, he'd break. Like he did to his horses, I was breaking him.

And him showing up at the club was a sign he was getting desperate. His clubs were hurting.

"Why are you so tense?" she asked, her finger tracing the crease between my brows.

I relaxed, pushing my father out of my head. I was good at doing that, had done it for years.

Lowering, I kissed the corner of her mouth on each side then lifted and rolled off her. Getting out of bed, I then dealt with the condom.

When I came out of the bathroom, she was naked on her side, perched up on her elbow watching me as I approached the bed. And I fuckin' loved it. I loved how her gaze trailed over me and there was a tiny smile on her lips.

"You have a lot of tattoos," she said, her voice a little scratchy and husky as if she'd just woken.

"Mmm." I slid onto the bed beside her, not ready to leave yet even though my phone was probably going crazy with texts and calls from the guys because we were late for brunch.

I bent one knee and put my arm above her head so I could play with her hair. She ran her fingertips over the tattoo on my neck. "Is this a hawk?"

"No. It's a black kite."

"That's a bird?"

She continued to trace the spread wings that curved up my neck. "It's a bird of prey. You see the tail?"

She nodded. "It's forked."

"Yes. What makes them distinct from others."

"It's beautiful," she whispered.

"My first tattoo. It was done in a guy's basement when I was seventeen. Ream knew him and he had done a few of his. The guy has his own shop now and is so busy you can't get in to see him for months. He did most of mine, but a few I had done while on tour."

"Why do you like them so much?" She traced one after the other over my shoulder to my pec then farther to my abdomen.

"They are pieces of me. Stories."

"This is my favorite." She dragged her finger down my arm over the stormy waters and thick dense clouds overhead. The sun's rays peaked through them, and specks of light hit the water. And below the water in the depths bloomed a flower, its petals closed, the stem broken.

An orchid.

Her fingers stopped on the flower and her eyes lifted to mine. She didn't have to say anything. Neither did I. The flower represented her.

The orchid lost in the depths of the river.

Like I'd been lost.

The stormy river where my brother died. Where my anger flourished and pieces of me drowned with him. And her... Savvy was the light struggling to reach me beneath the surface.

But the anger was controlled now. At least most of the time. And the orchid, she blossomed and came back to me.

She rested her cheek on my chest, her palm flat on my abdomen. "You scare me, Killian."

"I know." She feared who I'd been, the overprotectiveness, what was happening with my father. She'd been hurt and feared that happening again. "Will you come to brunch with me, not because you have to, but because you want to."

She looked up at me. "Yes."

I tilted to kiss her. My body sagged. I hadn't realized I was tense asking her, but I was.

"Is it at Logan and Emily's?" she asked.

"No. We get together at Crisis and Ream's adoptive parents on the last Sunday of every month. We used to go to Georgie and Deck's, but he's been busy with work."

"Georgie and Deck?"

I absently stroked up and down on her arm. "Mmm. We met Georgie and Deck when we were first starting out. She worked at a coffee shop Logan, Ream, Crisis and me used to hang out at. Now she owns two coffee shops." Her palm slid over my abdomen then lower, and my cock swelled.

"And Deck?" she asked.

I clenched my jaw as the tips of her fingers drifted lower still. "Ex-special forces. He has a company that deals with the scum of the Earth. Not so legal, but he's a good guy and would do anything for his friends. Fuck, he has. And his men."

"So, who will be there?"

155

"The guys in the band with their women."

She touched the ridge of my cock, and I sucked in air. "Fuck, baby."

She wrapped one finger at a time around the base of it. "Savvy, I'd like nothing more than to fuck you again, but we should go." I was never late and recently I'd been off schedule and doing things I never did, like right now, lying in bed after sex.

She trailed kisses down my chest, her grip tightening on my cock and I groaned, hardening.

She reached my abdomen, and her tongue swirled, wetting the surface of my skin while her hand slid up my cock and back down again. My hand went to the top of her head as she shifted over my thigh and lay between my legs.

Her thumb grazed the piercing, and I hissed, bunching her hair in my fist. "Jesus."

Her head lifted, mouth a breath away from the tip of my cock. "Killian?"

"Yeah," I managed to grind out, my body tense and on edge waiting for her lips to wrap around me.

"I never forgot you either."

Fuck.

My breath locked in my chest as her mouth enclosed around my cock.

Chapter Eighteen

Savvy

"OH, MY GOD, SWEETNESS, YOU MUST BE KITE'S GIRL, Savvy. I'm Sophia Wesson."

A well-put together woman rushed toward me wearing white pants and a light pink blouse with a brilliant smile and warm, welcoming eyes.

She put her hands on my shoulders then kissed both cheeks before pulling me in for a hug. She ran her hand over my hair. "Look at this gorgeous hair and face. So beautiful. And you're a dancer."

"Yes," I replied.

"Well, it's so lovely to meet you. I'm glad you could join us. Kite has never brought anyone over before." She turned to Kite and kissed both his cheeks. "You're late. I didn't think that was possible, but now I see why."

My cheeks heated, and Killian squeezed my hand reassuringly.

"Vincent told me you knew Logan and Kite in high school. That's wonderful."

I wasn't sure who Vincent was until Kite squeezed my hand

157

and said, "Crisis. Vincent is his real name, and his mom refuses to call him by anything else."

"I don't know why he doesn't use his real name." She ushered us through the house. "Everyone is already here and breakfast is nearly ready. Have you met the crew?"

"I haven't met Kat."

"Kite, the others are out back, I'll show Savvy around first."

God, Crisis and Ream's mother was so nice and funny. It kind of clashed with how she looked, very classy and straight laced.

"You good?" Killian asked.

I nodded.

He released my hand, and I watched him as he strolled away. God, it was hard to believe an hour ago I had him between my legs.

Killian Kane had fucked me. It had been... life changing. Just like his kiss eleven years ago.

I didn't know what to do with that yet. There was so much I didn't know about him and what worried me was if he'd ever share more than what was on the surface. I couldn't be with someone again who kept things from me. David had kept lots—women.

Killian did say he'd take me to his place, and I was also here, with his friends. And it wasn't because he paid me to be.

"Kat painted this," Sophia said as she showed me a painting above the mantel in the living room. It was a white horse galloping through the waves on a beach.

"It's beautiful."

"She has a rare talent and—"

"Mom, stop bragging about me," a young woman said as she sauntered into the living room with Haven. They each carried trays with glasses and a jug of orange juice and another with water and cucumber slices. "Hi. I'm Kat. Ream's other half."

"Savvy."

Haven smiled warmly, and we all walked through the house to the patio. The women set the trays down on a large iron table while Sophia talked about the guys practicing in the garage when they started out and how bad Crisis was singing.

"Do you know Vincent insisted on Easter egg hunts up until he was seventeen?" Sophia said as Emily came out of the house with a bowl of scrambled eggs. "Savvy, he was incorrigible. Ream wasn't into an Easter egg hunt around the backyard at seventeen, so Vincent told him we gave a hundred dollars to whoever collected the most eggs. A lie, of course. They raced around the backyard like bulls ramming one another in order to get to the eggs." She shook her head smiling as she looped her arm around Haven's waist and squeezed. "Then Killian and Logan showed up, and the four of them wrestled one another for the chocolate eggs."

I smiled. Killian racing around the backyard for eggs was hard to imagine. I'd never seen him laugh at school let alone race around looking for hidden chocolates.

My chest swelled because it was a part of him I'd missed.

"When Ream found out there was no money, he went at Vincent. What made it worse was my Vincent laughed the entire time. It took both Killian and Logan to break it up."

Kat turned to me. "Ream was a little volatile back then."

"A little?" Crisis strolled outside with a plate of what smelled like bacon. "Hell, the guy was a grenade."

"Vincent Wesson. Language," Sophia abolished.

"What?" he asked innocently. "It's hell. Not even a swear word, Mom."

Emily, Haven, and Kat laughed. I smiled.

I was introduced to Mr. Wesson, who manned the barbecue flipping sausages. Then my eyes hit Killian out in the backyard with Ream and Logan and a little boy who looked about eleven or twelve.

They were kicking the soccer ball around. Well, Killian was kicking it around, and Ream and Logan were attempting to get it from him.

He easily maneuvered the ball between his feet. It was hypnotic.

I was mesmerized by his agile, lean legs and tousled hair with strands hanging in front of his eyes as his head bent while he effortlessly kept Ream from getting the ball. He glanced up at the kid, who looked to be his partner, and kicked it gently to him near the makeshift goal. Then he bodychecked Ream.

The boy kicked it so hard, he fell backward onto his butt, but it shot right between the chalk markers on the wood fence.

"Score," the kid yelled, jumping to his feet and throwing his arms in the air.

Killian immediately jogged over and high-fived him then bent and said something to him. The kid smiled from ear to ear, obviously pleased with himself while Killian ruffled his hair.

"We're fostering him," Sophia said. "His name is Hendricks, and he's been bounced around homes since he was five." God, the poor kid. I knew the feeling, but luckily, it had only been a couple years and not until I was fifteen. I couldn't imagine being in the system from the age of five. "He loves soccer and the guys. He talks about Kite all the time, and he plays soccer with him every time he comes over. Even in the snow."

I rested my hands on the railing as I watched Killian, and my heart swelled. I never imagined him being like this with a kid. Or playing soccer. But there was something different in him when he was with Hendricks. Something in his eyes, it was almost... painful. Like it hurt.

He must have sensed me watching him because he raised his head and looked over.

His eyes locked on me, and my heart shot off. Saying something to the guys, he strode across the mowed grass toward me.

It didn't take long before he stood in front of me. Heated skin from the sun and running around, his hair in disarray... and he never looked sexier.

"You're really good with Hendricks."

He hooked my shoulders and pulled me into him. "He's a good kid."

I smiled. "You'd be a great dad."

He tensed, eyes narrowing. "I'll never have kids Savvy."

My heart dropped. Killian didn't want kids? Before I could ask why, he kissed me.

And it wasn't a quick, sweet kiss. It was a hard, deep, tongue-action kiss that had me sagging into him as my knees weakened.

When he broke away, I wanted to bury my head in the sandbox because everyone was watching.

"Ugh, gross," Hendricks said as he ran up the steps with the soccer ball under his arm.

The tension gone from Killian, he smirked then leaned back on the railing and positioned me in front of him, so my back was to his front. He looped his arms around me, and I rested my hands on his arms. It took me a few minutes before I relaxed, realizing that Killian had no qualms about letting it be known I was with him. But then, he hadn't before either.

We joined the conversation, which currently was Logan talking about how Ream threw Vincent in the pool a while back because he'd been hitting on Kat.

This, I found out, was before Ream and Kat were together and their relationship, or rather non-relationship, was combustible.

Brunch was nothing like I expected. Actually, I hadn't known what to expect, but it wasn't Killian laughing and joking around. There was still that underlying reserved part of him, but with his friends, the people he cared about, Killian was warm and easygoing.

"You fit," Killian said two hours later in the car.

"Huh?" I asked, turning my attention to him, although I had to admit it was rarely off of him even when he wasn't with me.

"You fit. It's like you've known them for years."

"I really like your friends, Killian."

"Yeah, but it's more than that," he said. "You can like people. They can like you, but you don't fit. But you do."

His eyes briefly met mine before he looked back at the road.

He was right. I hadn't felt like I was on the outside looking in on a group of friends who'd known one another for years. I was on the inside with them.

"I didn't know you played soccer. I don't remember you on the team at school."

He didn't look at me, but I saw it, the hands tightening on the steering wheel and the clenched jaw. "I wasn't."

"Oh." There was something there, but he didn't elaborate, and it was the part of Killian that I wasn't so sure about. "Well, you looked… sexy."

"Sexy?" His brows lifted as he briefly glanced at me, and I shrugged while chewing on my bottom lip.

"Yes. Incredibly sexy," I said and ran my hands down my thighs. "And before you ask, yes, I was wet. I'm wet now."

"Fuck," he said. Slowing the car, he turned into an alley then stopped the car. "Is your pussy throbbing? Aching? Does it want my cock, orchid?"

God, it was hot when he spoke like that. "Yes."

He unclipped his seat belt, reached over and grabbed the back of my neck and pulled me toward him.

His mouth slammed into mine.

My stomach dropped. But it was a good drop. It was the kind where you were excited but startled at the same time.

"Climb on my lap, orchid."

"It's in the middle of the day and we're in an alley." And it was a total turn-on—the spontaneity of having sex in a sports car, in an alley in the middle of the day.

"Mmm," he smirked. "The windows are tinted. No one can see us."

I awkwardly climbed over the gear shift and straddled his lap. He gave me no time to think, breathe, or even settle myself comfortably before his mouth was on me again.

Ravenous.

Fierce.

Uncontrolled as he savagely kissed me. One hand in my hair, he jerked my head to the side so he could deepen the kiss.

Shocked at this sudden assault, I was a rag doll, molding my body to whatever he demanded.

His hand went under my dress, and I heard a tear as he ripped my panties off.

I had no idea how he managed it, and I didn't care.

Killian was going to fuck me.

My back pressed painfully into the steering wheel, and my one foot was jammed awkwardly between the seat and the door, but it didn't matter.

I craved him. My need was so overpowering that control was nonexistent.

"Killian," I breathed against his lips.

"Yes," he growled. "Say my name. Again."

"Killian," I repeated and it came out like 'Illian as I panted.

He kissed me then urged my head to the side where he nibbled on my neck at the same time as he thrust two fingers inside me.

"Oh, God."

"Your pussy is so fuckin' wet for me, Savvy."

I lifted as much as I could with my hands on his shoulders, fingers pulling at his shirt as I rode his fingers. My head hit the roof of the car each time I rose, but I barely noticed it.

"Oh, God," I cried when he let my hair go and grabbed my hip instead to help me move.

Harder.

Faster.

He withdrew his fingers and pushed me back so my spine jammed into the steering wheel and the horn briefly sounded.

His hands went to his jeans, and I quickly shoved them aside, undoing his belt, buttons, and then released his cock.

He groaned, eyes closing, head falling back on the headrest. "Christ," he muttered. "Condom. In my wallet."

I reached for his wallet in the console and found a condom. I quickly tore it open with my teeth then rolled it on him.

I lifted then positioned above his cock and slowly lowered. A moan dragged from my throat as he filled me. God, it was like coming home. A home I didn't know I had. A home I'd never had.

His hands squeezed my hips so hard I knew I'd have bruises, but I wanted them.

I wanted his mark on me because this was what I'd been missing all my life.

Killian.

"Jesus Christ, orchid," he said in a ragged, breathless growl as I moved up and down on him.

This wasn't pretty or nice sex. This was hurting sex.

And it was amazing.

I sifted my hand through his hair and yanked on it while I thrust my hips. My other hand clawed at his shirt, and I heard the tear in the neckline as I yanked it down so I could touch his naked chest and his nipple piercing.

"Baby," he said as our bodies banged and hit together.

"Killian," I cried.

His cock drove me insane as I moved up and down. The silver barbell rubbed against the wall of my sex and caused my core to heat and build, and my womb to flare with tingles.

"Savvy. Fuck. Now," he groaned, his hands tightening on my waist. Throwing his head back, corded neck exposed, he closed his eyes.

Seeing him orgasm sent me over the edge and spiraling into my own release. I raised my arms above my head, palms flat on the roof as I tilted my hips into him one more time before I screamed, "Yes. Yes. Yes." Then I moaned as wave after wave pulsed. "Ohh."

I collapsed.

His arms wrapped around me and his mouth rested on my throat.

That was when the blue lights flashed in the rear window, and a loud brief siren rang into the air.

My eyes widened. "Shit." I scrambled off his lap.

"It's fine," he said with a chuckle.

He did up his pants, which took him a millisecond, while I had to try and flatten my hair and straighten my dress. And I couldn't find my panties. God, I no doubt looked like I'd just been fucked.

"Oh, my God." I closed my eyes, trying to control my breathing.

I'd never had sex in a car. Actually, the most risky, and I wouldn't even call it risky, was in the dance studio with a locked door and after hours.

There was a tap on Killian's window.

I groaned, lowering my head so the officer couldn't see Killian's bite marks on my neck or my red face from the scruff burn.

Killian pressed the button and the window slid down.

"Sir. Ma'am. Is everything okay here? You're blocking the alley," the officer said.

The fifty-something officer looked at Killian then to me and into the backseat then back to Killian.

"Yes. Thank you, Officer," Killian said. "We were just having a rather... heated discussion."

Oh. My. God.

The officer's eyes flicked to me. "I see. Are you okay, ma'am?" he asked.

"Uh, yes, Officer. Thank you," I managed to squeak.

"Would you mind showing me some ID, sir?" he asked.

"Of course," Killian said politely.

God, he could go from raw and rough to a complete gentleman in a flash.

Meanwhile, I was still in 'just been fucked' land with nerves darting off in every direction and my sex throbbing something fierce.

Killian reached over into the middle tray and opened his wallet, pulling out his driver's license.

The officer's gaze followed his movements, and that was when I saw my panties dangling from the parking brake.

Kill. Me. Now.

Killian cleared his throat, I think to cover his laugh because it was obvious the officer saw my panties and Killian was aware he did.

Asshole. I wanted to snatch them away, but that would only draw more attention to them.

Killian handed him his ID.

"Please stay in the car," the officer ordered.

The second he turned to go back to his cruiser, I snatched my panties, opened the glove box and shoved them inside.

Killian laughed.

"It's not funny," I retorted, glaring at him.

He reached over, hand cupping the back of my neck as he dragged me toward him and kissed me.

"He saw my panties," I continued.

"Yeah, but I think it was your red cheeks and 'just been fucked' hair that gave it away. The panties were a bonus."

I rolled my eyes. "Maybe he thought you were forcing me."

Killian barked out a laugh. "Baby, you were on top of me if you recall. And fuck, you were hot riding my cock."

"Sir."

My cheeks burned because the officer stood at the window, his hand out with Killian's ID, and he must have heard that last comment.

"Thank you, Officer," Killian said, taking his license and placing it in his wallet again.

Bastard wasn't even rattled.

"I didn't recognize you," the officer continued. "You're Kite from Tear Asunder."

"Yeah," Killian replied.

My brows lifted and I was surprised when the officer held out a pad of paper.

"Would you mind? My kids are huge fans."

Killian graciously took the pen and pad. "Pleasure. What are their names?"

"Jessica and Brandon," he replied.

Killian scribbled something on one page, flipped the page, scribbled again then passed the pad and pen back.

"Thank you. And sorry to disturb you and your girlfriend. But I'd advise next time, keep the alleys clear."

"Of course."

"Ma'am."

"Uh, thank you," I said.

"Kite. Great to meet you. And thanks again."

"Anytime."

The officer walked back to his car, got in and honked once as he backed out of the alley.

166

Killian started the car and pulled out.

"Do you do that often?"

"Which part?"

"Get caught having sex in a car."

"Never had sex in the car before," he said. "I don't like public sex. I'm private with everything." But he publicly dated me. We had sex in a car. He had me on his lap at Compass. He kissed me in front of all his friends.

He stopped at a red light and looked over at me, his expression serious. "Seeing you with my friends, Savvy. Seeing that you fit. Fuckin' irresistible."

He pulled up in front of my building, got out, then walked me up to my door. I wasn't sure if he was going to stay or not, but since he didn't park, I figured he wasn't. I put the key in the lock then opened the door before turning to him.

"Why haven't you ever dated before?"

"Does it matter?"

"Well, maybe not. I'm not sure what we're doing here or if I still have a job, but if we are doing something, then yeah, it's important."

He nodded. "We're doing something, Savvy. And I can't say you don't have a job at the club, even though I'd like to. And I've never wanted a relationship. The attachment."

"Why not?"

He hesitated and ran his hand down my arm to my hand. "No one ever measured up to you."

My breath hitched.

"I don't want to define this, Savvy. I just want you." He leaned in and kissed me. "Wanted you from the beginning. And I was pretty clear then what would happen if you ever came near me again."

"The beginning when?"

He slipped his hand under my hair, fingers gentle on the back of my neck. "When I kissed you for the first time."

My pulse spiked and my body heated. "We were teenagers, Killian."

"Yes. And I was too fucked up to have a girl like you. Never thought I could have you. I'm still fucked up, and you've had a taste of that." He leaned in, his lips next to my ear. "Breathe, Savvy."

"I can't," I whispered.

He half smiled then kissed me. It was brief, but it was all Killian—confident, casual, controlling, with a hint of fierce, raw emotion.

I wanted so badly to trust him, but I needed time to think. Today was overwhelming, and my head was spinning with Killian and what he did to me.

He released me. "I'll call you later."

I stood in the hallway, leaning against my door watching him as he jogged down the stairs.

"Did I win the bet?" My head snapped over to Trevor standing in his doorway smirking. "Because with that face, you were definitely just fucked."

"Oh, my God. I never made a bet." I opened my door and slammed it behind me, hearing his laughter.

Chapter Nineteen

Killian

I texted Savvy as I walked toward dick David's studio.

Will you stay at my place tonight?

A sleepover?

I chuckled, which was exactly what I needed before confronting her scumbag ex.

Yes. We'll order in. And watch a movie. Naked.

She didn't reply right away, and I imagined her tapping her finger along the side of the phone debating. I knew she was hesitant *real* dating me. Fuck, she was hesitant fake dating me, but there was no denying what was between us.

I hadn't been able to see her for two days as we'd pulled a couple of all-nighters recording at Logan's. But I'd called, texted and sexted. And the fuckin' girl was a natural at sexting, leaving me with a perpetual hard-on.

Sounds like a slumber party.

What kind of slumber parties have you been to naked?

LOL. Can I choose the movie?

Pick you up at 6

I pocketed my cell and walked into the dance studio. Marble floors. Leather couches. Artwork on the walls. Expensive artwork by the looks of it. There was one of those fancy coffee machines and a juicer with a bowl of fruits and veggies on a table in the waiting area.

And Savvy was living in a fuckin' shit building with more than likely drug dealers. Jesus.

I approached the reception desk where a young girl sat and smiled at me.

"Can I help you, sir?"

"David Knapp?"

"He's teaching a private lesson at the moment." She glanced at her screen. "But he'll be done in twenty minutes if you'd like to speak with him then." She tucked the few strands of hair that had escaped her bun behind her ear and tilted her head smiling. "Is there something I can help you with? I can book your daughter or son in for lessons with David or one of our other instructors. Daphne is here with a beginner class. You can go in and watch if you'd like."

If I ever had a daughter, which I wouldn't, not a chance in hell would I let her near scumbag David's studio. Fuck, I'd probably never let her out of the house.

The parents who waited on the leather couches had their eyes on me. I was accustomed to the stares, whether they recognized me from the band or they just eyed up my piercings and tattoos, I certainly didn't fit in this high-class dance studio.

And neither did Savvy. Not that she wasn't classy. She was in

170

her own right, but this place was cold and sterile. I pictured Savvy in a place where it was real and warm. Brick walls. Worn hardwood floors. No reception area, just maybe a laptop and benches for people to sit on while they watched. Everything out in the open, not behind closed doors.

But then dick David liked closed doors, didn't he? I wondered how long he'd been fucking other women behind Savvy's back.

"Which room is he in?" I asked, my jaw clenching.

Her smile dropped, and she nervously glanced at the double doors on the left before saying, "If you'd like to help yourself to coffee or juice, he won't be long."

But I was already making my way to the double doors. She called after me and then the click of her heels followed. "Sir, you can't go in there."

I threw open the doors and strode in.

The girl behind me gasped then quickly spun around and left. I didn't.

I shut the doors and stood with my arms crossed and legs braced as I faced the couple with half their clothes off. *She* was pressed against the mirrored wall. He was doing the pressing.

"I'd advise you leave," I said to the barely legal girl.

She quickly crouched, grabbed her top and held it in front of her, then ran through a changing room door on the other side of the room.

David didn't bother hiding the fact that he was doing a lot more than teaching. Or maybe this is what he taught. Fuck, Savvy had taken lessons with this asshole. She'd worked for him. She'd lived with him.

Christ. Had she fucked him in here? Had he had her up against the mirror?

I gritted my teeth thinking of his scummy hands all over her.

"Get the fuck out." David's shirt lay at his feet, but he didn't bother putting it on.

He obviously knew who I was. Good. The less time I spent here, the better. And I wanted him to know I was with Savvy.

I remained silent for two reasons. One I needed a second, and two because I wanted David to sweat. It wasn't hard to figure out why I was here.

He walked across the room to a bench where he picked up his phone. "I'm calling the police."

Fuckin' coward. "Please do. I'm curious to know how old the girl you were just about to fuck is?"

His head jerked up from his phone. "She's legal."

My brows lifted. "Maybe. But I'm betting the parents waiting outside for their kids in the next room have no idea what you were doing during one of your *private* lessons?"

David lowered his phone. "It's none of their business and it's consensual."

Fuckin' dickhead. I clenched my hands into fists, wanting nothing more than to beat the shit out of this guy. But I couldn't. All I punched was a bag now.

"Then it won't matter if I tell them."

He stiffened. "What do you want?"

I strode toward him. Immediately, his eyes shifted right and left as if contemplating his escape routes. "Simple. I want you to stay clear of Savvy." I stopped a foot away. "And by clear, I mean she no longer exists to you. You lose her number, her address, her fuckin' name. Show up at her apartment again, and next time I won't be this polite." I lowered my voice. "But first, David, you'll retract the lies you spread about her. And if you don't, I will make sure you never teach dance again."

He had the nerve to smile, although it was tight. And from the slight quiver in his voice, he was nervous. As he should be. "No one will believe you."

"Try me."

"You can't do that."

I smiled. "I can and I will. And I'd like nothing better than to ruin you like you did Savvy."

"Did she send you here?" he spat.

Fuck no. "Does it matter? The result is the same." I was uncertain how Savvy would feel about me being here, but David showing up at her apartment could not happen again. Luckily, Roman had been there and had recognized David entering the building. Luke had given him a picture of David in case he showed up.

This had to end, and Savvy working at the club had to end. I didn't like it. Yeah, I hated the guys looking at her, but it was more than that. Compass had a link to my father, and with the profit numbers Brett gave me, my dad's clubs had to be in the red.

He wasn't going to sit back and let that happen, so I needed Savvy as far away from that as I could.

She loved dancing and the club gave her that, but the warmth radiating from her eyes wasn't there. The passion was lit, but it didn't burn like I'd seen in the gym at school when she'd danced.

"Fix the lies—today." I then turned and walked away before I hit the bastard.

"Savannah is dancing at a club and fucking a rock star. That's not on me. No parent will want their kid taught by her. She's finished in this business no matter what I say."

I stopped, hand on the door handle. "Then you are, too."

"No one will believe you. I'm well-respected, and you're a drummer in a rock band who is fucking my ex-girlfriend."

I opened the door, which took a hell of a lot. All I wanted to do was turn around and put him on his ass. The only reason I didn't was because of Savvy. She wouldn't like it and I liked Savvy—a lot.

No. It wasn't like. It was love.

I probably always had, but I'd placed her in a compartment of my mind a long time ago where I couldn't find her. Where she was safe from me. From my anger and bitterness. The hurt.

And then she'd left.

She'd left and I'd let her go.

But Savvy came back to me, and she may not have known that was what she was doing, but that was what it was. And I'd do everything I could to keep her safe.

Luke was waiting outside, leaning against the side of the car. "Do I need to call Deck?"

I huffed. "No." If I beat the shit out of David, the police would be involved, and if the police got involved, I'd need Deck to help smooth things over. "Didn't touch him."

Luke's brows lifted, but he didn't say anything.

"Where are we with the horses? You hear from Danny?" The kid was supposed to e-mail today, but I hadn't heard from him.

Luke tossed me the car keys. "Five minutes ago. Your dad isn't purchasing any new horses." Which means he's watching his funds. "He may have something on a horse called Faith. But I haven't watched the video he sent yet."

I was driving as I hadn't wanted Luke to bring the limo and draw attention. I opened the door and looked at Luke over the roof of the car. "If we go after another polo pony, my dad is going to know someone in the stable is responsible. I won't risk the kid."

"Danny needs the job," Luke said.

"Then we find him something else." Emily knew enough people in the horse world to get him into another stable. I folded into the car, and Luke hopped in the passenger side.

I drove to the warehouse where Luke had left his car.

"She's staying here tonight," I told Luke before he got out of the car.

Luke nodded. "I'll call Roman. You going to tell her about today?"

"Yeah." David would do one of two things: retaliate thinking he could, or he'd do as I asked. Either way, Savvy would find out, and I wanted her hearing it from me.

Luke left, and I went inside to shower and change before picking up Savvy.

Chapter Twenty

Savvy

KILLIAN PICKED ME UP AT SIX, WELL FIVE-FORTY-FIVE because he was always early. He was a perfect gentleman, even though I kind of didn't want him to be. The most he did was a light touch on the small of my back as he guided me to his car.

He didn't waste any time when he drove out of my parking lot when he said, "I went and saw David."

I jerked, eyes shooting to his face. "You did?" I was uncertain how I felt about him doing that, but I wasn't exactly angry, more surprised. But then it was Killian and he'd been pissed when David had shown up at my apartment even if it turned into a good thing.

"He won't come near you again." His tone was abrupt, as if he was thinking about the encounter.

"Did you...?" I glanced at his hands on the steering wheel and when my gaze shifted back to his face, his brows rose.

"Did I punch him?"

David deserved it, but he'd also not take it well and I didn't want Killian getting into trouble because of me. "Yes."

"No. But he will be retracting what he said about you."

My chest swelled and I wanted to crawl into his lap and kiss him. Instead, I leaned over and kissed his cheek. "Thank you, Killian."

"You're welcome."

Five minutes later, he pulled up to a warehouse down by the docks and parked.

"Why are we stopping here?" I asked.

"My place."

I stared at the ominous building. "The entire building?"

He chuckled. "It's not as big as it looks." He climbed out of his car and I followed.

I wasn't so sure about that.

It was an industrial area, and the building was old, like one of those hundred-year-old factories. A lot of them had been converted into livable lofts, but not in the dock district as there was nothing around, and no one wanted to live here.

Except for Killian, it appeared.

He met me at the front of the car and slid his hand in mine, squeezing. "It's safe."

I half laughed. "You had my car taken to a wrecking yard because you deemed it unsafe. I doubt you'd walk me into a building that wasn't," I said as we walked across the gravel to a large metal door. "Still, it's a warehouse."

"I had it converted to be a living space. The building was in pretty good shape and empty. It used to be a storage place for ships' cargo. But it's been ten years since it was used, so I got it for a good price."

The more I thought about it, the more I realized this was exactly where Killian would choose to live. Private. Exclusive. Different and yet simple.

He opened the heavy metal door.

"You don't lock it?" I asked.

He shrugged. "Nothing to steal." He moved down the hall to a cage door where he parted the gate and shut it behind us. Then he pressed a button and the elevator clunked and groaned as it made its way upward.

It jerked to a stop, and he opened the gates that led right into his place.

I immediately noticed the distressed hardwood floors and a massive open space. And I meant *massive*. At least three thousand square feet of floors and nothing else. A dancer's dream. All it needed was a mirrored wall.

The walls were brick with substantial windows along the south side and looked out onto the water. The ceilings had exposed duct work and pipes, which was at least fifteen feet high.

But I didn't have time to take in much more as he shut the gates and moved into me. He backed me up against them, and they clanged.

"Two days is too long."

It was. I hadn't stopped thinking about him. It didn't help that he kept sending me dirty texts reminding me.

His hands locked around my wrists and he raised my arms above my head and pressed them against the gate. "Grab hold."

I did.

Then his mouth took mine.

I moaned against his lips. My heart pounded as his body leaned into mine, my back digging into the hard rungs.

His kiss was bruising and harsh, but in the intensity was sweetness, as if he couldn't get enough of me, yet it wasn't invasive.

It was finding what was lost.

He pulled back, hand cupping my jaw. "You on anything?"

"Yeah." I'd been on the pill for years. "And I had a physical after my relationship ended." I'd gone to the doctor immediately after I'd caught David cheating on me.

Killian bent as he kissed my neck and along my collarbone. "I don't want anything between us, orchid."

"Have you been checked?"

He lifted his head and his eyes locked with mine. There was something there, but like other parts of him, it was hidden. "I'm good, Savvy." He ran his hands down my body to my ass and lifted me up. I hooked my legs around his waist.

"Fuck. I'm starved for you." His voice vibrated against my skin, and I arched my neck, hands in his hair.

"Killian."

Like a tidal wave crashing into the rocks, all control disintegrated as clothes ripped off and it was a frenzy of mouths and hands.

My body was alive with thrums and electrical pulses, and I couldn't get enough of him.

God, I wanted him. All of him. Every single piece.

My panties were the last shred of clothing to be torn off before he slid his cock inside me.

"Jesus. Christ," he growled as he pushed his length inside me. "I fuckin' never knew... I never fuckin' knew."

"Killian." He held me up against the elevator gates, my thighs locked around him, arms looping his neck with my fingers in his hair.

He thrust while his mouth savagely took mine.

It was a wild, raw need. As if it had been eleven years instead of a few days since we'd been together.

"Bed," he murmured against my lips. Then while still kissing me, he carried me across the warehouse where I was lowered onto a mattress, and he followed. "Never wanted anyone else. Never."

His words were a haze as I arched into him and he tilted his hips and thrust into me, his hands on the mattress spanning just above my head. I ran my hands down his chest, his abdomen, then around to his back, discovering every crevice and hill beneath the palms of my hands.

"You're all I ever needed." His words were harsh from his raspy voice as he thrust again and again. "Just you. Just my orchid."

My body tingled and tightened at his words, and I came hard and fast. "Killian," I screamed, fingers scraping his back as my body convulsed.

"Fuck," he grunted then came with me.

Our bodies were taut and unmoving as we panted.

He collapsed his forehead onto my shoulder, and I slowly withdrew my nails from his back.

Neither of us said anything.

After a few minutes, he trailed kisses down my neck to my nipple where he dragged his teeth over one then the other before he rolled off me, taking me with him, so I was tucked into his side.

"Eleven years," he murmured.

I rested my cheek on his chest and absently drew circles on his abdomen. If I'd ever done drugs, I imagined this was what it was like. The high, as if nothing were real, just a haze of euphoria.

I tilted to look up at him. His eyes were closed and he appeared so peaceful. It was strange as with his friends he was relaxed and casual, but the look on his face now… the outer corners of his eyes drooped, the subtle lines above his brows gone—quiet.

Killian used to remind me of a hurricane raging over the ocean, with so much built-up intensity. But after all these years… it was like he'd found his way to the eye of it and it circled around him.

But at this moment the hurricane was silent.

I reached up and traced his lips. Soft, pliant to my touch. It was complete peace. And when he opened his captivating green eyes, the hardness and pain swimming in the depths was gone.

He opened his mouth and bent forward slightly to take my finger into his mouth. His lips closed around it and he made a low growl deep in his throat. "Put your finger in your pussy. I want to taste you again."

My heart pounded and I hesitated. When I didn't right away, he teeth clamped my finger. I withdrew it abruptly from his mouth, and his brows rose while he waited for me to do as he asked.

I slid my hand down my chest, abdomen, then to my sex while my eyes remained on his. Then gliding it between the wet folds to my entrance, I pushed my finger inside.

"Two," he said in a raspy voice as he watched me.

I adjusted and pushed another finger inside me, moaning.

Killian enveloped my wrist and gently pulled my hand away then lifted it to his mouth. "Come closer," he ordered.

I did.

"Put one finger in your mouth. Taste us. Your pussy's juices and my cock's."

I swallowed and did as he asked. He leaned forward and took my other finger in his mouth so our lips were almost touching as we sucked on my fingers.

"Fuck. I hope you were thinking of a porno tonight, baby. I don't think I can watch a chick flick."

"What about a drama?" I teased.

"Jesus. No." He fell back onto the bed, arm over his eyes.

"You said it was my choice."

"No, I didn't respond."

True.

His arm came around my shoulders and tugged me closer. "You can watch whatever you want as long as I get to play with you."

"And what does your play entail?"

"Whatever I want."

I remember Mars saying he was into kink and I wasn't too sure if his play differentiated from my idea of play. "Does your play hurt?"

He chuckled. "No, Savvy. Not tonight."

I bit my lip. "But sometimes it does?"

His hand lightly stroked up and down my back. "If that's what you want. If pain turns you on, Savvy." I didn't know. I liked when he was rough and when he tied the belt around my wrists. "Every person is unique in what they like."

"So you're into... BDSM?"

"I'd call it kink, but I used to go to a BDSM club. Although, it wasn't for sex, Savvy. It was a release of another kind."

"What kind?" I wanted to know more. God, I wanted to know everything about him. Yet, that scared me too because I was pretty sure Killian didn't want what I wanted. He'd never had a girlfriend. He lived in a warehouse. He had unresolved issues with his dad and told me he'd never have kids. Though I'd seen how amazing he was with Hendricks.

He sat up. "Stay. I'll order us food. Thai good?"

I nodded. "I love Thai." I was still thinking about the BDSM club he'd gone to and the fact that he'd avoided answering my question.

He was completely unabashed as he slid from bed naked and walked across the room. I watched his tight ass as he went to the washroom. He flicked on the light and only half closed the door.

He was such a contradiction. Completely open with his body, direct, honest, but much of him was hidden and private.

He came back to the bedroom and snagged his jeans off the floor to take his phone out of the pocket.

"Killian?"

He lowered the phone and like he always did, he gave me his full attention. "Mmm?"

"Are you really okay with dating? I mean for real."

The corners of his lips curved up. "Savvy, we're way past the dating stage."

I frowned. "How do you figure? Technically, this is only our second date. What stage are you referring to?" I asked.

He knelt on the bed and hooked the back of my neck, urging me closer to him. His lips an inch away from mine, he drawled, "The stage where there's no escape."

He kissed me, and I melted. God, this man could ruin me. He'd already ruined me for all other kisses when I was fifteen. But now... he could end this, and there'd be no one else for me. No one I'd want more than him. No one who could even come close.

And that was terrifying.

"I need to feed you," he said and climbed off the bed. He then walked into the kitchen as he called the Thai restaurant.

I leaned up against the headboard, holding the gray sheet to my chest as I peered around his place. I hadn't had the chance to before and I was a little shocked at the emptiness of it.

The living room, if you could call it that, consisted of an L-shaped, charcoal gray couch facing a big screen TV on the brick wall, and a metal coffee table.

To the right was the kitchen, with stainless steel appliances, granite countertops, and black cupboards. Simple, uncluttered, and it looked as if he'd just moved in. Except there were no boxes to unpack.

I crawled off the bed, wrapping the sheet around me as I walked toward the kitchen where Killian poured two glasses of wine. The sheet dragged behind me as my bare feet padded over the hardwood.

I realized what was missing. It wasn't just furniture; it was that there was nothing personal. And I mean nothing. No pictures or artwork. No accessories like throw pillows or statues. The only personal items visible were a set of drums over in the far corner of the warehouse-slash-loft.

The only thing that said anything about who Killian was.

"No time to decorate?" I asked.

"I've had time," he replied.

"Then you have something against furniture?" The two stools at the island, a couch, and a bed didn't constitute a living space.

He walked over to me on the other side of the island and passed me a glass of red wine. "I'm not particular about where I live, Savvy. It's not important to me. I like being able to walk away at any time."

I frowned, my heart pounding. That didn't sound like someone who wanted a home. A place where you smiled when you drove down the street knowing you were home. A place with memories scattered throughout.

"Walk away where?" I asked.

He took my hand and led me over to the couch. "It's just four walls that make up a shitload of bills, Savvy."

No home. That was what he meant. He could walk away because this wasn't a home. Nothing important was here and why he didn't bother locking his door.

No attachments.

"Your drums."

He shrugged. "They're replaceable. Everything in here is replaceable, except you." My breath hitched. "Sit." He held my wine as I sat on the couch. He handed it back, eyes trailing over me. "You're losing the sheet once the food arrives. I want you naked until you leave here."

"And when is that?"

"When I let you." He smirked, but I had a feeling he wasn't kidding.

The Thai food arrived, and Killian put on a pair of plaid pajama pants to answer the door, and I heard him speaking to the guy, but it wasn't English.

And holy shit it was hot as hell listening to him.

"You speak another language?" I asked as he set out the containers on the coffee table.

"A few words here and there."

"Of Thai?"

"Mmm. I love Thai food. Savvy, lose the sheet."

I released the luxurious material and it pooled at my waist. He eyed me for a second because the sheet still covered my lower half, then he turned and finished opening the containers.

Picking up the controller he turned on the TV, scrolled to Netflix, then passed it to me. "Whatever you want, orchid."

I smiled. While he went to the kitchen to grab napkins, I put on one of my favorite movies, *Guardians of the Galaxy*.

He came back and didn't even glance at the TV as he settled in behind me, so I sat between his legs, my back to his front. He positioned us so he leaned against the armrest and our legs were up on the couch.

Then he leaned over and pulled the coffee table closer. "What's your preference?" He gestured to the food.

"Anything."

He kissed the back of my neck, and I shivered. How the hell was I supposed to eat like this? His cock was hard and pressing into my butt while his one arm looped around my waist, fingers gently caressing.

He reached for a container and a pair of chopsticks. I thought he was going to pass them to me, but instead, Killian fed me a mouthful of curry pad Thai.

The music came on when Chris Pratt walked through the cave. Killian lifted his head and glanced at the screen.

He nibbled on my ear. "Fuckin' perfect."

183

And that was how we ate. Sitting on the couch, wrapped in one another's arms as he fed us curry pad Thai, mango chicken, rice noodles, and a few items with names I didn't know, but everything was delicious.

"Enough?" he asked when I shook my head to another spring roll.

"Yes, thank you."

He bit into the spring roll over the top of my shoulder so the crumbs would fall into the container. Who would've thought the sound of a crunch could be sensual.

But it was. Everything about this was. Him expertly using the chopsticks was attractive.

My sex throbbed and my body thrummed with anticipation when I considered his idea of play as we finished eating. But Killian set the container down and leaned back, his arms around me, one hand flat on my stomach and the other lower, inches away from my sex.

"Breathe," he whispered next to my ear. Then his pierced tongue ran the length of my neck and my belly flipped.

But he didn't do anything more than hold me and kiss my neck as we watched the movie. And eventually, I relaxed and snuggled into him. He threw his leg over the top of mine, and I loved the weight of it on me.

His chest vibrated as he laughed at something in the movie and I realized it didn't matter that his place was empty and bare.

Killian was what made this place warm and inviting.

It was him. The way he was. Who he was. I just wasn't sure if that who was right for me long term. If he was even thinking long term.

I noticed the punching bag over in the far corner. It was red and hung from a thick chain. I wondered if he used it and then re-membered his bruised knuckles. Had his knuckles been due to punching the bag or his father?

I looked at his right hand and ran my fingertips over his knuckles. They were calloused, and there was a hint of a scab still on the right index knuckle. I circled it, then slipped his hand in mine and lifted it to my mouth and kissed the wound.

He stiffened. "If you want to ask me something, ask, Savvy."

I lowered his hand and tilted my head to look at him. "Did you hit your father the other night?"

"Would it bother you if I did?"

I thought about it for a second. I didn't like fighting, but Killian had never done it for fun. There'd always been something driving him, and his father was part of that. "No. And yes." I rested my hand on top of his. "No, because after seeing Lucifer, I think he deserves it. And yes, because I don't want to see you hurt."

He snorted. "He could never hurt me, Savvy."

"But he has."

His chest rose and fell, and his arms tightened around me. "Yes. And now I'm hurting him."

"Compass? And the horses?"

"His clubs can't compete with Compass. We made sure of it. Best dancers. Brett's name. Safe. Clean. No drugs. He goes under, he loses everything."

No drugs. Killian had always hated drugs in school. "Why do you care? I mean if you don't like him, what does it matter?" I stroked his knuckles. "He makes you angry. Like when you were a kid." It wasn't a question. He'd already told me his father blamed him for his mom's death.

"The knuckles are from the bag and from Logan sparring with me. I took your advice, Savvy. I hit a bag instead of a person. Took me a while, but after the raid, shit changed for me." He slipped out from under me and stood.

I reached up and dipped my fingers in the waistband of his pajamas. "I liked you then, and I like you now, Killian. I'm just not sure if we want the same things."

His fingers curled around my wrist that was holding his pants, and he slowly dragged them down while I held them. His cock sprung free and his pants pooled on the floor.

"We want the same fuckin' things, Savvy."

"A home? Family? Kids?" I asked.

He scowled, jaw clenching. "It will work."

"Killian, I can't do it again. Be with someone for years and find out they don't want what I do."

"Don't ever compare me to that asshole," he ground out.

"I'm not comparing you to him. You're nothing like him. I'm being clear as to what I want, and I want a home."

"You can't deny that you want me."

"I'm not. I do." But eventually that wouldn't be enough.

"Just you. That's all I need. And I need you right now." His eyes trailed down my naked body then back up again to meet my eyes. "You ready to play, Savvy?"

My eyes widened and my breath locked in my throat. I nodded.

He shook his head. "No, baby. I need words. Unless of course my cock is in your mouth or you're gagged."

Holy fucking shit.

My sex pulsed, throbbed, quivered and my voice crackled as I said, "Yes."

"Good. Finish watching the movie. I'll clean up first."

He was going to leave me like this? My body aching for his touch while he cleaned up—naked.

"I'll help," I said, rising and the sheet falling to the floor. I sure as hell couldn't concentrate on a movie now.

"Like fuck." He hooked my waist when I went to grab a few empty containers. "Sit. Watch your movie." He smirked. "Or watch me. But I want you here on the couch waiting for me." He ran his hand down my body to my mound and slid his fingers on either side of the folds. "Christ. Soaked."

I arched into him moaning as his finger circled my entrance, but he didn't put it inside me. Instead, he dragged his wet fingertips up my body all the way to my mouth. He didn't have to ask this time as I opened my mouth. He slipped his finger inside and I tasted myself.

"Sit," he urged.

I did.

He put his hands on my thighs and gently spread them apart. "Stay like that."

"What?"

"Legs apart, baby."

I opened my mouth to tell him I couldn't because, God, I ached for him and keeping my legs open was painful without him touching me. But I clamped my mouth closed, and he chuckled before turning and giving me a good view of his ass as he collected the containers and took them into the kitchen.

Chapter Twenty-One

Killian

I TRIED NOT TO LOOK OVER AT HER ON THE COUCH, LEGS PARTED, chest rapidly rising and falling, face flushed under the dim ceiling lights. Putting the containers in the bin, I took my time wiping off the counter that didn't need wiping and rinsing out the sink.

She wanted kids. A family. A home.

I wanted to give her that, but I didn't know if I could. I'd never considered any of those things before, but with her... maybe after shit settled with my father there was a chance? Fuck, losing her wasn't an option.

When the credits rolled on the TV, I walked over and picked up the controller and shut it off. Without looking at her, I strode back into the kitchen.

Silence. That was what I wanted. Just the sound of her breathing. Opening the freezer, I took out an ice cube tray and bent it so the cubes popped free then put them into a bowl.

I heard the slight hitch in her breath at the sound of the ice cracking. I was betting she was an ice virgin. Good.

I knew I wasn't her first with sex, but this was something much more than fucking. It was incredibly intimate and sensual. It was about trust and losing yourself to the other person. Submitting. Trusting.

I didn't have a candle, which I'd have preferred, but I had honey, and it would have a similar effect when heated. I reached up into the cupboard and took out the honey. After squeezing some into a glass, I placed it in the microwave.

While I waited for it to heat, I looked over at Savvy who was very quiet on the couch.

My body stilled as I stared. Christ, so fuckin' perfect.

Her eyes were closed, head tilted to rest on the back of the couch as if she were sleeping, but I knew she wasn't.

Not with her legs parted and her hands resting on her inner thighs as if she was debating whether to touch herself.

She was listening, and when the microwave dinged, there was a subtle jerk of her body. I padded across the space to my closet and took out one of my ties. Then I picked up the bowl of ice and the glass of honey and went back to her.

"Keep your eyes closed," I instructed while placing the bowl and glass on the coffee table. "I'm going to blindfold you with my tie."

The pulse in her throat beat faster. "Okay," she replied, remembering the rules to give me words. I could read her body, but it was important that I had her verbal consent because her body might want it, but not her mind.

I leaned over her, being careful not to touch her as I placed the silk material over her eyes and gently tied it. Her hands rose and she touched it.

Her apprehension rose from the way her body stiffened, so I ran my hand over the top of her head. "Relax, orchid. I'd never hurt you."

"I know."

"But you're still scared?"

She nodded. "Yes. A little. I've never been blindfolded before."

I liked that she admitted that to me.

"Lie down on the couch, Savvy."

I was silent while she shuffled around to lie back, putting her legs up. Once she was settled, I stirred the ice cubes with my finger, so she'd hear them clinking.

"I used to watch you dance in the gym before class."

She gasped, and her hands went to the blindfold to pull it off, but I reached out and took hold of her wrists. Slowly, I lowered them to rest on her thighs, and she opened her mouth to say something. "Shh. Just listen and feel."

She swallowed. I picked up an ice cube and droplets of water dripped on her skin as I held it over the top of her abdomen.

She sucked in air, her muscles tightening.

"I'd watch you dance by yourself through that tiny window every Monday, Tuesday, and Friday." I lowered the ice cube to her nipple, circled it, then moved to the other before trailing a cold path down her body to her clit where I rested it there and let it melt from the heat of her body.

Her legs quivered. My cock was rock-hard, and I wouldn't be able to take as long as I wanted before I needed inside her. But I had to give her something as she was uncertain about us.

I sifted around in the bowl for another ice cube and brought it to her mouth. She parted her lips, and I wet the surface before slipping it into her mouth with my fingers holding it. She sucked on it, and I watched her throat as she swallowed the small amounts of liquid the ice offered.

"When I watched you, it was like I could breathe. The anger inside me evaporated like the ice. It melted away with the heat of your body as you danced." I withdrew the ice from her mouth and slid it down her skin to her inner thigh. With my other hand, I grabbed a handful of cubes and placed them on her stomach before I picked up the glass of warm honey.

I tested it first to make certain it wasn't too hot by placing a small amount on my wrist. I dipped my finger in again so it was coated with the thick sugar then traced across her lips.

A moan escaped her throat.

"Lick your lips, Savvy."

Her tongue slowly slid across the plush surface and it took every ounce of control I had not to fuckin' kiss her. But I had to share one more thing with her.

"I'd never met you, but I knew what kind of person you were from the moment I saw you with Daniel consoling him." A small sound escaped her lips. "And when I was near you, it was like... the hatred and anger, all of it was gone."

I bathed my finger in the honey again then drew around her nipple before I bent and licked the erect nub before drawing it into my mouth.

She arched into me, and I put my palm on her stomach to keep her in place, the ice now a pool of water that dribbled down her sides.

"I stayed away from you, so you wouldn't be ruined by me. I couldn't chance you getting hurt when you were made up of all the goodness I'd lost." Two wet stains appeared on my blue silk tie over her eyes. "I didn't want to care. Caring and losing again... I couldn't do it. But I already did care, Savvy. It was too late."

Her breath came in short gasps as if she was trying to stop herself from crying, while at the same time, trying not to be aroused by what I was doing to her body.

"What I said at the cemetery about your mother was cruel, but I didn't know how to be nice anymore. I wanted everyone to hate me. But you didn't. You believed in me. I don't know why, but I felt it." I tilted the glass and poured honey between her breasts and watched the thick golden sugar trail a path to her belly button. "When you left, I changed. And a lot of that had to do with you. And the guys in the band. The music." I inhaled a deep breath. "I swore never to find you because I knew if I did, I'd never let you go. I needed you to come to me, Savvy." I swirled my tongue around her belly button then followed the honey upward. "And you did. And this time, I won't let you go."

She blindly found my forearms and tugged me closer. "Killian. Kiss me. Please. I need you to kiss me."

I tore off her blindfold and hooked her back, dragging her hard up against me. Then our mouths collided.

She moaned beneath my bruising assault. Her hands in my

hair, the glass of honey forgotten as it spilled over her body between us.

I growled low in my throat as I crawled onto the couch, taking her with me so we lay on it together. The glass fell on the floor, forgotten. The ice melted in the bowl, forgotten. The honey sticking to our skin, forgotten.

But what wasn't forgotten was the taste of her salty tears as I kissed her. The same as eleven years ago. And I couldn't get enough of her.

It was dangerous, the way I felt about her. Powerful. Intense. Consuming. And yeah, it was obsessive.

"Fuck, Savvy. Fuck." I growled as I stroked my cock up and down her sex before settling it at her entrance.

She held my head in her hands as I drew back and our eyes locked. Tears stained her cheeks as she smiled at me.

And it was a smile that lit her eyes and warmed my chest.

"I never forgot you, Killian. The orchid was a piece of you I took with me. I thought that was all I'd ever have of you."

I kissed her again, and her hands slid down my forearms that kept me perched above her.

I tilted my hips and slid inside her. The anticipation, the constant arousal, the need... it finally interlocked into a wild craze of limbs and mouths.

Harder.

Faster.

Deeper.

I thrust, and she met my movements with her own. Our bodies smacked together, honeyed skin sticking each time.

We rolled right off the couch onto the hardwood floor, her on top of me, my cock still deep inside. The small of my back hurt, but it wasn't from the landing, it was the glass I fell on that shattered and cut into my skin. But no chance was I stopping this.

I grabbed her hips. "Ride me, Savvy."

She sat up, lifted slightly then came down on my cock.

Over and over again.

I watched as her head tilted back and her eyes closed as she rode me.

Fuck, I'd never get enough of this. Of her. And it didn't even have to be sex. Just being with her.

I grabbed her ass with one hand, fingers in her crevice and it urged her on harder and faster.

"Yes," she cried.

I gently applied pressure to her tight puckered ring and slowly the resistance eased and my finger slid inside.

"Killian," she panted. "Oh, God. Yes."

My finger slid in and out as she rode me hard on the floor. I met her thrusts with my own so I sank deeper.

"Christ, orchid. Christ." Every muscle tightened as my orgasm exploded into a roar of firecrackers.

Her core squeezed my cock, thighs clamping and her fingernails scraped down my chest as she came, too, then collapsed on top of me, so her head tucked into the crook of my neck.

My finger slid from her ass, and she moaned and kissed the hollow of my throat. I wrapped my arms around her and held her to me until our hearts returned to normal.

"Have to move, baby." We sat up together, her arms coming around my back.

I winced when she touched the glass embedded in my back. "Killian?" She scrambled off my lap to take a look. "Oh, my God. The glass."

"Don't move." I climbed to my feet then picked her up in my arms.

I carried her into the kitchen and set her on the counter, but that didn't last as she hopped off and ran into the bathroom. "Killian." She peeked around the corner scowling, with a facecloth in her hand. "Come here."

My girl had boss in her. I inwardly smiled as I strode into the bathroom and her boss became more boss as she took over. I remembered she had first aid training and she still volunteered at the hospital.

"Turn around and put your hands on the counter." I chuckled, listening to her, but did as I was told. "God, I can't believe you didn't say anything." She examined my back. "It looks like there are three shards in your back. Where are your tweezers?"

"Savvy, I don't have tweezers."

"Such a guy," she muttered under her breath, and it was cute. "I guess you don't have disinfectant either?"

I did because of my knuckles when I punched the bag too hard. I reached under the bathroom sink and pulled out the bottle and gauze.

"I'll try and use my fingernails," she said and put her hands on my waist firmly as if to make sure I knew this is where she wanted me.

I liked this side of her. Fuck, I liked all sides of her. And I didn't want to spend another night without her. It was fast. Fuck, it was supersonic, but I'd waited eleven fuckin' years. Now that she was here, I didn't want her going back to that apartment. But she was already hesitant after dick David and pushing her could push her right out the fuckin' door.

Savvy gingerly removed shards of glass the size of fuckin' rice grains from my back with her fingernails. I stood quietly and waited while she played nurse. She'd always had this nurturing quality about her. Something I'd been drawn to, maybe because it was something I lacked. When Emmitt died, caring died with him—until Savvy.

"Do you have any salve?" she asked.

"In the cupboard above the toilet." When she went to walk away, I turned and grabbed her by the hips, tugging her backward into me. I kissed the back of her neck. "Thank you."

"You're welcome."

"I don't want you to go." I meant ever, but I couldn't tell her that. She wasn't ready.

She smiled. "I'm just getting the salve."

"Yeah," I murmured, letting her go.

She went and got the salve then applied it to the wounds before her hands settled on my hips.

"Killian?"

"Yeah, baby."

"At Compass, you said you knew every single way my body moved. It's because you used to watch me dance."

"Yes."

"I never saw you. Not once."

I turned and softly stroked up and down her arms. "If you did, would you've stopped?"

"Probably. You scared me. And you weren't very nice." She reached up and touched my cheek. "But you're nice now. When you're not being bossy."

I cupped her chin. "This is going somewhere, Savvy."

"Do you ever *not* get what you want, Killian?"

"Yes, for eleven years."

Chapter Twenty-Two

Savvy

I ROLLED OVER TO SNUGGLE INTO KILLIAN'S WARMTH, BUT ALL I found was a cold mattress.

Sitting up, the sheet held to my chest, I scanned the warehouse for him. It didn't take long to figure out what he was doing when I heard the smacks of his fists hitting the hard leather.

The punching bag was at the far end of the warehouse, and there were no lights on, but the sun was rising and peeked through the windows, offering a soft orange glow across the room.

His muscles flexed with every hit. Tattoos expanding over his biceps as he drew his arm back, hand curled into a fist as he plowed into the bag. Over and over again, skin glistening with sweat.

Unable to look away, I stared breathlessly as he bounced on the balls of his feet. Agile and beautiful. I'd never seen him fight in school, but as I watched him now, I realized why no one could beat him.

There was a fierce concentration on his face. Determination. A hardness. There was anger too, but it was controlled. As if he had a leash on it and held it back.

With each punch the anger lessened. As if he was hitting more than just a bag. He was hitting someone and beating him down. And with it the anger.

But there was more to the haunting sound of him punching the bag. It was the pain beneath the anger. A pain so deep that it was what drove him to do this. Not the anger.

Naked, I crawled from bed and walked toward him, my heart breaking as I continued to watch him. Hit after hit, his face a mask of intensity.

He was so focused on the bag, he didn't notice my approach until I lightly touched his waist as he was about to swing. He tensed then grabbed the bag with both hands to steady it.

It took a second before the strain in his muscles eased, and he lowered his arms, turned and inhaled a ragged breath. His pulse throbbed in his neck, and it was obvious he'd been at this for a while.

"Savvy." His expression softened, and he ran his hand over my head to the nape of my neck. "Did I wake you?"

"No." I reached up and placed my hand on his heated chest. "Do you do this often?"

His brows furrowed and it contradicted his half smile. "When I can't sleep."

I stepped into him, chin tilted up and my other hand curling around his forearm. "You're beautiful fighting."

His jaw clenched. "It's not fighting, Savvy. It's working out."

But it was fighting. He fought something. I saw it in his expression. His body. In every hit. I just didn't know what he was fighting. His father? Himself? Or something else?

What worried me was that he still hid behind the wall and I didn't know if I was strong enough to get through to the other side.

But how could I expect him to give me that part of him when I was holding back? In order to have all of him, I had to give him all of me and risk the pain of getting hurt again.

And as he held me in his arms, the sun a soft glow on the side of his face, the week-old scruff along his jaw and a bead of sweat dripping down his temple, I knew there was no walking away from him.

He was worth the risk.

The hidden. The complicated. The man who had demons behind the captivating green eyes, but within the depths also lived a man who cared. Who protected. Who made my heart skip a beat and my breath stop.

He leaned forward and kissed me, his fingers fisting in my hair. I sagged into him, my bare skin instantly damp and heated by his. No matter how amazing it felt in his embrace, he was still tense in his arms. His touch.

Whatever kept him awake and made him hit the bag still lingered.

He pulled back. "Going to shower, baby."

He didn't ask me to join him, and I saw the conflict on his face as he continued to battle whatever was bothering him. Releasing my hair, he stepped back, but I moved with him.

"Killian?" His brows lifted. "Don't go." I slid my hand down to the sparse hairs on his pelvis then lower to his workout shorts where his cock was already erect.

"Let me shower first."

I shook my head. "No. I want you here. Right now." Against his bag. Where I suspected a lot of his demons lived. I wanted him to think of me when he punched the bag instead of whatever hunted him.

His eyes flicked to his bag chained to a steel beam.

Neither of us said anything, and I waited to see if he'd let me in enough to do this.

"Stay here." He strode into the kitchen, and I heard a drawer open and shut and then he walked back with what looked like rope dangling from his hand. My heart skipped a beat and belly thunked, but it was a good thunk. An excited thunk.

"Give me your wrists," he said, stopping in front of me.

There was no hesitation as I held them out in front of me. He was deliberate and methodical as he tied my wrists together with the rope like he knew exactly what he was doing. Like he'd done this before.

"You've done this before?"

"The ropes, yes," he said without looking at me. Something was wrong. He was being cold and avoiding my eyes.

"Killian?"

"Raise your arms above your head," he ordered.

"Killian?" I repeated as I did as he requested. He reached the chain and threaded the end of the rope through a link, and I felt the tautness on my wrists. "Are you going to look at me?"

His chest was against mine as he knotted the rope, so my arms were hitched above my head and my back was against the hard leather of the bag.

"Killian. Look at me." I said, but he still didn't. "See me." Because whatever he saw now wasn't me. It was too precise and unemotional. Something had shifted from the bag to him tying me up. "Killian," I whispered. "Please."

His arms lowered and his hands glided down my arms to my waist where his fingers spanned them. His eyes were closed, and his lips pressed firmly together.

"Does this remind you of someone else?" I asked.

His eyes snapped open. "There is no one else."

"Then what's wrong?"

He clenched his jaw. "Jesus, Savvy. You. It's you. It's this. You asking me to do this. You knowing what I need when I'm supposed to be the one giving you what you need." He bowed his head, and I wished I could hold him. Touch him.

"What I need is you." I waited until his head lifted and our eyes locked. "Just you and whatever comes with you. The hurt. The pain. The anger. The sweet and the caring. All of you."

My sex tweaked because the look in his eyes was heated and possessive. He reached for me, and my breath hitched, and goose bumps popped before he even made contact.

And when he did make contact, it was his thumb tracing the plump surface of my lower lip then to my chin, neck, collarbone and to the crevice between my breasts. His eyes followed his caress until he stopped at my belly button. "You don't know all of me."

"I know," I replied.

He nodded, then his finger continued its path to my sex, and I sucked in a lungful of air as he slipped into the wetness. "Never have I been with someone. Not like you."

Lowering his head, his lips a breath away from mine, he inserted his finger up inside me at the same time as his mouth took mine.

Warmth invaded, and the chain clanked as I yanked on the rope. The hard leather of the bag swayed into my back and pushed me closer to him. He groaned and grabbed me around the waist, deepening the kiss.

Having the weight of the bag at my back and him at my front, both pressing into me, was cathartic. Unable to get away. Not wanting to, but being vulnerable to him... it was erotic and overwhelming and intense.

It was trusting him completely. A giving of myself, letting go and surrendering to him.

He broke away and yanked off his shorts then checked my wrists and rope before he hitched me up in his arms. He used one hand to position his cock and the other to hold my ass.

I wrapped my legs around him. "Hard, Killian. I want you to fuck me like when you hit the bag."

His brows lowered for a second. "Savvy," he growled and then he kissed me again, as he pushed his cock deep inside.

But he didn't move.

Instead, he kissed me while I curled my hands around the rope, using it as leverage to hold my body up. But I didn't need to. Killian's arms held me.

And he'd never let me go. I just wasn't sure if that was literal or not. But right now it didn't matter.

"I tried, baby. Fuck, I tried, but I couldn't."

"Tried?"

His cock pulsed inside me and my body throbbed with need, but I didn't move as he rested his forehead against my chin. "Sex."

My chest tightened and heart pounded. He couldn't be saying what I think he was saying. "Killian? I don't understand."

He lifted his head and his eyes met mine. Those ice green eyes that reminded me of the Popsicles my dad and I ate on the porch.

"I've been with a lot of women. Mostly play. Bondage. But other things at the BDSM club. Two girls at once, fuck, it was easier when it was two girls, but I never fucked them. Never did my cock go inside them. You're the first, Savvy." My eyes widened and I gasped. "I tried once after you left. But I couldn't do it. All I saw was you."

"Killian." My insides melted in a heat of... what? Love. Did I love Killian?

He briefly kissed my quivering lips. "I didn't want to ruin the image of being inside you. So, I kept that for myself."

Oh, God. A tear escaped and rolled down my cheek. He saw it and kissed it away.

"Now that I have you and the image is real... fuck, I can't let you go again."

"I'm not going anywhere, Killian."

He groaned and tilted his hips. His cock sank deeper and I closed my eyes.

Then there were no more words as he fucked me against the bag. With each thrust, the bag moved away and then swayed back into me.

It was hard. Fast. And just when I thought my wrists couldn't take it anymore, he reached up and yanked on the loose end and the rope released.

I wrapped my arms around his neck and kissed him. He met my fierce need with his own as he carried me to bed then lowered me, his lips never leaving mine.

Then Killian made love to me.

It wasn't wild and raw. But with each thrust, each touch, each kiss, it was the building of something more. Something neither of us could get back. Parts of us, maybe.

My mind spun with his words repeating over and over in my head. And in some ways, it hurt because I'd been with other men. I'd thought I was going to spend my life with David. I'd had a plan.

If he hadn't cheated on me, if I hadn't needed a job so desperately, I may have never gone to Killian. God, to think I'd have missed this.

Afterward, we lay in one another's arms for a long time. My cheek on his chest and his arm over me as he gently caressed my back.

I traced one of the tattoos on his side as I spoke. "Ms. Evert, my last foster mother, asked me once what was so important about the orchid. I guess she wondered why I wanted to save it because I'd had it for a year as I went from foster home to foster home and it had never bloomed. It was kind of pathetic looking, actually." His caressing stilled, and he tilted his chin to look at me as I did him. "I told her about you. How you fought. What you said to me. How you found me at the underground fight and saved me from getting caught. Then at the cemetery. Even what you told me about your dad." He didn't say anything. "She was the only person I told about your kiss that day. You know what she asked me? If I'd be sad if the orchid died.

"I told her the orchid was home." His arm tightened around me. "At the time, it was. It was what came with me to each foster home, and when I looked at it, even as pathetic as it was, I smiled." I trailed my fingers along his torso. "I told her I'd never let it go and she said you must be someone really special.

"I remember thinking about you when it bloomed and wishing you could see how beautiful the orchid became. Ms. Evert wanted me to put it in a nicer pot, but I liked the cracked pink one. It was you, Killian. The orchid. The pot. Damaged and hurt, but fighting to survive. And I guess I thought if I looked after it, you'd be okay."

He kissed me on the top of the head. "Fuck, baby."

I sat up so I could look at him. "I've always wanted a home. Somewhere I could settle and decorate and make memories. You know, like notches in the tree outside marking the kids as they grow. I've always wanted lots of kids." His brows lifted at that. "Well, at least two so they could protect one another." His body tightened and a darkness blanketed the brilliant green in his eyes. "I know you don't want kids, Killian."

He sat up, taking me with him, then lifted me so I straddled his waist, his hands on my hips. "I don't. And, Savvy, no matter how much I want you, I can't give you that."

I nodded, my chest tight as I tried to hold back the tears. Because I didn't know where that left us except on different paths.

He inhaled a ragged breath and his gaze held mine, tortured and pained. "I had a brother." I tried to conceal my reaction, but my body stiffened and eyes widened. "In Ireland. Emmitt. He was a year and a half younger than me. A really good kid, and I swear he had your good bits scattered all through him, Savvy. There wasn't a mean molecule in his body even when he had a reason to be mad at the world." He closed his eyes, tilting his head back to rest on the headboard. "But not Emmitt. He accepted who he was and accepted everyone else and who they were."

I sought out his hands, linked our fingers together and rested them on my thighs. He squeezed, and I knew this was really hard for him to talk about, but he was giving me this. A part of him.

"He even accepted my dad, although he didn't always like him, but not for what he did to him, but for how he treated me. Emmitt had Tourette's and our dad thought my brother could control the spontaneous blinking, but of course, he couldn't. He'd make him practice in front of the mirror for hours which only made it worse. But it was football where my brother found his place. His freedom. God, he was so good at it and was going to go far and my dad knew it. Everyone did. He was a natural, and it's where he was happiest, with a ball between his feet."

Tears streamed down my cheeks. I knew where this was going wasn't good and it pained me to hear his voice crack as he spoke.

"He was teased all the time. Bullied constantly by kids in school. Kids on the other football teams. I tried… fuck, I tried to protect him from it. I was his brother. I was supposed to protect him."

He swallowed as if he were having trouble getting the words out. "I was kissing some chick. That's why he walked home alone so I could stay late in class with the girl." He released one of my hands and ran it down his face before he rubbed the inner corners of his eyes. "I found him on my way home later. He was face down in the river. Dead."

I choked back the sob, biting my lip so hard I tasted blood.

"A few days later, three kids confessed that they'd chased him through the fields, throwing sheep dung at him. It was raining, and he slipped on the wooden bridge and fell through the rope rungs into the river. They took off instead of helping him. The fall didn't kill him. The coroner said he was likely unconscious and drowned."

I reached up and stroked the side of his face, unable to say anything. It had to be over fifteen years ago, and from his expression, it was like it happened yesterday. He carried so much guilt and pain with him.

For something he wasn't responsible for. "You fought the bullies in school because of Emmitt."

He nodded.

Oh, God. He blamed himself, and it was his way to try and ease the guilt. No wonder he'd been so angry all the time, and why I never saw him with any girls. "What happened to the kids?"

He shrugged. "Nothing. It was deemed an accident. A year later my dad moved us to Toronto."

Sorry, wasn't enough for losing someone. No words were. "Your brother, he sounds like an incredible person. I wish I'd met him."

"Me too, Savvy." He lifted me off his lap and climbed out of bed, then offered his hand. "Shower." He was closing the subject. "Then we'll go for breakfast before you go to the hospital."

"Okay."

I was volunteering and then working at the club. He'd yet to mention me working there, but I was pretty sure it was on his mind. And I was pretty sure he wasn't happy about it.

I wanted to ask him more about Emmitt, about what happened to his mom, about the animosity between him and his father. Had it stemmed from Emmitt's death? But it wasn't the time, and I didn't want to push him.

"Are you with the band today?" I asked as he led me into the bathroom.

"Yeah, we're working on a new song for the album. I don't know if I'll be at Compass, but Luke or Roman will be there if I'm not."

I stopped before he reached into the shower to turn on the water, and he turned to look at me. "Thank you, Killian. For sharing Emmitt with me."

He pulled me into his arms and while holding my chin, he kissed me.

It was a drunk butterfly kiss. A kiss that went from the tip of my toes to the top of my head. A kiss that gave me the piece of him he'd kept from me.

Killian Kane had let me in.

Chapter Twenty-Three

Killian

I SMILED WHEN I READ THE TEXT FROM SAVVY.

When are you coming?

Fuck, I liked that. I liked that she missed me and it had only been eight hours since she left my bed. I'd dropped her off at the apartment then went to Logan's to record for the day. She was going to work on her résumé which made me fuckin' happy. I'd tried again to give her money to open her own studio, but Savvy had simply laughed.

I'd spanked her ass then fucked her from behind.

She was at Avalanche with Frankie and the girls from Compass celebrating Bree's breakup with her boyfriend. I guessed that was a good thing.

I typed back.

On my way, baby.

"You're serious about her," Logan said.

Eme was out of town for a couple days at a horse clinic she was giving, so Logan had decided to come with me to Avalanche.

"Yeah." For three weeks, I'd woken to her scent as I held her in my arms. Fuck, getting this chance with her… it was all I'd ever wanted and didn't think I'd get. And now the images I'd carried with me were real. "Always have been. Just couldn't get there. But this shit with my dad… I can't have it touch her." I dragged my hand over my head. "What you went through with Emily… Christ, I don't know how you both survived it. My father doesn't come close to yours, but if he touches her… I don't know what I'd do. Fuckin' kill him and end up in jail."

"We'll make sure that doesn't happen, Kite. What Eme went through because of me… fuck, it will haunt me for the rest of my days. It killed me. Every fuckin' day it killed me. But nothing wins against love. It wins every single fuckin' time."

"He's losing his horses," I said. "Emily said the SPCA is doing a thorough investigation."

The Society for the Prevention of Cruelty to Animals had removed another horse, Faith, from his stable. Emily had the mare at her and Logan's farm along with TK, my informant. He was more than happy to leave my dad's stable and now worked for her; she was teaching him her way to be with horses. A natural way.

Word was my father was giving up polo and his horses were for sale. I thought I'd feel happy about the fact he was crumbling, but it was more of a relief for the horses. There wasn't the satisfaction I'd expected to feel that he was scrambling to keep his nightclubs alive. Because the fact was, I no longer cared. All I cared about was Savvy, and I wanted this to end. To walk away from the club business. Forget my father.

"You have Shield on her?" Logan asked as Luke pulled up to the pub.

"Roman is at her apartment when she's there, but she's at my place most of the time."

His brows lifted. "You at least put up some fuckin' pictures and make it look normal? Maybe buy a throw pillow or two."

I snorted. "She has me."

Logan chuckled as he opened the door and got out. I followed.

Savvy wanted a home. Fuckin' kids. Notches in the trees. Pictures. Things I couldn't give her. I'd live wherever the fuck she wanted, but I couldn't walk into my house and see memories in picture frames.

I had to be able to walk away. Not from her. But from a place. It was my control knowing everything was disposable.

Logan texted Matt, and he opened the back door of Avalanche for us.

"Matt." I shook his hand, and he slapped me on the back before he did the same to Logan.

"You hear from my sister?" he asked Logan.

"They landed in Florida about an hour ago."

As we walked down the hall toward the bar, Matt asked about the spread the magazine was doing on the band next week. We had to fly to New York for a couple days for the photo shoot and interview, and I planned on Savvy coming with me. Although, she didn't know it yet.

My eyes scanned the crowd searching for Savvy, and when I saw her, my chest swelled. Fuck. Her cheeks were flushed, and her eyes danced as she laughed at something.

I froze as I stared at her. Needing a moment to just watch her without her knowing I was. Like I used to do in high school.

Fuck, it was hard to believe she was mine. That she'd placed all her good bits in my hand and trusted me with them.

Christ, I wanted to pick her up and toss her over my shoulder and take her home.

Home.

I'd never called a place home before. But Savvy made it home.

"Kite?" Matt said.

I jerked my eyes from Savvy to Matt who held a beer for me. "Thanks."

He nodded to the group of girls. "Didn't realize the woman you're dating is best friends with Mars."

I frowned. "You know Mars?"

He nodded. "Met her at my gym a few weeks ago. But it wasn't the best introduction."

"Scaring off the women again, Matt?" Logan said, grinning.

He snorted. "A female going to the gym by herself at three in the morning is fuckin' stupid."

"And you told her that," I said. Matt was single, and he was likely still single because all he focused on was Avalanche and looking after his sister, Kat. Although he didn't need to do that anymore as she had Ream, and Kat could look after herself. I got it though as he'd raised her since he was eighteen after their parents had died. I'd be the same way if Emmitt had lived.

Logan shook his head. "I hope you weren't interested because calling her stupid would put a dent in your chances of dating her."

Matt's gaze shifted across the bar to where Savvy stood. Beside her was Mars. And from the way Matt was looking at her, he was interested. Although as far as I knew Matt was never interested in a girl for long.

"Don't hurt her," I said. "I don't want Savvy pissed at you because you fucked her best friend and never called."

Matt didn't respond; instead, he clanged his beer with ours. "Need to go check on the band. Fuckin' lead singer is a complete ass. I'd kick him out of here if I had another band on standby." His dark brows lifted. "Want to call Ream and Crisis? Impromptu show?"

"No," I said. I wanted to spend time with Savvy. I had eleven years to make up for. It was then I saw her head turn in my direction, and my heart stopped.

The look in her eyes. Fuck. It was like everything I wanted to say to her was written there. Desire. Need. Want. Trust. And yeah, love.

"Jesus," I muttered under my breath.

She smiled and my heart kick-started again. I made my way toward her and she whispered something to Mars, who looked over at me, and she smiled and winked at me. Then Mars's gaze shifted to the far right in the direction Matt had gone.

Savvy set her fruity drink on the bar top as I reached her. I ran my hand down the curve of her back to the cusp of her ass. Cupping her chin, I bent and kissed her.

"Savvy," I murmured against her lips. "Fuck, I missed you."

She laughed. "I saw you this morning."

"My point exactly." I glanced up at Mars, Frankie, and the girls from Compass saying hi to all of them. "Going to steal my girl for a minute."

Bree wiggled her brows. "You hear that, Hijack? He called you his girl. Yep, I need to find me a guy like Kite."

"Hijack?" She laughed, and I slid my hand in hers then weaved through the crowd. Logan was at the bar sitting with Vic, one of Deck's special-ops guys who was nursing bottled water.

"Where are we going?" she asked, her heels clicking behind me.

I opened the bar flap then closed it behind us before walking through the swinging doors into the back.

As soon as I was sure we were alone, I shoved her against the wall. Then I kissed her like I really wanted to kiss her when I'd seen her, but couldn't.

I grabbed her wrists and slammed then up against the wall above her head. "Move in with me," I growled.

She drew back, but she couldn't go far. "Killian. I can't."

I nipped her lower lip then kissed her again. My piercing clanged against her teeth as our mouths moved. Fierce. Violent. Hungry.

"Move in, Savvy." This wasn't like the car where I could just get rid of her apartment. She had concerns after her dick ex, and I got it, but I didn't have to like it. I wanted to know she was at my place. Our place.

I pulled back, my gaze heated. "I want you with me."

She was panting from the bruising kiss and her lips were swollen. "I can't."

"Damn it, I don't like you there." I not only didn't like her in that building, I wanted her with me. I wanted to wake up with her. Go to sleep with her every night.

She reached up and stroked my scruff with her fingers. "You can't put me in a bubble, Killian. Just like you couldn't with Emmitt." My jaw clenched and I released her wrists, backing off.

"Emmitt has nothing to do with this." But it did. I hadn't protected him and the need to protect Savvy was overwhelming.

She placed her palm over my heart. "He'll always have something to do with it, and that's a good thing, Killian. I just don't know if you realize how much he is part of everything you do."

"I don't fight anymore."

"But you do, Killian. You're fighting yourself. Your father. The demons in that bag. You're constantly fighting who you are by trying to control everything else. I'm not going anywhere, but I can't move in with you. Not right now."

"I hate you in that place," I said, moving back into her and caressing her cheek with the back of my finger.

She rested her hands on my waist. "I know. But it's not forever, and I received a reply from a dance studio."

It was like a load of cement dropped from my shoulders. "Fuck, that's good news."

She smiled. "I hope so. I like your club and the money is great, but the hours suck, and it's exhausting."

I weaved my fingers in her hair and pulled her into me as I kissed her again, my other hand grabbed her thigh to hitch it on my hip. She was wearing a black cotton dress and it easily lifted as I slid my hand along her inner thigh to her panties.

She gasped against my mouth when I touched her. "Killian."

I groaned, pressing her hard into the wall as I deepened the kiss, my finger sliding through her wetness before I shoved it up inside her. She tilted her head back, arching her neck. I kissed along her chin, then down the curve of her neck.

"Fuck you, Matt," some guy yelled.

"Christ," I muttered, breaking away from Savvy and lowering her leg to the floor. I blocked her body with my own as she readjusted her dress then turned toward the booted feet coming in our direction.

"You signed a contract. You can't walk out," Matt shouted at the other end of the hall.

"Watch me," the guy replied.

"You leave, you'll never play in this city again."

It was obvious this was the lead singer, Matt mentioned. He was tall, lean, looked about seventeen or eighteen and had tattoos inked down his right arm. He wore a white T-shirt, ripped jeans, and motorcycle boots. He also had what looked like motorcycle gloves in his hand. His unruly dark hair went with his wild daunting eyes that were currently focused on me.

"Problem, asshole?" he said.

I stiffened, and Savvy's hands resting on my back curled into my dress shirt. "Yeah, you walking out on Matt is a shit move. Don't want to play tonight, but looks like I am." Because I'd never leave Matt in a lurch, none of the guys would. I'd have to put a call into Crisis and Ream, and after eight hours of recording, I was betting neither wanted to drive to Avalanche and do a gig. But they would.

He came to an abrupt halt a few feet away. I saw the realization hit his eyes when he recognized me, but it only seemed to piss him off more. "I have shit that's come up."

"More important than your career?" I asked. Because like Savvy knew firsthand, word spread in the industry fast and another bar wouldn't touch him if he walked out like this.

His eyes narrowed. "Yeah. My sister dyin' in the fuckin' hospital."

Savvy gasped.

Matt had caught up and overheard him. "Why the hell didn't you say anything?"

"Because it's none of your business. It's no one's business, but mine." He strode down the hall, slammed his palm into the swinging doors and was gone.

"Fuck," Matt muttered. "He didn't say anything. All he said was he had to go."

"Who is he?" Savvy asked.

"Gavin Chase," Matt replied, then headed back the way he came. "I have to announce to the bar he's not playing tonight."

"Let me talk to his band," I said. Matt stopped and looked over his shoulder. "If they know any of our songs, Logan and I can play with them." I was okay on the guitar and could play in a pinch, but the singing wasn't my thing.

"Fuck. Thanks, Kite." Matt jogged down the hall and disappeared into one of the rooms.

I turned, placing my hands on Savvy's waist and squeezing. "You okay to stick around for a while. Hang with the girls?"

She nodded, but her eyes were tearing and one slipped down her cheek.

"What the fuck?" I wiped it away with the pad of my thumb.

She half smiled. "I like you."

"And you're crying because of that?"

"A lot," she added. "Okay, more than a lot."

"Savvy," I growled, then tugged her into me. "I fuckin' love you." Then I kissed her again.

Chapter Twenty-Four

Savvy

TONIGHT HAD BEEN MY LAST SHIFT AT COMPASS. I'D MISS THE girls and dancing, but I was excited about my new job. I hadn't told Killian yet because I wanted to surprise him when he arrived back from New York.

I'd told Frankie last night and gave her my two weeks' notice, but she'd insisted tonight be my last night so I could start my new job sooner. She also knew Killian wasn't pleased about me working here.

I called Ali, the woman who owned the dance studio, this morning and let her know I could start right away. The salary wasn't as good as Compass, but it didn't matter. It was enough to live on, and once I built up a clientele, my salary would also increase.

My phone vibrated, and I took it out of my purse as I walked up the last flight of stairs to my apartment, Luke behind me.

Just landed. I'll see you in an hour.

Can't wait to see you.
You too, baby. Luke with you?

LOL… yes. Luke would have to be dead before allowing me to walk into this building alone.

Baby, you're sitting on my face tonight and that pussy is mine. After I spank that sweet ass.

My sex clenched at the thought. Killian pushed me sexually, but hell, it was a good push. Freeing. He excelled with the ropes and had tied me up the other night with my legs positioned over my head and secured to my wrists, while my wrists had been secured to the bed rungs. Then he'd leaned over me and slid his cock inside. Slow. Deep. So incredibly deep that—

"Miss Grady?"

I jerked from my thoughts and realized I was standing outside my door with Luke standing beside me.

God, he'd only been gone two days. How did I survive eleven years without him?

He consumed my every waking and sleeping thought. And he didn't make it any easier when he sent texts like the last one.

"That was Killian," I told Luke. "They've landed. But I'm sure you already know that." Killian had asked me to go with him, to New York, but I'd had the job interview, although I hadn't told him that. I'd said I wasn't a fan of flying.

His eyebrows knitted together as he glanced at his phone. "No. Roman hasn't messaged me yet. But good to hear. He will be coming here?"

I smiled. "Yes, so you don't have to wait around."

"I'll wait."

I put the key in the lock and went inside. Luke waited until I turned the lock before I heard his footsteps jog down the stairs.

Flicking on the lights in the kitchen, I grabbed a bottle of water, then sipped it before pouring a little into the orchid on my windowsill. It really did need a new pot and now that I was with Killian, I was okay with parting with the cracked pink one.

The floor creaked behind me, and I spun around. I managed a half scream before a large calloused hand covered my mouth and I was quickly yanked up against a hard, unrelenting body.

I screamed again, but it came out as a muffled moan. I kicked and struggled against his arms, but I was like a ragdoll to him as he easily dragged me toward my bedroom.

Oh, God. No. Please no. I twisted against his fierce hold, but his arms were like steel and my arms were locked to my sides. I slammed my foot down onto his boot, but it was like hitting cement.

"Stop fighting, damn it," the man growled in my ear. "He just wants to talk to you."

He? Who? What was he talking about? Why were we going into my bedroom?

Fear raced through me. If I could make enough sound, someone would hear me. Trevor. God, Trevor would hear me if I could scream or make enough noise.

But whoever had me trapped in his arms knew that, and his hand smothered my mouth. I was having trouble breathing as I dragged in air through my nose.

When he went to shut the door, I elbowed him in the ribs. He grunted, but his hold remained.

"Relax," he barked. "She's a feisty one. Like one of your mares."

Mares? Like a horse? My eyes scanned my dimly lit bedroom and hit the man sitting in the rocking chair in the far corner. My lamp beside the bed was on, but it offered little light. All I could see was his profile in a soft yellow glow. They'd shut the curtains, and the rest of the room was left in complete darkness.

But the light was enough to know who it was.

Killian's father.

The monster in the closet. And the bogeyman under the bed. At least that was what I used to think of him. Now, all I saw was a weak, pitiful man who had been cruel to Killian, which seemed more significant since knowing about Emmitt. And someone who hurt defenseless animals.

"Are you going to be quiet?" his dad asked. He sat in my rocking chair and it groaned as he slowly rocked.

I nodded, but it was a lie.

His eyes shifted to the man holding me and he gave a curt nod. The hand slid from my mouth but the second my mouth opened, a fist plowed into my side, and the wind knocked out of me. I bent over, tears filling my eyes as I fought for air.

My captor hauled me up, and something was shoved into my mouth, so I was forced to drag in air through my nose. "Don't make this hard on yourself," he whispered into my ear.

Fuck you.

"Savannah Grady. The trailer trash with the druggie mom." My eyes snapped to his, heart pounding. He recognized me? How did he know who I was?

"I thought it was you at the club, but I wasn't sure until I had someone check into it. Just like your mother, dancing for money."

I had no idea what he was talking about.

"How do you think she had enough money for the drugs? Waitressing?" He laughed, the chair continuing to rock as he spoke. "She worked for me. In one of my clubs, but the dancing involved was a little more… well, interactive."

No. My mom didn't dance. She hated dancing and was always telling me I should give it up. That I didn't have the right body for it.

Oh, God, had she been trying to convince me not to dance because she didn't want me to end up like her?

He clucked his tongue, shaking his head back and forth. "It's a shame what happened to her. I heard it was the drugs, not the accident that killed her. She was a beautiful woman and made me a lot of money. I bet Killian pays you well, too. Does it include you fucking him?"

I struggled against my captor and managed to kick his shin, but all it did was get me another fist, this time to the ribs and I bent over, breathing heavily through my nose. I swallowed back the bile in my throat.

"Did Kill tell you about his brother and his mother?" He stood and strode toward me. My chest rose and fell erratically. "His brother was going to be famous. A football star. But Kill was always jealous of him. That's why he let him walk home alone that day. He knew the kids were bullying him." God, he was insane to believe Killian would do that. Why did he hate him so much? "From your expression, I see he's told you. That's a surprise. He never talked about Emmitt. Even when I forced him to look at his picture and tear it up." My stomach lurched. "Did he tell you his mother overdosed after Emmitt died?"

The drugs. It was why Killian had been so against drugs in school and at Compass. He'd lost his mother the same way I had.

"So, he didn't mention his mother? I guess you don't know he's not my kid either. That he's a bastard." He reached out, and I flinched but was unable to move away from his touch as he ran his finger along the curve of my neck.

I stopped breathing, my insides curdling. I was afraid I'd throw up and suffocate on my own vomit.

He picked up strands of red curls, rubbing them between his thumb and forefinger. "I told your mother once I liked your red curls." My heart skipped a beat. Oh, my God. "She didn't like that. I think she was afraid I'd put you in one of my clubs. I may have if you hadn't left."

He dropped the strands of hair. "You're stubborn like her. I like that. The spirited horses always turn out to be the best, once you break them."

I'd been right about his dad. There were no good bits. No wonder Killian warned me at the cemetery not to trust everyone. Because he'd grown up with this man.

"Remove the gag," he ordered, then scowled at me. "Scream, and you'll lose your front teeth."

I coughed as my captor pulled the gag from my mouth and tossed it on the floor. Everything in me wanted to scream, but I knew if I did, I'd never get enough out before his threat became real.

218

"Killian will be furious when he finds out you came here. One of his men is outside right now. You'll never get out of here without him seeing you." Furious was an understatement. And it worried me what Killian would do.

He laughed. "Why do you think we're here? You know what he was like, don't you, Savannah? I wonder how he'll feel when he sees the bruises on you." The bruises? His eyes flicked to my captor and the steel arms released me. I staggered to the side of the bed, away from both of them. "I suspect he'll revert back to his old ways and that façade he hides behind will break."

Before I had time to process what he was talking about, his fist barreled into my stomach, and I fell to my knees on the floor, the wind knocked out of me. But it didn't stop there as the bulky guy looked over his shoulder at Killian's father and with a nod from him, he grabbed me by the hair then slammed his fist into my face. My lip split as I bit my tongue and blood pooled in my mouth and dribbled down my chin.

I grabbed the duvet, trying to pull myself up, but collapsed on the floor again, my head spinning from the blow.

The shadow of my abuser backed off, and Killian's father took his place, crouching in front of me. I jerked back when he reached to touch my swollen lip and fell on my ass, my spine hitting the nightstand.

"A rock star who has a violent past and beats his girlfriend." He tsked. "I wonder what the media will have to say about him now?"

"He'd never hurt me," I spat. "Killian would die before he laid a hand on me."

He stood towering over me. "Maybe so. But the media will spin it my way, especially when I tell them about his arrest at the raid. Juvie. And the kids he beat up. I wonder how many of them would talk now?"

"Why? Why do you want to hurt him?"

"Because he ruined everything," he shouted. "She was my wife. Mine. And she thought she could take Kill and leave me—for him. My own brother. I'd never let that happen. Never."

Oh, God. Killian was his brother's child. The uncle whom he lived with after his father left him in juvie. Did Killian know? Did his uncle?

I couldn't imagine what it was like for Killian to grow up with a man who held such animosity for him. And it wasn't his fault. Then to lose his brother and his mother and be left with this man.

Tears stained my cheeks. "Don't hurt him. Please."

"I don't plan on hurting him," he sneered. "He'll do that all by himself. That façade he plays so well will crumble and Kill will end up exactly where he was meant to be… in jail."

"At least you'll be dead. Because he's going to kill you."

My words bounced right off him as he quirked a smile. "I see why he's infatuated with you. You're exceptionally beautiful when you're angry." He turned and headed for the door, pausing to say to his crony, "Don't be long. Meet me on the roof."

I scrambled to my feet and managed a half scream before he grabbed me and cut off my air with his arm hooking my neck. I kicked out at the lamp on the nightstand, and it crashed to the floor.

Please, Trevor. Anyone.

"Fuck," he growled. He abruptly released me, and I staggered back, sucking in air. I didn't see his fist come toward me until it was too late.

I hit the floor and everything went dark.

Chapter Twenty-Five

Killian

I called Savvy in the car on the way back from the airport, but it rang then went to voice mail. It was two in the morning and she may have fallen asleep. I smiled, thinking about my mouth on her pussy.

Fuckin' two days. It had been hell without her, and the guys had noticed. I'd let Logan deal with the magazine, which was normally my deal. I'd even gone to my hotel room early both nights so I could talk to Savvy. There was nothing sweeter than Savvy saying good-night to me in her honey voice over the phone.

Logan and Ream both lived out of the city, so Roman was driving them and Crisis left his car at the airport.

I called again. No answer. I pressed End and sent her a text that I was five minutes away. I didn't have a key to her place, so as much as I'd love to wake her with my mouth between her legs, I couldn't.

"Okay, what's the deal with this chick Savvy?" Crisis asked, glancing over at me. "You've been with a lot of chicks, man, but this is different. She's either really fuckin' good in bed and is into your ropes and shit or she's permanent."

I slipped my phone back in my pocket. "Both."

Crisis slapped the heel of his hand on the steering wheel. "I fuckin' knew it. Ream owes me a case of beer."

I shook my head. "You guys made a bet?"

He shrugged. "Yeah. He thought you'd never last." He glanced at me. "Your track record sucks, so he had the advantage, but you bringing her to my mom and dad's place, that sealed it. Kite, man, we've lived together. I saw you bring chicks home. Never with the same one twice. Never. But this one, you bring to family dinner, to Logan's, to your vacant warehouse that you don't call home." He huffed. "And it's not. Fuck, man, you need to sell that place. Or at least decorate if you want to keep a girl like Savvy. Or get a cat. Something to say you're normal living in that place."

I chuckled. "I'm not getting a cat."

"If she's so permanent, why didn't you say that at the interview with the magazine?"

They'd mentioned Savvy because of the pictures of us floating around, but nothing much had surfaced yet, and I wanted to keep it that way. At least until this shit with my father was over, and I planned on ending it sooner than I'd thought.

I'd decided to sell my half of Compass to Brett. If my father's nightclubs went under, then I didn't want to be part of it. I didn't give a shit anymore. He wasn't important and I was making him important.

Savvy was important.

Emily and the SPCA were dealing with the horses. Even if I was walking away from this, his continued abuse of horses had to stop.

Crisis pulled up in front of Savvy's building, and I unclicked my seatbelt. "Waited a fuck of a long time for Savvy. Only girl my cock has ever been inside and she will be the last. Clear enough for you."

I opened the door and got out.

"What the fuck?" Crisis shouted leaning over the seat. "Kite? What the fuck do you mean? Jesus, man. Are you serious? Christ...."

I shut the door.

"You owe me a phone call tomorrow." I heard him curse as he drove off.

Luke walked up, and I shook his hand. "All good?"

"She's been home half an hour."

"And already asleep because she's not answering her phone," I said. "She has to buzz me in." She was giving me a key to her place tomorrow. Non-fuckin'-negotiable.

Luke frowned. "You called her?"

"Yeah. Why?" I took out my phone to see if she'd texted me back. She hadn't.

Luke looked up in the direction of Savvy's third-floor apartment.

My back stiffened. "Luke?"

"Her kitchen light is still on."

"And?"

"Been watching her a long time. She never leaves lights on when she goes to bed. And you said she knew you were coming?"

Because Savvy was concerned about the hydro bill, and yeah, she knew I was coming. My heart pounded and stomach coiled as I pressed her number again and listened to it ring as we jogged up to the front door.

Luke pressed her buzzer. No answer.

"Jesus." Everything inside revolted as a million thoughts plowed through me. Nothing could happen to her. She had to be okay. I couldn't lose her, not Savvy too.

I yanked on the doors, but the one good thing about this place was the front door locked. I banged my fist into the glass. "Damn it." I looked at Luke. "Her neighbor Trevor. Buzz him."

Luke scrolled through the names while I paced back and forth.

Trevor answered. "What the fuck? Do you not know my fuckin' rules. No one buzzes me after midnight." The air went silent.

"Fuck." I buzzed this time and as soon as it clicked when he picked up, I spoke. "It's Kite. Buzz me in."

"Why didn't you say that the first time?" Trevor replied.

The buzzer sounded, and Luke threw open the door and we

ran inside. My heart was in my fuckin' throat as we raced up the three flights of stairs.

I didn't bother knocking on Savvy's door or asking Trevor for a key. I slammed my shoulder into it, splintering the wooden frame, and the door burst open.

"What the hell is going on?" I heard Trevor shout from across the hall. Luke grabbed my arm to haul me back, and I glanced at the gun in his hand.

"Kite. Let me check it out first," Luke said.

"I can't." I jerked my arm free and moved through her apartment, eyes scanning the couch first, praying that maybe she'd just fallen asleep. But the truth was, I already knew. I felt it.

"Savvy?" I yelled, running for the bedroom, Luke beside me.

The second I stepped into the room and saw her it was like being slammed in the gut with a wrecking ball, then a chainsaw ripping open my chest.

"Noooo!" I shouted, tumbling to my knees beside her, my hands running the length of her body as I tried to see where she was hurt.

She lay on her stomach, her head to the side, hair covering her face, and blood splattered across the floor.

"Don't move her," Luke ordered as he held his phone to his ear. He was talking to someone, but his words were muffled as my mind gyrated with fear.

"Fuck. Savvy. Baby." I brushed her hair away from her face and neck and felt for a pulse.

I closed my eyes as a wave of relief poured over me when I felt the thump beneath the pads of my fingers. "She's alive."

A shadow cast over me, but I didn't look to see who it was, all I saw was Savvy and... fuck, Emmitt. Facedown in the water, blood splattered on the rock where he'd hit his head.

But there'd been no pulse.

Savvy was breathing. She was fuckin' breathing. "Where the fuck are the paramedics," I shouted.

"Any second," Luke said as he crouched beside me and took her wrist to check her pulse.

"I swear. I didn't hear anything. Fuck. Fuck. Fuck. I heard her come home and…" Trevor went on as he paced the floor, his eyes shifting to Savvy every time he turned.

I grabbed the blanket at the end of the bed and lay it over her while I held her limp hand in mine.

I heard sirens. Footsteps. There were people bustling into the bedroom, and I couldn't focus on anything but her.

"Kite. They need to take her." Luke dragged me back so the paramedics could put a neck brace on her, then they rolled her onto the stretcher.

Christ, this was my fault. I brought this into her life. I ran my hand through my hair as I watched Savvy being carried out of the bedroom.

My hands shook and my body trembled. "I did this. I did this."

"We don't know what happened. A lot of scum come into this building, Kite." Luke said.

This was my father. Her place wasn't robbed; nothing was disturbed. This was him.

Luke put his hand on my shoulder. "I called Crisis. He's meeting you at the hospital. I'll stay here. Talk to the police."

I didn't even realize I'd walked downstairs as Luke spoke. I climbed into the ambulance with Savvy, and my hand found hers.

"She'll be okay," Luke said as the doors shut and the ambulance's siren blared.

"Sir?" Why? Fuck, why would he go after Savvy? Why hurt her? "Sir? We need her arm, sir."

I glanced at the paramedic beside me who held a cotton swab in his hand. "Her arm, sir."

The moment I released her hand, it was like I was letting her go. That she was slipping from my grasp. "Christ." I put my head in my hands and closed my eyes, but the second I did, images of Savvy lying motionless on the floor haunted me.

I didn't protect her.

"She's going to be okay, right?" I asked the paramedic, my voice barely distinguishable.

"Don't know about internal damage, sir. We'll know more when they take her in for radiographs. But she's stable. Heart and lungs clear. Blood pressure steady."

I nodded, running my knuckles down her cheek. "I'm sorry, Savvy. Fuck baby, I'm so sorry."

The ambulance stopped and I moved out of the way as the paramedics wheeled her in and I followed until they disappeared behind swinging doors and a nurse stopped me.

"Kite."

I stood staring at the door, my limbs frozen.

"Kite, man." Crisis's hand settled on my shoulder, but I didn't move. I couldn't.

My mind was an infestation of emotions. Emotions I'd kept locked away, and now like a raging river hitting a cracked dam, they were leaking through me.

I didn't know how to react. I was afraid to react. Fuck, this wasn't me. I had control. For years, I had control.

But the dam had broken and behind it was the boy who'd lost his brother. A boy who was reminded day after day that it was his fault for not protecting him. That it was his fault his mother had died and the family was ruined.

Memories buzzed like wasps around me. Reminding me. Hunting me.

I inhaled a ragged breath and turned to face Crisis. "I have to go."

"Whoa. Kite." He grabbed my arm. "Where? Haven is on her way. And I called Logan. He and Emily will be here soon with Ream and Kat."

Fuck, I couldn't breathe. My chest was tight and my head felt as if it was going to combust. I had to get out of here before the anger boiled over.

"Text me when you know something."

"Jesus Christ. You're leaving? You just blurted out that she's the first fuckin' chick you stuck your cock in and you're leaving? What the hell, man?"

The hospital doors hissed as they opened. The second the air hit me, I inhaled deep lungfuls of air.

I was being pulled away from Emmitt's body.

Cold, wet, and alone. The river raging like I was. My father stood on the bank glaring at me. The hatred in his eyes. Hatred I'd been subjected to for years until I got out. And I got out because of Savvy. Saving her at the raid had ended up saving me.

He hurt Savvy. He fuckin' hurt her.

It was the crack in the pink pot. It burst wide open and was spilling out onto the ground.

"Kite, where the fuck are you going?" Crisis shouted. "Kite!"

I strode across the parking lot to the street and hailed a cab.

Chapter Twenty-Six

Savvy

I WOKE TO THE SOUND OF BEEPING AND TRIED TO SIT UP, BUT THE second I did, agony shot through my ribs.

"Savvy? Thank God."

I blinked, attempting to focus, but everything was blurry. "Mars?" A warm hand lay on my forearm and gently squeezed. "Where am…?" I sucked in air as the memory came back like a movie reel on fast forward. Killian's father. His hatred for Killian. My mother.

"You have a concussion and broken ribs, but you're going to be fine," Mars was saying.

"Killian?" God, where was he? He'd been on his way to my place.

"I don't know where he is."

I groaned, sitting up, and the beeping accelerated on the machine. "What do you mean?"

"Luke came by the hospital to check on you and told us he and Kite found you on the floor in your bedroom. Kite rode in the ambulance with you, but Crisis said he left as soon as they took you in."

"No." My heart raced. This was exactly what his father wanted.

He'd be ready. Killian would be arrested if he went after him. "No. I have to find him." I yanked on the intravenous in my arm, and Mars stood, her hands locking my arms at my sides.

"Savvy. Stop. You can't do anything. And you need to rest. Killian can look after himself."

"I have to go. I have to get out of here" I winced when I tried to push her hands off me, but my ribs objected. "I need to talk to him, damn it. Luke. Where's Luke?"

"I don't know. Maybe looking for Kite? Savvy, you need to lie back and settle down."

I couldn't. He'd been worried about his father. That was why he'd put his security on me. All his father cared about was his reputation. How he appeared to everyone else. He was the complete opposite of Killian. God, Killian wasn't his real son. It was why he never cared about him. Killian was a constant reminder of his wife's cheating. Her wanting to leave him.

"Mars, can you get me Logan's number?" He knew Killian. He knew about his fighting.

"I can do better. He's out in the waiting room with everyone else. The nurses are fighting over who gets to work the nurses' station in the waiting room."

"They're here?"

She nodded. "Yeah. All night."

"All night? How long have I been unconscious?"

"You were brought in around two-thirty. It's nine now."

Which meant Killian had been gone for six and a half hours. "I need to talk to Logan."

"Okay, but you're really not supposed to have visitors. I lied and said I was your sister. But Logan—"

"Is my brother."

She nodded. "Okay." But before she let me go, she pursed her lips together. "You promise to stay in bed?"

"Yes," I replied.

"Okay," she said, then left to go get Logan. It was only a minute later that he strode in. I doubted the nurses believed he was my brother, but suspected they'd pretty much say yes to anything he wanted. As he approached, he wore a fierce scowl and his body was tense.

"How are you feeling?" he asked.

He stood beside the bed, and if I didn't think Logan was intimidating before, he certainly was now towering over me while I was hooked to machines and in a flimsy, backless hospital gown.

"Good," I replied. His scowl deepened. "It hurts, but I'm fine. It was Killian's father. He was waiting for me at my apartment. He must have known you guys went out of town and I'd be there. He wants Killian to go after him. You have to stop him from—"

He huffed. "That won't happen."

"But—"

"That won't happen," he repeated.

"But—"

"Savvy. Kite won't go after him. Okay?"

My heart pounded and the machine beeped frantically. "How do you know that?"

"Because I know Kite. He's fuckin' pissed as hell right now, and I'm betting his knuckles are taking a beating, but it's not because he's gone after his dad, even though he deserves it." Logan sat on the edge of the bed. "Kite won't because of Emmitt."

"You know about Emmitt?"

He nodded. "Yeah. No one else does though. I had a shit father, too, and Kite helped me with that a while ago when I was recuperating from… well, let's just say I took a beating. That's when Kite told me what happened in Ireland." He touched the back of my hand. "He never planned to go after his dad, Savvy. They've had no contact for years. But when Kite was in the car accident with Haven and Luke, he was all over the media. I guess his dad seeing all the focus on Kite… it stirred the shit back up.

"His contacted him and I don't know what was said, but it had to be bad because Kite's hands were beat pretty bad for weeks. That's when he decided to open Compass with Brett. Financially hurt him."

Logan sighed. "His dad fucked him up, Savvy. He drilled into him day after day that he killed Emmitt, destroyed the family. I don't know all of it, and that's for him to tell you, but a twelve-year-old kid living that shit… it stays with you.

"Everyone said Emmitt was going to be the famous football star of Ireland. Him dying was his father's dream shattering. Ironic that the other son became the famous one." He squeezed my hand and stood. "Get some sleep. The police will want to talk to you tomorrow. I'll let you know as soon as we find Kite."

Tears filled the rims of my eyes and one spilled over to slide down my cheek and drip onto the white sheet. "How am I supposed to lie here not knowing if he's okay?"

"Because you love him and that's what he'd want you to do, Savvy."

I woke to the mattress dipping and then the weight of an arm sliding across my abdomen. My eyes flew open, and for a second I had no idea where I was or who was holding me until his whispered voice vibrated next to my ear.

"Shh. It's just me."

Killian. A wave of relief washed over me, and it was as if I'd been holding my breath for hours and could suddenly breathe.

"Where did you go?" I glided my hand down his arm and stopped when my fingers touched the material wrapped around his knuckles. "Killian?"

I tried to sit up, but he gently squeezed my side. "Stay. Let me hold you, Savvy. Please. I need to hold you for a minute."

There was so much pain in his graveled voice that it was as if pieces of my heart chipped with each word. "Okay."

Lying on my back, Killian's body curled into mine, I listened to his breathing slow until he fell asleep.

I watched him, watched as the crease between his eyes and the tightness of his plush lips eased.

Vulnerable. That was what Killian was right now. I'd never imagined him this way, but I realized it was always there, just hidden behind everything else.

A kid trying to crawl out from under the guilt his father placed on him. And he did. He was an incredible man who fought against the pain and the anger and became this successful, protective, and loving man. That never died with Emmitt and became saturated by his father's cruelty. It was just harder for him to show. To trust his heart to someone.

But he'd given it to me, and I'd protect it. He needed me to protect it.

When the sun peaked over the horizon and an orange glow lit the room, Killian stirred, and his arm tightened around me. I winced from the bruises, and he immediately loosened his hold and opened his eyes.

"Fuck, sorry."

"Kiss me, Killian," I whispered.

He leaned over, careful not to put any weight on me, and his mouth found mine. It would always find mine. There was only one, and Killian was it.

His kiss was slow and gentle as to not hurt my split lip. But it was just as warm and passionate as always, making my belly flutter. He lifted and the crease between his eyes deepened.

"Savvy."

Right there. It was in his voice. The way he said my name... hesitant and without that lilt at the end. My heart skipped a beat and my stomach dropped.

"It's going to be okay," I said.

He stiffened.

"It's going to be okay," I repeated.

"I'm the one who should be telling you that." He shifted onto his back. "But it's not, Savvy." I sat up, gritting my teeth at the pain and moved so I was on my side facing him. He scowled at me. "Baby, don't move. Fuck, the doc said you had... that he broke your ribs."

He'd spoken to the doctor? When had he done that? "It's going to be okay," I repeated, hoping he'd listen if I said it enough times. That he'd believe me.

"He broke your ribs, Savvy." He raised his voice, but not enough to alert the nurses.

"It was his hired hand. And it's only one rib." I laid my hand on his chest. "Killian. Where did you go? Logan said you weren't at the warehouse."

"I wasn't."

"But your hands."

"I had to fight, Savvy." He said the words like they were poison, and I realized why when he continued. "Really fight. The bag wasn't enough." His jaw clenched. "I went to an underground fight."

Oh, God. Logan said Killian swore to never fight another person again. But he broke that promise last night. "Why?"

"It was either that or kill my father."

I ran my hand lightly over the bandage on his knuckles. He said his father. But his uncle had been his real father. Did he know? Would it matter?

"He told me... he said he wasn't your real father." His body stiffened. "Your uncle was." He didn't move. "Killian? Did you know?"

It was a while before he answered. "I didn't know for sure, but I suspected. He hated me even before Emmitt died. Before I got into trouble. But he'd never admit I wasn't his. His reputation was everything to him and his wife cheating on him wouldn't have looked good." He paused. "I don't know if my uncle knew or not and it wouldn't have mattered to him. He called me his son and... he was like a father to me."

"I'm glad you had him, Killian." I ran my hand up his chest to rest over his beating heart.

He didn't say anything more for a while and I felt it... the coldness descending. His body tense. The silence. How his arm no longer held me. He was distancing himself.

"It's going to be okay."

His jaw tightened and then he threw his legs over the side of the bed and sat on the edge, his hand running overtop his head. "Savvy...."

My pulse raced with panic because I knew what he was going to do. I shook my head, tears pooling. "No. Killian. No."

"I can't give you a family. I just can't do it."

I sat up, pain forgotten as another type of pain lanced my heart. I settled my hands on his shoulders, my cheek against his back.

"Don't let him win."

"This has nothing to do with him. It has to do with me. Who I am, and I can't give you what you want."

"You're saying this now, but in a few weeks or months, it will get better. We can survive this. I don't want anyone else. There is no one else."

"There's always someone else."

"No. There isn't. And you damn well know it. Just you. Only you."

He stood and my insides coiled as he turned and I was met with a mask of cold. "He will never touch you again."

I choked on a sob as he walked to the door. The wall had slammed down over his emotions. "Fight for me, damn it. Stop fighting everything else and fight for me. For us."

He opened the door.

"Killian." He hesitated a split second and then was gone. "I love you," I whispered as tears streamed down my cheeks.

Chapter Twenty-Seven

Three weeks later

Killian

I STOOD ON THE EDGE OF THE RIVER AND SKIPPED THE STONE across the surface of the water.

One.

Two.

Three.

Four.

It sank beneath the surface and I sifted around with my feet on the spongy grass for another flat stone. I picked one up and rolled it between my fingers as I heard the steps approach. I didn't turn around. Didn't care who it was.

"Kite."

I stiffened then drew my arm back and whipped the stone.

One.

Two.

Three.

Logan came up beside me, casually tossing a stone in the air. He stared across the surface of the water. We both did. Silent. Listening to the gentle splash as the water hit the rocks on its way downstream.

He threw the rock he was holding, and it skipped once then sank. "Too round," I said.

"Didn't skip stones much in the compound growing up."

I passed him a flat stone. "Like you're slicing the water. Flick the wrist." I skipped another and Logan watched.

He frowned as he concentrated, then tried again. Three skips.

We did it for a while. Nothing else said between us, just the stones, the river, and us. But I knew he didn't fly all the way to Ireland to skip stones.

"This where he died?" Logan asked.

"Yeah." Five feet away. The rock he'd hit his head on was still there, but the water level was lower now. "How did you find me?"

"Same man who found Emily and me in Mexico," Logan replied.

Deck. "Is he here?"

"No. Luke's with me. And he's pissed you left without telling him."

I bet. I'd asked him to organize twenty-four-hour security on Savvy, but didn't tell him I was leaving. After I'd watched Mars pick Savvy up from the hospital, I'd taken the first flight out.

The police had released Seamus after questioning, just like I knew they would. There was no proof it was him who assaulted Savvy. No witnesses. They couldn't hold him. He was too careful. But it didn't mean I'd let him walk away with his head held high.

Logan tossed another stone. "He's gone, Kite."

My muscles tensed, my shoulders sagging at the same time. "Vic." It was a statement because I already knew. I'd talked to Deck and Vic about what needed to be done.

Vic did what other men couldn't stomach. He was good at extracting information. Obtaining confessions. My father wouldn't last long with Vic.

Vic had no sympathy. No remorse for what he did. And he'd make my father hurt for what he did to Savvy.

"He didn't kill him," Logan said. "That you?"

I nodded.

"So he's to leave the country and never come back?"

"Yes." That was what I'd discussed with Deck and Vic. And if you were ever in Vic's custody and he threatened you, you'd take it seriously and never put a fuckin' toenail in the country if he told you to.

"So Vic was your idea?"

"Yeah."

Logan nodded. "And the 'leak' to the press?"

I frowned. "What leak?"

"Some inside scoop about the abuse of his horses and his girls at his clubs. They're now all talking to the police. Corruption. Payouts. They're doing a thorough investigation and have frozen all his accounts. He's ruined and even if he hadn't *disappeared*, he'd be in jail for a very long time."

The two things most important to him—his reputation and wealth. Both stripped from him. Bastard had done it to himself.

I didn't know how to feel. Satisfied that he finally got what was coming to him? That it was over and I didn't have him lingering like a black cloud over my head? I sure as hell wasn't happy.

But I felt nothing. Fuckin' nothing.

I'd felt nothing but cold since I'd walked out of that hospital room. It had been the hardest thing I'd ever done. Hearing her call my name... the choked sob.

Fuck, I wanted to give her everything. A family. A home.

But when I'd seen her on the floor... not knowing if she were alive or dead—my worlds collided. Past and present. Control. Anger. Pain. Grief. It was everything I felt when Emmitt died and what did I do...? I went to an underground fight. I lost control. I broke, and I feared what would happen if we had everything and it was ripped from me again.

What it would do to Savvy.

Logan crouched and picked up a pebble, rolling it between his fingers. "Kite, she doesn't look good," he said. "Emily went and saw her and... she said she looks like she hasn't slept in weeks."

I closed my eyes and curled my hands into fists as I stared at the river splashing over the rocks. "She still living at Mars's?"

"No. She moved back to her apartment a few days ago. And working at the dance studio." Logan stood and tossed the pebble into the river. "Trevor was there when Emily came by."

I clenched my jaw. "Good."

"Cut the bullshit, Kite," Logan barked. "It's not fuckin' good. She's not fuckin' good. Nor are you. Do you know she dropped the car you gave her at your warehouse? Mars says she doesn't eat, and Bree, Frankie, and even Greg have been by to see her. You know why? Because you're over here in Ireland running away from a fight. A fuckin' fight you need to make, Kite."

I turned to glare at him. "And what happens when she gets hurt again and the bag isn't enough? What happens when my kid gets beaten up in school by bullies? What the fuck do you think will happen then?"

"I think you have a good head on your shoulders and you'll do what you have to." Logan bowed his head and stared at his feet. "I never told anyone this. But you need to hear it. When Emily was taken... I watched her tied up and hanging like a fuckin' carcass then whipped. I stood there and watched and did nothing. Do you have any idea what that's like? And that was day fuckin' one. The woman I loved begged me to help her and I didn't."

My stomach twisted. "You couldn't."

He shook his head. "Doesn't matter. Wouldn't. Didn't. Couldn't. It's all the same. I put her through the worst hell imaginable and her forgiving me was at zero percent. But I fought for her. I fuckin' fought and I never gave up. Because love wins every time, Kite."

He slapped me on the back. "Stop worrying about the details. Get your ass back to Canada, Kite."

I watched him walk across the field to where Luke leaned against a tree with his arms crossed.

I don't know what Logan said to him, but Luke pushed off the tree, and they walked toward the road.

Crouching, I picked up a handful of stones and sifted through them for the flat ones and let the others drop to my feet.

I drew my arm back and whipped the stone across the surface of the water.

One.

Two.

Three.

Four.

Five

Six.

"Need to go, buddy."

Chapter Twenty-Eight

Savvy

THE MUSIC FLOWED THROUGH ME, SOFT AND HAUNTING, AS I danced. I didn't think. The emotions the music evoked moved my body.

Every day I thought it would get easier without him, but it wasn't. Because every day was one more day I'd lost being with him. But even though it hurt like hell to wake up in the morning and know he was gone, I did it. I wasn't giving into the pain. I wasn't giving up on us and I was fighting for me, too.

The music grew darker and louder, the beat pounding through my body. The tears slipped down my cheeks as the story, my story, lived and breathed in the music.

When the song ended, I was on my knees beside the window, hair covering my face, chest rising and falling.

When the music ended, that was when it hurt the most. That was when my heart bled.

I spent as many hours as I could at my new job teaching dance, but no matter what I did, Killian lingered. He was all around me, and I couldn't let him go.

"Do you ever go home? Or sleep, for that matter?" Ali asked from the doorway. She was the opposite of me, fragile and dainty, the look of a ballerina, which she'd studied for years before switching to contemporary dance.

I sat back on my butt, knees bent, arms hooked around them. "Not much of a home to go to." Because my home was somewhere in Ireland right now. When Emily came by to see me last week, she'd told me he'd been there for a few weeks.

Maybe it was a good thing. I could stop listening for his footsteps coming up the stairs of my apartment buliding and stop glancing at my phone hoping I'd see his name pop up.

Emily offered to take me to see Lucifer, Clyde, and Dale, but seeing the horses was a reminder of Killian. But it was more than that. Emily and Logan were Killian's best friends, and as much as I liked them, I couldn't be friends with them.

"I had an e-mail today about David Knapp," Ali said. "You... dated him for a while, right?"

I heard the hesitancy in her voice and no doubt she'd heard the rumors David spread about me. "Yeah. We lived together and I worked at his studio."

"And you're not friends now?"

I snorted. "I found him in bed with one of his students."

Ali's brows lowered as she crossed her arms over her chest. "I knew the rumors had it wrong the moment I met you." Yeah, David turned the tables, making me look bad and he the victim. "Then I guess you won't be sad to hear his studio has closed and he's gone bankrupt."

"Wow, really?" At one time I think David loved me. Or at least he believed he did. He'd been affectionate and kind, and we'd had a good relationship. At least that was what I'd thought. But even with him cheating on me, I still didn't wish ill on him. He was passionate about dance, and I knew the studio was important to him.

"Yeah, my friend e-mailed me and said he's moving back to Vancouver." David grew up in Vancouver. Ali smiled. "Gotta love karma. See you tomorrow. Lock up?"

"Yeah. You mind getting the lights?"

Ali flicked the switch and I was left in darkness. I heard the door quietly shut behind her and then the front door beeped as it opened and closed.

I watched the cars pass by the window as their headlights offered a kaleidoscope of light across the studio.

My gaze stopped on the shadow of a man leaning against the building across the street. It was impossible to see his face as he wore a baseball cap low over his eyes. But as I stared at him, tingles of awareness tap-danced across my body, and my heart pounded.

Killian?

He was here?

Watching me.

I didn't move. Neither did he. And I didn't know if he knew I saw him or not. But it was when he stopped staring in my direction, and he bowed his head that my heart broke.

Killian.

I closed my eyes, holding back the tears as the ache swelled. The pain. The hurt for him.

When I opened my eyes, he was gone.

For six nights he watched me from across the street, and I danced knowing he watched me. It was freeing and painful at the same time. I put everything I felt into the movements, hoping that maybe he'd understand the story I danced. That maybe he'd see my love for him.

Each night when the song ended, I turned off the lights, sat on the floor and held my breath.

Hoping he'd smile.

Hoping he'd cross the street.

Hoping he'd not walk away.

But he always did.

I didn't know how to reach him without pushing him farther away, but I wasn't giving up on us. He loved me. That didn't just go away. It bore into your soul and lived there.

And maybe I'd never have kids with Killian, but I'd have him and the family that came with him. A family who had welcomed me into their arms without hesitation.

I left the studio early tonight, unable to face another night with him watching me then leaving. Because that was what it was. Him leaving me again and again. As I walked up to my apartment building, the hairs on the back of my neck rose, and I felt his eyes on me.

He was here.

I didn't look though. I opened the door and jogged up the three flights of stairs then went into my apartment, straight into my kitchen and picked up the orchid from the windowsill.

It had to stop, and this was the only way I could think of to do it. To make him react. To do something. Either walk away for good or come back to me.

This was our beginning.

When I'd lost everything and was scared and alone, Killian had given me a piece of him to take with me.

And he knew how important the orchid was to me.

"What are you doing with that?" Trevor asked as he propped up against his doorframe, arms crossed.

"Pushing him," I said.

He chuckled. "About time, cupcake. Let me know if you need any help."

I carried the orchid downstairs and out the door, then walked the length of the building to the garbage bin. I lifted the lid and tossed the orchid inside.

The lid slammed shut and the sound echoed through the parking lot.

Eleven years I'd held onto the orchid, and somehow even unconsciously, it was holding onto Killian, too.

Walking away was hard. I wanted to go back and grab the orchid. Save it. Save us.

I looked straight ahead, uncertain if he'd seen me or not, but knowing either way, I had to do it.

"What the fuck are you doing?"

My body sagged at the sound of his voice behind me. It was as if he just handed me a piece of my heart back. His words didn't matter because I knew he'd be angry. I wanted him to get angry.

I slowly turned, and even though he had dark circles under his eyes and his lips were pursed, and his brows were dangerously low, he was the most beautiful sight I'd ever seen.

God, I missed him. The urge to throw my arms around him was overwhelming, and I had to look away for a second to collect myself.

"Savvy, what the hell?" He stayed six feet away as if he didn't trust himself to come any closer.

"I don't want it anymore," I said, lifting my chin and trying to appear as if him being here didn't affect me.

"Bullshit," he said.

I shrugged. "Does it matter? It's gone, and I'm moving on." But I wasn't. He was my home. Wherever that may be, and however long it took to get there, this man was my home. He was just fighting it. But that ended now. "And stop watching me, damn it."

His jaw clenched and his back stiffened. "I can't. I fuckin' can't."

Oh, God. I wanted to wrap him up in my arms and take away all the pain he'd suffered. As a kid unwanted by his father. As a teenager lost to the anger that consumed him. As a man who controlled his emotions and buried his pain.

"Well, you know what, I can't stop hurting. I can't stop missing you. I can't stop feeling like I can't breathe. And I can't stop loving you. But I've accepted it. I've accepted that my love for you will never die and I'll have to live with that. But I sure as hell don't need you stalking me and reminding me of it." I turned, swiped my fob over the pad and the front door unlocked.

"Savvy."

I threw open the door.

"Savvy," he growled.

I stepped inside, but I didn't make it far before his hand grabbed my arm and he yanked me aside, pressing me into the glass. "Damn it, Savvy. You can't throw the orchid away."

He may have said orchid, but I knew he was saying us.

My heart pounded, and my belly fluttered as he held my wrists on either side of my head against the glass. His eyes blazed, but the green was alive and burning. The ice chips had melted.

"Kiss me," I said. "Kiss me goodbye. Then do what you're good at and walk away and hide behind your wall."

His eyes narrowed and his grip tightened. It hurt, but I wanted the pain. I wanted him to hurt.

"Kiss me," I repeated. For a split second I thought he was going to let me go as he loosened his grip, but then he swore beneath his breath before his mouth slammed against mine.

It was like jumping off a waterfall and having no idea when I was going to hit the pool beneath. Not caring. I just wanted this feeling to last forever.

His kiss was starved.

Determined. Bruising. Uncontrolled. And within all of that was love. It was him loving me without borders.

"Savvy," he murmured against my lips. He released my wrists, and I wrapped my arms around him. He pulled back and cupped my chin, his eyes smoldering with desire, but there was a hesitancy within the depths. "I can't give you everything you want."

"You already have, Killian. I have a home in you. A family in you. The gift of loving you."

"But kids...."

I weaved my fingers into his hair. "We'll get a dog."

There was a hint of amusement in his eyes, and I sagged into him. He would be okay. All the emotions he'd buried for so long were raw and still hurting him, but he'd be okay. We'd be okay.

He reached into his pocket and pulled out a ripped, crumpled piece of paper that looked like it had been soaked in water. He smoothed it out on the glass window and I saw my writing. My words. It was the note I'd written to him when I'd left that day in the rain. I remember thinking he'd never see it.

I hope one day there'll be a next time.

Thank you for the orchid Killian.

I'll never forget you.

Savvy

"Killian," I whispered. Two tears trailed down my cheeks and he wiped them away with the pad of his thumb. Killian had found my note. He'd kept it like I'd kept the orchid.

"I may have kept myself from you, but you were always with me, Savvy. And fuck, I love you." His kissed me again before he picked me up in his arms and I hooked my legs around his waist. But he didn't carry me upstairs; he carried me to his car then walked away.

"Where are you going?" I called.

"To get the fuckin' orchid then I'm taking you home."

Epilogue

One year and five months later

Savvy

I CAME OUT OF THE BATHROOM WITH A TOWEL WRAPPED AROUND me to see Killian awake and leaning up against the sleek black headboard, one leg bent and a book balanced against his thigh.

The gray sheet bunched low on his hips, and my eyes flicked to the sparse trail of hairs disappearing beneath the material.

I'd woken up with him every morning for the last year and a half and there wasn't a single day he didn't look totally fuckable. But what did me in this morning were the thin-rimmed glasses perched on his nose that totally clashed with his tattoos and piercings, but made him look sexy as hell. And he damn well knew I thought it was sexy as hell.

Killian flipped his book closed, and I jerked at the abrupt sound. "You didn't wake me."

"If I did, we'd be late. It's almost ten."

He tossed his book aside, and it landed with a thump on the wooden platform surrounding the mattress. We'd picked out the new bed together several months ago along with sheets and a few throw pillows. The one side of the bed had a row of four large glass squares that lit up with soft green lights. The headboard was solid and black, and had an iron bar running the length of it that curved down both sides.

The iron bar had been the custom part of the bed that Killian had told me in great detail how he was going to use it when he tied me up.

"You could have woken me with your wet pussy on my face or my cock in your mouth," he drawled.

He removed his glasses then leaned over and placed them on the nightstand. The sheet slipped farther and my sex pulsed. Would I ever get enough of this man?

Killian's pull ate the space between us and even ten feet away it felt as if I were right next to him.

Last night, he'd stripped off his clothes, crawled into bed then wrapped me up in his arms and fell asleep. He and the guys had been working long nights on the album to get it finished this month. I'd gone to the recording studio with him a number of times, and watching him on the drums was magical.

I walked to the cupboard, my feet sinking into the new white shag carpet that he'd shown up with last month. It was a slow process, and I let him be the one to decorate the warehouse, but he was. There were now throw rugs scattered throughout, and he'd put in an enormous mirrored wall in the open space for me to dance, along with a stereo system that we could play as loud as we wanted since there were no neighbors.

"Drop the towel and come here, Savvy." His voice was quiet and steady, almost soft.

My body was the complete opposite as it thrummed with desire, excitement and anticipation of his touch. I paused, my hand on the door handle.

I turned around and faced him. I shouldn't have because there was no way I was denying him anything. Inhaling a quivering breath, I approached the bed.

"Straddle me," he said.

I knelt on the mattress, threw my leg over his waist, then slowly lowered so his hard cock settled against my wet folds. I shifted forward rubbing him against me, and he groaned.

His eyes met mine. "Fuck, I love you," he said as his hands spanned my waist. "Never a day will go by that I won't love you. And never will there be a hint of uncertainty that you belong anywhere else but right here."

There wasn't a peppering of goose bumps across my skin; it was a horde of them, and they didn't pepper; they assaulted. "And I don't ever want to be anywhere else."

He cupped my cheeks then tugged me in for a kiss, but I placed my palms on his chest, holding him off.

"We need to be fast. You have to shower before we go."

He frowned. "We're not being fast."

"If we're late again, we'll never hear the end of it from Crisis."

"Fuck him," Killian growled as he dragged me closer.

"I think I'd rather fuck you."

He slapped my ass—hard. I squealed to get away, but he rolled, careful not to hurt me as he shifted so he was on top of me, his hands pinning me down. "You think?"

I bit my lip, trying not to laugh. "Well, he's pretty charming and so cute with little Melody."

Killian huffed. I wiggled underneath him

"And you're good with Drum."

He slapped my ass again. "Drum is a fuckin' dog."

I smiled. "But he's your dog."

"Ours."

"No, Drum is yours, Killian. He doesn't leave your side and looks up at you like you're God. You take him everywhere you go and he sits on your lap when we're on the couch."

"Savvy, I can't leave him here by himself while you're at work, and I have a better lap. He's smart."

I secretly smiled because despite how he played it, the little black Pomeranian with tan over his eyes was Killian's dog even if he'd adopted him for me. There'd even been a picture of him carrying Drum under his arm that went viral. He thought it was ridiculous. I thought it was the sexiest shot I'd ever seen of him.

I wanted to have it blown up and framed on our wall, but Killian wasn't quite there yet with having pictures displayed. And maybe he wouldn't ever be. But I didn't need pictures. I had him.

As if knowing we were talking about him, Drum jumped up and down beside the bed. Killian reached over the side of the bed and picked him up and set him on the mattress. Drum danced around in circles then dug in the sheets and plopped down in a tiny ball closing his eyes.

I laughed, rolling my eyes.

Despite what he thought, Killian had good bits in abundance. He may not trust easily, or let others see who he really was, but those he let in, he would give his life for.

He shifted his hips so his cock rubbed up against my clit. I moaned and arched my back. "What would you prefer? I fuck you slow in your ass or hard in your pussy?"

"You're giving me a choice?"

"No, baby. I'm doing both. I just want to know your answer."

I dragged my teeth over my lower lip, and his eyes smoldered. "I'll let you know."

He growled before his mouth crashed down on mine and then he did exactly as he said.

We were a half hour late arriving at Sophia and John's for brunch, and everyone was already sitting on the patio eating, including Matt and Mars. We apologized, and Sophia smiled, shrugging it off and saying it was no big deal while Crisis tried to get a rise out of Killian by asking why we were so late. Of course, Killian didn't react to Crisis's teasing while my cheeks burned.

Now, we were playing croquet and Hendricks was winning. The

only rules we had were to get your ball through all the hoops first and hit the final peg.

Tear and Drum trotted out onto the grass while Crisis and Haven's eighteen-month-old daughter, Melody, followed holding with both hands the slobbery red ball that Tear just had in his mouth.

"Angel, don't put your fingers in your mouth after holding that," Haven called then said to me, "She is so going to put her fingers in her mouth."

I smiled. Melody was adorable and having just learned how to walk, she went wherever her little chubby legs could take her.

"Logan. Really?" Emily groaned. Logan's ball had hit hers and knocked it into the garden.

He smirked. "Have you ever known me to let you win, Mouse?"

She walked over to him, her hand protectively on her bulging stomach. Then she stood on her tiptoes and whispered something to him. He placed his hand on her stomach and after a second, his eyes lit up.

Emily and Logan had married in February. A winter wedding with Clyde and Dale pulling a beautifully decorated blue-and-white sleigh that had carried Emily to the front doors of the church. Kat had been her maid of honor, with Haven and Georgie as her brides-maids. Georgie had put blue streaks in her hair to match the blue-and-white theme.

Matt had walked Emily down the aisle as she didn't have a fa-ther, and Matt was like a brother to her.

Logan had looked absolutely stunning in his tailored suit and blue tie and gold cuff links, but it was Killian who had stolen my breath away as he stood beside Logan as best man.

His suit had been perfectly tailored to his tall, lean stature with the same pin-striped, blue-and-white tie as Ream, Crisis, and Deck, who had stood as groomsmen. He'd been mouth-wateringly sexy and when he'd caught me staring at him, he'd winked and grinned.

I'd melted and my sex had pulsed, and then I'd had to sit there beside Crisis and Ream's mom with wet panties while I'd watched Killian at the altar.

Ream, Matt, and Crisis took their shots and then Kat, who purposely went after Ream's ball and smacked it off course.

Ream hooked her around the waist, lifted her off her feet and kissed her. "Oh, baby, you're forgetting how good I am at mini-golf. This croquet shit is easy, but it's cute you're trying to beat me."

Kat smiled, running her finger along the scruff on his chin. "Do you know what it would be like living with you for the next week if I beat you? I'm trying to lose. I'm just making your game more challenging." Crisis laughed while Ream grunted. And Sophia and John looked at one another smiling.

Killian stood with his arms looped around me from behind, while I rested my head on his shoulder. He kissed the top of my head. "You're up, orchid."

I still found it difficult to believe he was mine. That after all these years, the sixteen-year-old kid who'd scared me, saved me, and was my first kiss, was now the man who loved me.

I peeled myself from his arms, lined up my mallet and hit the ball. It went straight through one of the hoop things. "Woot," I said, smiling.

Haven and Mars high-fived me.

I was losing pretty bad, but I was having fun doing it. And so was everyone else. I'd realized that despite the money and fame of the band, they knew where they came from and it never stopped them from doing the simple things like brunch at Mom's and playing a game of croquet. I'd heard they also spent time at Ream's cottage where they raced go-carts and played mini-golf.

Family. This was what I'd always dreamed a family was about. The love, the teasing, even the arguing. I loved it all and Killian had given it to me.

He also gave me a dance studio for Christmas. He'd bought another warehouse close to ours and had it renovated. The walls were brick, the ceilings were exposed to the ducts, and he'd had beautiful hardwood floors and huge mirrors along with a music system installed like he'd done at our place.

There was no way I could refuse his outlandish gift and besides, it was the most thoughtful gift he could have given me.

"Melody, don't play in the dirt, honey," Haven called. Melody had forgotten about the ball, Tear, and Drum. She was now digging a hole in the garden and piling the dirt in the skirt of her dress.

Crisis glanced over at his little girl and laughed. Then he dropped his mallet and jogged over to her, crouched and ran his hand over her blonde curls. Then he helped her pile more dirt into her dress.

Haven rolled her eyes, but her face shone with love for both of them. "These moments… I swear I couldn't love that man any more than I already do."

I peered over at Killian, who lined up for his shot, his expression focused, but his body relaxed. I couldn't love Killian any more than I do—he fit me.

Drum ran up to him just as he swung to hit the ball and distracted him. He missed.

Crisis, Ream, and Logan laughed their asses off, but unlike his band mates, Killian wasn't competitive and it didn't bother him.

He crouched to pat Drum, who panted, tongue hanging out of the side of his mouth because he was missing one fang tooth. We didn't know his age as Killian had adopted him from a Pomeranian rescue, but they told him he was six or seven years old.

Killian stood and his gaze drifted to Melody, Crisis, and Haven, who sat on the ground with them. We never talked about kids. I knew he didn't want them and I'd accepted that. I had a family, and Killian and I'd never regret giving up having them.

"Oh, my God, Tear. No," Emily shouted as her dog took off with her ball and Drum chased him, panting. Everyone laughed.

Except Killian. He was stalking toward me, his expression calm, but serious.

When he reached me, he put his finger under my chin and his thumb grazed my lower lip. "Love you, Savvy."

I placed my hands on his chest, smiling. "I love you, too."

He leaned in and kissed me, soft, gentle, and brief. "I'm going to have to fuck you more often."

I laughed. "Are you not satisfied with our sex life, Killian?"

"Mmm," he murmured against my mouth as he kissed me again.

"I'm more than fuckin' satisfied, but if I want you carrying our child, I need to fuck you more often."

My mouth dropped open and eyes widened. "Our child?"

He kissed me again, this time deeper, and my knees weakened. But it wasn't only from the kiss. It was from the excitement sparking through me. Killian wanted a baby.

He drew back and wiped the tear spilling down my cheek. "Can't promise you I won't be overprotective. We're going to have to check school districts for the best ones. And I don't want to live in the warehouse with the kids. They need to be close to a park or somewhere they can play sports and we should—"

I cupped his cheek. "Killian. You're going to be an amazing dad. And maybe we can talk about that once I get pregnant."

I looped my arms around his neck and pulled him down for another kiss.

"Stop kissing your girl. It's her shot," Crisis shouted. "You already held up brunch because you were fu—"

"Crisis!" Sophia reprimanded. "Don't you dare."

"His ass needs kicking," Killian said.

I laughed. "It does."

He grinned. "Be right back, baby."

The End

Acknowledgements

This book has been an incredibly long process. Probably because I wrote the book twice. After the first book, I decided it wasn't right for Killian, Savvy or myself. I didn't LOVE it. So, I tossed it and started again. It was the hardest thing I've ever done in writing, but I'd have it no other way.

When I wrote 'The End' on this book, it was cathartic. I cried. I laughed. I was relieved. This was Killian and Savvy's story and this was how it was meant to be told and I loved it. This was the book readers deserved from me.

There is one person who has been vital on the journey this book has taken. My content editor, Kristin. Her insight. Her support. Her incredible patience. When I lost my way, she led me back on the right path. When I was stuck in the mud, she threw me a rope, yanked me out, set me on my feet, and gave me a push. When I lost faith in myself, she believed in me.

Kristin has been with me since my first published book and I'm honored and grateful to have her as a content editor and call her a friend.

Thank you to the readers for being so patient and understanding when I decided to re-write *Kept from You* and delay its release a few months.

To all the girls in my group 'Nash's Naughty Fillies'. Many of you have been with me since the beginning and I've even had the incredible pleasure of meeting some of you in person. Thank you from the bottom of my heart for all your support.

Thank you to my editor, Becky at Hot Tree Editing, and Donna, for your understanding and patience when I switched books on you, then constantly e-mailed because I had a deadline and was panicking.

Thank you to my agent, Mark Gottlieb and Trident Media

Group, and to everyone at Audible as well as the narrators who have been fantastic with the audio versions of this series.

Stacey, every book you format has been perfect, but it's not only that you make my books look beautiful, it's all those little things you do for me between books. The minor changes you do at the drop of a hat. Responding to e-mails within minutes, if not seconds and how flexible and willing to help any way you can. You are amazing! Thank you, Stacey.

Elaine, when I thought I booked *Kept from You* in for proofing and realized I didn't, my heart dropped. But you fit me in anyway. Thank you so much. I owe you. How does me visiting with London, Fable sound?

Thank you to the amazing Debra, The Book Enthusiast Promotions, and all the bloggers who are vigilant about spreading the word. My books wouldn't be seen without you!

I was fortunate enough to obtain the cover photo from the incredibly talented Wander Aguiar Photography.

Wander, your photographs are exquisite and I'm honored to have one on my cover and I hope to have many more. Thank you to Nick Bennett, the brilliant cover model, for being my Killian.

And finally to my one of a kind beta readers, Lana, Midian, Susan, and Jill. I put a rush on this and you rose to the challenge, setting everything else aside in order to read *Kept from You*. Your insight and feedback helped tremendously and I value each of you so damn much! Thank you.

Hugs,

Nash xo

About the Author

Nashoda Rose is a *New York Times* and *USA Today* International bestselling author of twelve novels, including the Tear Asunder series, the spin-off Unyielding series, and her paranormal Scars of the Wraiths.

She lives outside of Toronto where she enjoys hiking with her Newfoundland dog London and riding her horses.

Goodreads: www.goodreads.com/author/show/7246093.Nashoda_ Rose

Facebook: www.facebook.com/pages/Nashoda-Rose/564276203633318

Website: www.nashodarose.com

Instagram : instagram.com/nashodarose

E-mail: nashodarose@gmail.com

Subscribe to the Newsletter

Made in the USA
Monee, IL
05 April 2022